BLOOD SPORT

Fargo had hoped to avoid a fight. Now that it had been thrust on him, he had a hankering to stomp the wagon boss into the plank floor. A fist clipped his cheek and he retaliated by sending Perkins sprawling with an uppercut. Someone grabbed his arm, and Fargo discouraged him with a jab to the jaw.

Max Perkins was recovering and coming back for more.

Springing around the table, Fargo ducked a clumsy punch to the face, then landed one to the pit of Perkins's stomach. Perkins tried to overcome him with brute strength, never realizing, in his folly, that Fargo was not only faster and more skilled at trading blows, but considerably stronger, as well.

Within seconds, the wagon boss lay sprawled on his back on the floor with Fargo over him, fists clenched, hoping Perkins would try to rise so he could knock him down again.

Fargo had not paid any attention to what was going on around him, a mistake he regretted when he heard the click of a gun hammer, and the hard metal of a gun's muzzle gouged his temple . . .

A GIANT
TRAILSMAN
ADVENTURE

IDAHO
BLOOD SPOOR

by

Jon Sharpe

A SIGNET BOOK

SIGNET
Published by New American Library, a division of
Penguin Group (USA) Inc., 375 Hudson Street,
New York, New York 10014, USA
Penguin Group (Canada), 90 Eglinton Avenue East, Suite 700, Toronto,
Ontario M4P 2Y3, Canada (a division of Pearson Penguin Canada Inc.)
Penguin Books Ltd., 80 Strand, London WC2R 0RL, England
Penguin Ireland, 25 St. Stephen's Green, Dublin 2,
Ireland (a division of Penguin Books Ltd.)
Penguin Group (Australia), 250 Camberwell Road, Camberwell, Victoria
3124, Australia (a division of Pearson Australia Group Pty. Ltd.)
Penguin Books India Pvt. Ltd., 11 Community Centre, Panchsheel Park,
New Delhi - 110 017, India
Penguin Group (NZ), cnr Airborne and Rosedale Roads, Albany,
Auckland 1310, New Zealand (a division of Pearson New Zealand Ltd.)
Penguin Books (South Africa) (Pty.) Ltd., 24 Sturdee Avenue,
Rosebank, Johannesburg 2196, South Africa

Penguin Books Ltd., Registered Offices:
80 Strand, London WC2R 0RL, England

First published by Signet, an imprint of New American Library,
a division of Penguin Group (USA) Inc.

First Printing, February 2006
10 9 8 7 6 5 4 3 2 1

Copyright © Penguin Group (USA) Inc.
All rights reserved

 REGISTERED TRADEMARK—MARCA REGISTRADA

The Trailsman

Beginnings . . . they bend the tree and they mark
the man. Skye Fargo was born when he was eighteen. Terror was his midwife, vengeance his first
cry. Killing spawned Skye Fargo, ruthless, cold-
blooded murder. Out of the acrid smoke of gun-
powder still hanging in the air, he rose, cried out
a promise never forgotten.

The Trailsman they began to call him all across
the West: searcher, scout, hunter, the man who
could see where others only looked, his skills for
hire but not his soul, the man who lived each day
to the fullest, yet trailed each tomorrow. Skye
Fargo, the Trailsman, the seeker who could take
the wildness of a land and the wanting of a woman
and make them his own.

1861, the unexplored mountains of Idaho—where the lust for gold was not the only lust, and blood was spilled as freely as whiskey.

Prologue

The three of them had been riding hard for many days. Always to the north, always pushing their mounts more than was wise. Countless times they glanced over their shoulders or twisted in their saddles to anxiously scan their back trail.

Fear rode with them. Fear in their faces and in their posture. The men tried to hide it but they did not fool the woman, and their fear fed hers. She was young and pretty, and always flashed a smile at the handsome young man who rode in front of her whenever he looked back, and because he was very much in love with her, he always returned her smile. But neither their smiles nor their love erased their fear.

"It has been two weeks," the woman commented one morning as their weary horses climbed a switch-back to a high ridge. "Surely we can take a couple of days to stop and rest?"

"Not until we reach Canada," said the young man she loved, "and even then I won't feel entirely safe."

"Maybe we are going about this all wrong, darling," the young woman remarked. "Maybe Europe would be better. Give me civilization over these mountains any day."

Some of the peaks were so high, they seemed to scratch the sky. Starkly beautiful, their scenic wonder hid a host of deadly dangers that made them some of the most formidable in all of North America.

The woman's admirer frowned. "We talked it out,

remember? Once we reach Canada, we can lose ourselves wherever you desire."

The third member of their small party, who wore a perpetually glum expression, spoke for the first time that morning. "Canada is a ways off yet and our horses are about played out. We're not in much better shape. We need to stop and rest like Tabor wants, Gideon."

With marked vigor the first young man shook his head. "Not with those devils after us, we can't, Asa."

"Maybe we have lost them," Tabor said.

"Do we dare take that chance?" Gideon responded. "Need I remind you what will happen if they catch us? You mean too much to me to risk losing you."

"I appreciate that. But it won't do us any good to ride our mounts into the ground. Asa has our best interests at heart."

Gideon scowled at his friend, then let out a long sigh. "I suppose the two of you are right. But I don't like it. I don't like being delayed one little bit."

Tabor, however, liked it a lot, and clapped her hands in girlish glee at the prospect of a long overdue rest. Her oval face, highlighted by exquisite eyes framed by extremely long eyelashes, split in a wide grin. "Wherever we stop, it has to be by water so I can take a bath."

"Bathing isn't important," Gideon sulked.

"Maybe not for you," Tabor said. "But I never went a day in my whole life without taking one until we started out. I'm sweaty and itchy and dirty and my hair is limp, and if I don't get to bathe soon, I will scream."

"Women," Gideon said, but he said it light-heartedly.

"You could stand to take a bath yourself, mister," Tabor scolded. "You are not exactly a rose. Either of you."

"Oh, thanks," Asa said.

"It's this damnable wilderness," Gideon said, surveying the countryside. "How anyone can stand to live in this godforsaken wasteland, I will never know."

"The Indians have lived here for ages," Tabor pointed out. "They were around long before the first white man came."

"Don't remind me of the heathens. We have been lucky so far in not running across any, but our luck can't hold forever. When we do, they're bound to be hostiles, and we'll be in a worse pickle than ever."

Tabor clucked at Gideon. "I never realized how big a worrywart you are. What other secrets have you kept from me?"

"Poke fun if you want. But hostiles should not be taken lightly. They will scalp Asa and me, and you will spend the rest of your days skinning animals and keeping a warrior warm at night, whether you want to keep him warm or not."

"Gideon!" Asa exclaimed.

"It's all right," Tabor said. "His bluntness is one of his traits I admire most. It shows he is honest at heart, and always says how he truly feels."

"There is such a thing as tact, you know," Asa said, but he dropped the subject.

Gideon was about to face to the north when movement in the far distance arrested his interest. Rising in the stirrups, he shielded his eyes from the glare of the sun and studied the source of the movement. Or, rather, the eleven sources, for there were eleven riders strung out in single file, and there could be no doubt who the eleven were and why they were there. "I thought we lost them," Gideon said in mild despair. He spoke softly, so neither of his companions would hear, but in the near absolute stillness of the woodland, he might as well have shouted.

Tabor twisted, and cried out, "They're still after us!"

"Did you think they wouldn't be?" asked Asa. "They won't give up this side of the grave."

"What do we do?"

"We stand and fight," Gideon proposed.

Now it was Asa's turn to scowl. "The three of us against the eleven of them? Do you have a death wish?"

"If you have a better idea," Gideon said, "I am open to suggestions."

Asa's silence betrayed his lack of one.

"So," Gideon declared, "either we forge on, and you have already pointed out how tired our horses are, or we lie in wait and ambush the devils and pray we kill enough of them to discourage the rest."

Tabor had a retort, if Asa did not. "Listen to yourself. You talk about killing as if you do it all the time. When the truth is that none of us has ever taken a human life."

"There is a first time for everything," Gideon philosophized. Bending, he slid his rifle from its saddle scabbard. "I would be a poor excuse for a future husband if I let them get their hands on you."

"There has to be another way."

"I repeat," Gideon said, "if you have one, let me hear it. If not, I'm tired of running, tired of hiding. I want to end it once and for all."

"Don't we all," Asa said. He shucked his own rifle. "So where and how do we go about it?"

Gideon scanned the terrain ahead. "That bluff looks promising. They'll be easy targets but they won't be able to see us."

The bluff was sixty feet high, the south side a sheer cliff sprinkled at the base with boulders of various shapes and sizes. In search of a way to the top, they rode to the east side, then to the north, where fate smiled on them in the form of a game trail up a gradual slope to the crest.

"This will do nicely!" Gideon eagerly gushed. "Beloved, you stay with the horses while Asa and I get ready for them."

"I don't like being left alone."

"Be sensible," Gideon urged. Roughly square, the top of the bluff was forty yards long from east to west and perhaps thirty from north to south. "We'll be close enough for you to spit on."

"Ladies do not spit," Tabor said. Nor did they wear mens' clothes, as she was.

"Ladies do not kill, either, and someone has to keep our animals from running off and stranding us afoot," Gideon insisted.

Reluctantly, Tabor waited at the north side of the bluff, holding the reins, while her two escorts hurried to the south rim, crawling the final few yards so as not to silhouette themselves against the blue vault above.

"I only hope this works," Asa commented as he fed a round into the chamber of his rifle.

"How can it not?" Gideon asked, gleeful that at long last they would soon have their pursuers right where he wanted them.

Asa's eyes were troubled. "The advantage of surprise isn't enough. There are too many."

"Not if we wait until they are right on top of us," Gideon proposed. "Not if we wait until we can see the whites of their eyes." He sighted down his Volcanic Arms carbine but the riders were still much too far off. "Wait for me to fire. Then shoot them down like the curs they are as fast as you can work your weapon."

"We can't drop them all."

Gideon lowered his carbine and arched an eyebrow. "Must you always be a fount of gloom? The few who are left are bound to turn tail and run."

"You don't know that," his friend noted. "It depends on how much we are worth to them."

"I swear," Gideon groused. "You're worse than a rainy day when it comes to—" He rose on his elbows. "Look! They've stopped! What do you think they are up to?"

A quarter of a mile out, the eleven riders had reined up in a half-circle. A talk of some sort was taking place. Presently the foremost rider detached himself from the rest and came on alone, his head to the ground, reading the sign.

"He's tracking us," Asa said. "We should go now, while we still can."

"That's their tracker. If we kill him, we might be able to shake them." Gideon flattened, his chin on the cool metal of his carbine.

"They're too close," Asa objected. "Please. For once, listen to my advice. Let's ride. If not for my sake, do it for hers."

"Don't you dare," Gideon said. "I would do anything for Tabor. But we have been given a golden opportunity. We must exploit it."

Asa was not pleased, but he did not make more of an issue of this friend's decision. Hunkering, he cradled his Spencer Repeater and felt his palms grow slick with sweat. He was terribly nervous and more than a little afraid.

Gideon was too excited to be scared. He could not wait for the riders to come within range. It was all he could to keep from leaping to his feet and banging away.

The renegade tracker was no fool. He rode slowly, with frequent glances at the trail ahead and the surrounding vegetation. A swarthy Indian, or maybe a half-breed, he wore a brown band around his head, and had long black hair that hung to his shoulders. His face bore the stamp of a cruel nature accented by a slit of a mouth.

More sweat broke out on Asa, on his brow and his neck. He resisted an impulse to wipe it off. Any motion, however slight, might forewarn their enemies. He swallowed and found that his throat was dry. All his spittle was gone. Worse, his temples were pounding as if to the beat of a blacksmith's hammer.

6

To young Tabor the wait was more than her nerves could endure. She began to pace. She had lost sight of the two men when they went to ground in the high grass at the cliff's edge, and she dearly yearned for a glimpse of her beloved. She loved him so much, thinking about him brought an ache to her chest.

"It's my fault," Tabor said aloud, bowing her head. "This is all because of me."

Gideon's gaze was glued to the dusky-hued warrior. He had met a few Indians, tame ones, as they were called, who lived on reservations and had taken up white ways. But he had never run into a savage specimen like the stocky killer riding slowly toward them. He should be scared. He should be terrified. But he was not. Instead, he felt a strange sort of calm. Maybe it had to do with Tabor, and his willingness to sell his life to protect hers.

The tracker was a hundred yards out. Suddenly he stopped and studied the bluff. His instincts were much keener than those of civilized men, and it was plain they had warned him something was amiss.

Keep coming! Gideon wanted to shout, but did not. Pressing his cheek to his rifle, he aligned the rear sight with the front sight and fixed the front sight on the tracker's chest. He had never killed before but he would for Tabor's sake.

Asa was in a panic. Images of what the other cutthroats would do swirled like so much chaff in a gale. He turned to whisper to Gideon that he had changed his mind, that they should fan the wind before it was too late. But before he could open his mouth, a rifle boomed like thunder and that which Asa feared the most came to pass.

1

Fort Hall got its start as a trading post in 1834. It became a stopover on the Oregon Trail. Some emigrants liked the area so much they decided to stay, and before long the trading post had grown into a small but thriving settlement.

In 1849 the Secretary of War established a military post several miles to the north and gave it the name Cantonment Loring, after Lieutenant Colonel William F. Loring, who oversaw the building of the post. But no one called it Cantonment Loring. They called it Fort Hall. It lasted less than a year. After the post was built, and manned, the army decided it was in a poor location, and abandoned it.

The settlers chuckled but were not worried. By now the original settlement had reached the point where the settlers need not fret about an Indian attack.

For their part, the tribes in the region were not happy about the influx of whites. They were even less happy after a white man discovered gold on Orofino Creek. Suddenly whites poured in from all over, and mining camps and new settlements and towns sprang up. Inevitably, clashes occurred. Lone travelers and small parties sometimes disappeared without a trace.

One of those lone travelers this bright summer morning was Skye Fargo. By his reckoning he was ten miles southeast of the original settlement, and he expected to arrive by midafternoon.

A big man, Fargo had broad shoulders, a lean waist,

and the muscular build of someone who spent nearly all his time in the wilds. He was uncommonly handsome, as many a filly would attest. His piercing lake blue eyes, which could chill an enemy with an icy glare or light with mirth during his revels at saloons, now squinted against the harsh glare of the sun as he scoured the countryside.

No one who did not stay alert lasted long on the frontier. The price paid for a lapse in vigilance was one's life. Hostiles, outlaws, beasts, and the elements themselves conspired to make the life of the unwary as short as an Irishman's temper.

In Fargo's saddlebags was the letter that had brought him. He was in Denver, indulging in cards, whiskey and women, although not necessarily in that order, when the letter caught up with him.

Fargo had almost ignored the letter's request. He figured that by the time he got here, those he was expected to find would be long dead. But ten thousand dollars would buy a lot of cards, whiskey, and women. So he saddled up and headed northwest, and now, after a long, tiring journey, he was almost at his destination.

A white hat so dusty from the trail it appeared to be brown was perched on his thatch of hair. Like most frontiersmen, he preferred buckskins. A Colt was strapped to his hip, a Henry rifle was snug in the saddle scabbard. Also, like most frontiersmen, he carried a hideout in his right boot, in his case a double-edged Arkansas toothpick that had saved his hide more than once.

The Ovaro rounded a bend in the trail, and Fargo drew rein.

Ahead sat a wagon, one of the countless prairie schooners that made the arduous trek to Oregon Country on a regular basis. A bent-backed turtle on wheels, this particular turtle was crippled. The driver had strayed too far to the side of the trail and struck a boulder hidden by the brush. Several spokes had broken. Now the driver was about to replace them, and was hunkered beside the busted wheel, setting up a jack made of heavy iron-bound wood.

Ordinarily, it would have been none of Fargo's business. But in this instance, his interest was piqued, and he sat there a minute, waiting to see if someone else would appear. When no one did, he gigged the stallion forward and drew rein a few yards out. "Howdy, ma'am."

The woman was so engrossed in the jack that she had not heard the dull clomp of the Ovaro's hooves. Now she whirled and rose. Her right hand dropped to a revolver at her waist. Her dress was plain homespun, her shoes as plain and well worn. But there was nothing plain about the woman herself. Lustrous blond hair framed a face that any man would give a second look. Nor could her plain dress hide the tantalizing curves underneath.

"What do you want, mister?"

Fargo smiled and pushed his hat brim back. "I thought you might want some help fixing that wheel."

"You thought wrong," she informed him, her hazel eyes burning with suspicion. "I can manage on my own, thank you very much."

Fargo shrugged. "I suppose so. But two can get the job done faster than one, and a heap easier."

"I've made it this far by myself. I can make it the rest of the way."

The confirmation that she was traveling alone surprised Fargo, and impressed him. "How is it you don't have a husband tucked away under that canvas?"

Her back stiffened and she said testily, "How is it that you poke your nose into the personal affairs of others? Be off with you before I get mad and shoot you out of that saddle."

"Shot a lot of people, have you?" Fargo asked, and swung down. Instantly she drew her revolver and trained it on him.

"That's far enough."

Fargo stepped to the broken wheel and squatted. "Three spokes need replacing. I hope you packed spares."

"Didn't you hear me?" the beauty demanded, backing up a step. "Get on your pinto and light a shuck. I mean it."

"Of course you do." Fargo reached for the jack. It had a toothed iron rack, a pinion wheel, and a pawl to lock the rack in place once the axle was high enough. Judging by its condition, it had not been used much.

"What in God's name is the matter with you?" the woman snapped, fingering the trigger of her Remington. *Get back on your damn horse.*"

"He can use the rest," Fargo said, and bent to slide the jack under the prairie schooner.

"I'll shoot. So help me I will."

"Do you always go around killing folks who offer to help you?" Fargo aligned the jack. "Wherever you hail from must be a real friendly place."

The woman's exasperation brought a flush to her full cheeks. "Ohio is plenty friendly, I'll have you know." She stamped a slender foot. "Damn you, anyway! Why won't you listen?"

Fargo smiled at her. "Because you're as lovely a woman as I've seen in a coon's age, and I would be a fool not to make your acquaintance." He quickly added to soothe her anxiety, "But don't worry. I'll lend a hand with the wheel and leave you in peace, if that's what you want."

"Of course it's what I want." After a few moments she replaced the Remington in its holster and said almost apologetically, "A woman can't be too careful. You understand, don't you?"

"I wouldn't trust me either, not around someone as pretty as you," Fargo replied, and was rewarded with a soft chuckle.

"You're sure something—do you know that? I didn't catch your name."

Fargo introduced himself, and to make small talk

and further put her at ease, he mentioned, "I'm on my way to Fort Hall on business. But another half an hour or so won't make a difference."

"Then aiding damsels in distress isn't what you do for a living?"

It was Fargo's turn to chuckle. "You might think so, given how attracted I am to damsels."

"Something tells me you have to beat them off with a stick," the woman said, and she was not entirely joking.

"Do you have a name or should I just call you Ohio?"

A grin spread across her face and she hunkered at his elbow. "I'm Lucille. Lucille Harper. But most folks call me Lucy." She watched him adjust the iron rack. "I can pay you for your help. I have a little money."

Fargo glanced sharply at her. "Don't tell that to anyone ever again. Out here there are some who will slit your throat for a few measly dollars."

Lucy's forehead pinched and she regarded him intently. "You sure are a strange one. You haven't known me three minutes and you act as if you're truly concerned for my welfare."

"I've seen too many people die for stupid reasons," Fargo said sourly, applying himself anew to the task at hand. "People like you who come out here thinking the same rules of conduct apply that apply back east. But there are no rules west of the Mississippi. It's kill or be killed. You would do well to remember that."

"Oh, honestly, Mr. Fargo," Lucy said, "you make it sound as if my life is in my hands every minute. Yet I've had a pleasant enough journey. The wagon train I'm with is filled with nice people. And those we've met along the way have been equally nice."

"Where did this wagon train get to?" Fargo asked. It was customary for a train to halt when someone broke down. Stragglers were easy pickings for the many two-legged wolves that called the wilds home.

"Everyone was so eager to reach the settlement, I

13

just couldn't let them linger on my account. But the captain of our train, Mr. Perkins, said he would come back and help me. I expect him any time now."

As if on cue, hooves thudded, and a rider came from the west, a brawny man in a brown jacket and a short-brimmed hat. On spying Fargo he jerked his head up and applied his spurs.

The jack was in place, so Fargo began turning the handle. He did not look up when the bay came to a stop.

"What is this, then, Miss Harper? Where did this fellow come from?"

"He stopped to help me," Lucy said.

"Oh really? Well, we don't need any help, so he can be on his way."

A hand fell on Fargo's shoulder and clamped tight, much tighter than was called for under the circumstances.

"Did you hear me, friend? Off you go. I'm Max Perkins, the wagon boss of the wagon train Miss Harper is with, and she is my responsibility."

Fargo slowly shifted and tilted his head back. It wasn't often that he took an immediate dislike to someone, but he took an immediate dislike to Perkins. The captain had an air about him—the sort of air a weasel had when it was about to pounce on a hapless chicken, or the air of a sly fox who was being too devious by half. "Move the hand or lose the fingers."

"What's that?" Perkins stepped back. "Did you just threaten me?" His left hand moved, exposing a Smith & Wesson. "I don't know who you think you are but that kind of talk has gotten many a jackass buried."

"Mr. Perkins!" Lucy exclaimed.

"You heard him," the wagon master said, and a grim aspect came over him. "I won't tell you again, mister. On your horse and on your way, or by the Almighty, I'll throw you on it."

Unfurling, Fargo faced him, his own hand close to his Colt. "How long have you been a wagon boss?"

The unexpected question caused Perkins to blink. "Why do you ask? What does it matter?"

"I've met most of them." Which Fargo had, in his capacity as a scout and sometimes a guide. "I've never heard of you."

"I'll have you know this is the fourth train I've guided," Perkins declared, "and I took each and every one through with no disasters."

"How many emigrants have you lost?"

Perkins made a sniffing sound. "I don't see where it concerns you, but I've lost a few. It happens. The dangers on the trail are many, and I can't be everywhere at once."

"How many?"

The wagon boss glanced at Lucy Harper, then planted his legs wide apart and growled, "Enough. I am in charge here."

"You're not in charge of me." Fargo had a fair idea what was coming, and he would be damned if he would stand for it. "Why not catch up with your train while you still can?"

"How dare you threaten me!" Max Perkins lunged, his thick fingers seeking Fargo's throat even as his left knee drove at Fargo's groin.

"No!" Lucy cried.

Quick as thought, Fargo sidestepped. He swatted Perkins's hands aside, then delivered a punch to the gut that doubled the wagon boss over and left him wheezing and sputtering.

"Please, stop this!" Lucy tried again. "There is no need to fight. It's silly."

Fargo agreed, but then, he had not started it. Perkins was the one who should let it drop. But some men were as stubborn as mules; they only learned the hard way. Or was it that, having overstepped himself, the wagon boss refused to back down and look bad in the eyes of Lucy Harper?

"No one manhandles me," Perkins hissed, and came in low and quick, his fists clenched.

Fargo avoided a wild swing and dodged an uppercut. He flicked a jab that jolted the wagon master on his heels but it was not enough to discourage Perkins from pressing the attack.

"I'll stomp you! You hear me?"

It was impossible for Fargo not to, Perkins roared it so loud. He blocked a blow, countered, blocked another, slipped a third. The wagon boss was big but he was ungainly, a bear who relied on his bulk and his strength instead of his brain.

Fargo lost his hat to a backhand he ducked. He connected to the ribs and caught Perkins on the left cheek hard enough to split the skin. Perkins sprang back, out of reach, and Fargo said, "Had enough?"

"Not by a long shot" was the angry retort.

"Suit yourself," Fargo said, and waded in. He had no taste for this but he wanted to end it quickly. A solid right to the jaw should have brought Perkins crashing to the ground but the wagon boss gritted his teeth and unleashed another uppercut. Sidestepping, Fargo retaliated with a flurry that forced Perkins to give ground. Out of the corner of his eye, Fargo glimpsed Lucy Harper with a hand pressed to her mouth and the other pressed to her bosom. The distraction cost him. His side was seared by pain; then a fist clipped his chin. Concentrating, he blocked yet another punch, then scored with several in a row. He put all he had into the last one and lifted the wagon master clean off his feet.

Perkins crashed to earth and lay in a daze. He was breathing heavily. Scarlet drops flecked his lower lip and chin.

"Now have you had enough?" Fargo demanded, standing over him.

"Never!" Perkins snarled, but he made no effort to rise.

That was when Lucy stepped forward and pushed

Fargo back. "Enough! I can't believe two grown men are acting so childish! And for what? Over who gets to fix a broken wheel?"

Perkins rose onto his elbows and spat blood. "You are my responsibility, Miss Harper. It's my job to help, not his."

"It makes no difference to me so long as the job gets done," Lucy said. "I don't mean to hurt your feelings, but I think you should go and let Mr. Fargo tend to the wheel. He stopped first, so I can't rightly turn him down."

"Sure you can. He's not a member of our train," Perkins persisted. Sitting up, he rubbed his jaw. "If you want him to do it instead of me, then I refuse to take responsibility. If anything happens, it's on your head."

"I would not have it any other way," Lucy said.

Glowering at Fargo, Max Perkins pushed to his feet. His cheek was beginning to swell, and before the day was out, he would sport a number of bruises. "All right. I've done all I can. But I don't like it. I don't like it one bit."

"Why not stay until he's done?" Lucy proposed. "Or better yet, the two of you can work together."

"Nothing doing," Perkins declared, and walked to his horse. Taking hold of the reins, he gripped the saddle horn and swung up. He was mad as hell and trying not to show it, but failing. "I credited you with better judgment," he told Lucy. "We'll talk more at Fort Hall."

Fargo did not resume work until the wagon boss was out of sight. Lucy was silent until he began to pull the wheel off the hub.

"I'm not stupid, you know."

"Who said you were?" Taking hold of the rim, Fargo wriggled it from side to side.

"That wasn't about who should help me," Lucy said. "Perkins has had his eyes on me ever since I signed on in Westport. I've been civil but I could do without the nuisance." She paused. "I reckon it comes from being female and single. But I do wish men could take a hint." She paused again. "Thank you."

Fargo nearly fell when he gave another tug and the wheel popped off like a cork out of a bottle. He set it flat and raised his head. "You're not out of the woods yet. It's a long way from Fort Hall to Oregon, and he's liable to be more of a nuisance."

"Maybe not," Lucy said hopefully. "Maybe he'll hate me for not taking his side."

"And maybe he'll make your life as miserable as he can to get back at you." Fargo figured the man was petty enough.

"It's not as if I have a choice. I must get to Portland."

"Where are your tools?" Fargo asked, rising. As she turned to get them, he said, "It's early in the season yet. You can always wait at Fort Hall for another wagon train to come along."

"I paid in advance for the right to travel with Perkins," Lucy said. "One hundred and fifty dollars—the going rate. There are no refunds. It's in the contract I signed. I won't get a cent back if I switch trains."

It took longer than Fargo anticipated to repair the wheel. He had to remove two of the felloes to get at the spokes, and one of the pegs was jammed fast. Meanwhile, Lucy told him about her life in Ohio; she had been raised on a farm, the fourth of seven siblings, and was now en route to join her oldest sister, who had married and moved to Portland.

"My parents were scandalized by me wanting to strike out on my own. They were sure I'd fall prey to hostiles or die of hunger or thirst or have my virtue compromised." Lucy giggled. "You would think I was a child, how they carried on."

"What will you do when you get to Portland?"

"I haven't thought that far ahead. Jobs are scarce, but so are females, so I figure I won't have a problem finding

18

one. My sister and her husband have offered to put me up until I can find a place of my own." Lucy idly stretched, arching her back, and her bosom swelled against the fabric of her dress. "I had to do it. I had to get away. To see something of the world. I didn't want to milk cows and feed chickens the rest of my life."

"We do what we have to," Fargo said. He had axle grease on his fingers and stooped to wipe them clean on the grass.

"I tried to tell my folks that. I tried to make them understand that what made them happy did not necessarily make me happy. They expected me to marry one of the local boys and settle down and do as my mother had done. But I just couldn't. I felt trapped, like there were invisible walls around me." Lucy bit her lower lip. "Thank God my older sister had already moved away. It gave me an excuse to follow in her footsteps."

Fargo had most of the grease off but there was still some between his fingers.

"Listen to me, will you?" Lucy grinned. "Prattling on to a total stranger. You have to excuse me. I haven't been able to socialize much on this trip and I'm half-starved for someone to talk to."

"What about the other emigrants?"

"Oh, the men are friendly enough. Some are too friendly. But their wives don't take kindly to them associating with an available woman. They don't take it kindly, at all." Lucy's shoulders drooped. "You would think I was a hussy, the way some have treated me."

"You should have the wheel checked by the blacksmith at Fort Hall," Fargo advised, and turned toward the Ovaro. "I'll be on my way."

"Wait!" Lucy exclaimed, much louder than was called for. "What's your rush? I was sort of hoping you would escort me in. In fact"—she hesitated, a pink tinge creeping up her face—"I was hoping you wouldn't mind riding up in the wagon with me. I'll make it worth your while. I have a flask of whiskey. For medicinal purposes only. But you're welcome to some if you would like."

Fargo grinned. "How did you know I was a drinking man?"

"Most men are. I never could stand the taste, myself. It burns going down something awful." Lucy smoothed her dress. "So what do you say? Would you mind my company a while more yet?"

"I'm not loco," Fargo said, and proceeded to tie the Ovaro to the rear of the wagon and climb onto the seat.

Lucy was waiting, the reins in hand. Next to her was the flask. "As promised," she said, and clucked to the team. The dust-caked mules lumbered into motion, and the wagon creaked and began rolling.

Fargo opened the flask and tipped it to his lips. It was whiskey, all right, and not the cheap coffin varnish peddled at most saloons and taverns. He savored his first drink since Denver, letting it rest in his mouth before he swallowed. "Smooth as silk," he complimented her.

"That might be, but it smells like something that came out the hind end of a horse."

"Sniffed a lot of them?" Fargo teased, and she laughed. "Are you sure you don't want some?" When she shook her head, he treated himself to a second swallow and then a third.

"If you drink it all, no harm done," Lucy commented. "I can always buy more at Fort Hall."

Fargo admired how the sunlight played over her fine features. She had exquisite full red lips that reminded him of ripe strawberries. "How long is the wagon train stopping over?"

"Mr. Perkins said we can spare four whole days, the longest any of us has had to rest since we started out. I'm told there is a general store, and I'm low on essentials. But what I most want is a long, hot bath." Lucy caught herself and blushed again. "Sorry. It wasn't proper of me to mention that."

Fargo could not decide if she truly was prim and proper, or whether she was extending a subtle invite. "Mention it, hell. I'll help you find a tub and fill it for you and scrub your back after you climb in."

Lucy giggled a trifle nervously. "My mother would throw a fit if she heard you be so forward."

"It's not your mother's back I want to scrub."

Lucy's hazel eyes filled with warmth and amusement. Just then the wagon gave a lurch and her left leg moved a few inches, brushing his. It all seemed perfectly innocent, but Fargo noticed she did not move her leg away.

"You say the darnedest things," Lucy informed him. "But I must admit, I find myself growing fond of you anyway. And I can't thank you enough for your assistance with the wheel."

Fargo waited for her to say, *"I don't know how I can ever repay you,"* but she was not that obvious. She had her standards.

"Isn't it lovely here?" Luch breathed deep and surveyed their surroundings. "The Garden of Eden all over again."

The trail wound near to the gurgling river. Colorful birds flitted among the trees, and here and there wildflowers grew. A butterfly flitted by on gossamer wings. When they rounded the next bend, several does bounded for cover.

"I'm almost inclined to spend the night out under the stars," Lucy mentioned, "if only I didn't want that bath so much."

"There's always the river," Fargo said. "You can take your hot bath tomorrow or the next day."

"I suppose I could," Lucy slowly drawled. "But what about you? You must want to go on in to the settlement."

Fargo gazed at her shapely thighs and felt a stirring down low. "It can wait one more night."

2

The clearing was bordered on one side by the Snake River and on the other by a wall of vegetation. From where Fargo sat by the crackling fire, he could hear the hiss of water break on boulders along the shore, and every now and again the splash of a late-feeding fish.

The sun had set an hour ago in a blaze of red-and-orange glory. Full night had yet to descend. A few stars sprinkled the darkening firmament but it would be a while yet before they dominated the heavens.

Fargo's conscience was pricking him. The letter said it was urgent he reach Fort Hall as quickly as practical. But he had been on the go for weeks, and both he and the Ovaro could use a little rest. The pinto was tethered with the team and contentedly grazing.

"Want more coffee?" Lucy Harper asked. "It will be a while yet before the stew is done."

"Sure," Fargo said, holding out his battered tin cup. The tantalizing aroma of the fresh brew set his stomach to growling.

"That was some shot you made bringing down that rabbit," Lucy complimented him. "It must have been all of a hundred yards."

"When a person is starved, their marksmanship improves," Fargo joked.

"Mine could improve from now until doomsday and I still would not be half as good as you are." Lucy sat on a short log Fargo had dragged over by the fire for that express purpose. In her palms she held her own cup, already full, and now she smiled and took a sip. "How do you like it?"

"Some of the best coffee I've ever had." Fargo repaid the favor, even though it was not quite as hot as he liked and she had used a bit too much sugar.

As if Lucy were privy to his thoughts, she remarked, "It's too sweet, I know. But since I was knee-high to a foal, I've always had a horrible sweet tooth. When I was a girl, I was forever getting into trouble for taking sugar from the sugar bowl without permission. One time my mother was so mad, she rapped my knuckles with a spoon."

"I like sugar, too," Fargo said to be polite. Just not as much.

Lucy gazed serenely at the sky. "Isn't it wonderful here? Nature in all her marvelous beauty."

"It's nice," Fargo allowed. "But never forget that under the beauty lies a lot of dangers."

Lucy scrunched her luscious lips in disapproval. "Why is it men are always so darned practical? Can't they ever appreciate beauty for beauty's sake?"

Fargo liked how her dress clung to her shapely legs, and the sweep of her bosom when she sat back. "Oh, I appreciate my share of beauty."

"So you claim, but I've yet to meet a man who doesn't think life is out to get him. Men are always looking at the somber side of things."

"That's because life *is* out to get us," Fargo observed. "From the moment we're born, we're waiting to die."

"What a morbid view," Lucy said. "I'm glad I don't share it. Why, if I was as gloomy as that, I'd put a bullet in my head to end my misery."

She was smiling as she spoke but Fargo had never seen anything humorous about suicide. To change the subject, he asked, "Are you sure Perkins won't come back to see what has delayed you?"

"After I made my feelings plain earlier? I very much doubt it. He has his pride. Plus there is Mrs. Swanson to keep him occupied."

"Who is she?"

"The wife of one of the emigrants. She and the wagon boss were extremely friendly from the very start. People whispered behind their backs. Her poor husband has no idea what is going on right under his nose."

Yet another reason Fargo had no hankering to marry. The irony did not elude him. But then, he never tried to trick women into believing he wanted more than he did.

"I would never do what she does if I had a husband," Lucy was saying. "I hold marriage vows sacred. When a woman says she will be faithful, she should stick by her word."

"Promises are easier to make than to keep." Fargo swallowed more coffee and studied the surrounding tangle of vegetation, which could hide anything from a hostile war party to a hungry grizzly.

"Is something wrong? Why do you keep looking around?"

"I like breathing," Fargo said.

"Oh, bosh. Not once this entire journey have I so much as set eyes on a fearsome beast or a single Indian. If you ask me, the perils of wagon travel are greatly exaggerated. I was half-convinced I would never reach Oregon alive."

"For every wagon train that makes it through without a problem, there are plenty that lose lives along the way," Fargo mentioned. "I've guided a few, so I should know." On the last train he was with, one man drowned while crossing a flood-swollen stream. On another train, a woman had gone off to pick flowers by herself, in defiance of the rule that no one should ever stray from the train alone, and that was the last anyone saw of her.

"Be that as it may, I won't have to worry about a thing once I reach Portland," Lucy said.

"Except all the men who will come courting. Women are rare there. Beautiful women even rarer. You will be the one who has to beat suitors off with a stick," Fargo predicted.

"I've never had a shortage of admirers, I admit." Lucy sighed. "It can be tiresome at times, but a woman can't help how she looks."

Was it Fargo's imagination or had the undergrowth across the clearing moved? From under his hat brim, he stared at the spot but did not see anything.

"You men have it so easy," Lucy commented. "You don't have women pawing you all the time. Or giving you suggestive looks. Or both."

"Women have their ways of making their interest known." Fargo was lifting his cup when the brush seemed to ripple to the passage of a fair-sized form. Holding the cup in front of his mouth so his moving lips could not be seen, he whispered, "Listen, and listen good. We have company. In about a minute I want you to ask me to fetch some blankets from your wagon. Wait several minutes. Then get under your wagon and stay there until I return or until sunup, whichever comes first."

"Why? What is wrong?"

"Just do as I told you and everything should be fine." Fargo took a sip, then set his cup down. With his chin tucked to his chest, he whispered, "Whatever you do, stay under that wagon. No matter what you hear. If I yell for you to run, you do just that. Run and hide and don't show yourself until you're sure it's safe."

"You're scaring me."

"I'm trying to," Fargo said. "You're more likely to do what I say and not get yourself killed."

"It could be nothing but a deer," Lucy offered.

"Deer generally don't come near a fire," Fargo set

25

her straight. Nor did most other animals. But man, with his unquenchable curiosity and his insatiable appetite for violence, was drawn to a campfire like a moth to a flame. "We'll find out what is out there soon enough."

Lucy surprised him by reaching over and gently covering his hand with hers. "Be careful," she whispered, then made light of her concern by saying, "I wouldn't want anything to happen to you after all the trouble I went to making the stew."

"The blankets," Fargo whispered. "Do it loud but not too loud."

Obliging him, Lucy requested, "Would you be so kind as to fetch a few blankets from my wagon?"

"Sure." Fargo rose and ambled to the prairie schooner. He climbed in the front, then quickly clambered over her neatly piled possessions to the back. Belly down, he slid off. From there he swung over the side and dropped lightly to the ground. With any luck, whoever or whatever was watching them had not spotted him.

After grabbing his Henry, Fargo hunched low and went down the bank to the river's edge. Heading west, he soon came to the woods. The lurker was north of the clearing. As silent as an Apache, Fargo cautiously stalked his way from tree to tree until he was sure he was close to where the brush had moved.

Squatting, Fargo probed the darkness, his every sense strained to the utmost. He was about convinced that he had gone to all that effort for nothing when soft rustling drew his attention to an inky silhouette perhaps a dozen yards from where he was crouched.

Fargo could not tell who or what it was other than that it was not a stump, a log, or a bush. It was alive, and it was circling to the east with a degree of stealth that rivaled his own.

His first thought had been that Max Perkins had returned, but now he was not so sure. Perkins did not impress him as being all that versed in woodcraft. And whoever or whatever was spying on them possessed more than average skill.

The silhouette shifted slightly, and Fargo clearly discerned two legs and arms. So it *was* a person, and the dull glint of metal warned him the intruder was armed with a rifle.

Fargo had an easy shot. He could not tell exactly where the heart was, or the head, for that matter, but there was no doubt he could hit the man. But he did not fire. He was not the kind to shoot first and consult a corpse later.

Lucy was still by the fire. She was drinking coffee and humming to herself. No one would suspect she was putting on an act.

The figure stopped. The rifle rose.

Fargo had figured he was the one the lurker was after. But there could be no mistake; the figure was aiming at Lucy Harper. With the realization came instant action. Fargo jerked the Henry to his shoulder, sighted as best he was able in the gloom, and since he already had a round in the chamber, all he had to do was thumb back the hammer and squeeze the trigger.

Unfortunately, manufacturers had yet to invent a rifle that did not click when the hammer was pulled back. The distinct sound carried to the dark figure, and in the next heartbeat, the lurker spun and the night belched smoke and lead in Fargo's direction.

As the rifle went off, Fargo dived flat. He answered in kind but he was prone and no longer had a clear shot. Pushing onto his knees, he was all set to fire again but there was no one to shoot. The would-be killer had melted into the vegetation. He hesitated, unsure which direction to take, when suddenly two more shots cracked like bullwhips and slugs missed him by a cat's whiskers.

Again Fargo responded, firing at the muzzle flashes.

27

He saw the figure bolt to the northwest. Rising, he gave chase. He risked a glance at the clearing to assure himself that Lucy had done as he instructed and was pleased to see she was taking cover under the prairie schooner.

A twig snapped. The lurker had thrown stealth to the breeze and was in full flight. Even so, Fargo soon noticed that his quarry was not making as much noise as most people would while blundering blindly through a forest in the dark—more proof that whomever he was up against was no common pioneer.

A target presented itself, and again Fargo snapped the Henry to his shoulder. But the instant he did, a pine came between them and he had to lower the Henry again. He covered fifteen yards in long, lithe bounds, then abruptly drew up short as it dawned on him that he had lost sight of the assassin—and the woods were completely still.

Hunkering, Fargo felt beads of sweat break out on his neck and brow. He had nearly made a fatal blunder. Whoever was out there might be waiting for him to run right into their gun sights.

The quiet played havoc with nerves. Fargo could practically feel the other's presence. But all he could do was wait for the killer to give himself away.

The seconds stretched into minutes. Not so much as a leaf stirred. The wind had died, which was in the killer's favor as much as it was Fargo's. Whoever moved first chanced a bullet.

The wait became interminable. The whole time, Fargo scarcely breathed, and willed himself not to blink.

Then a new element intruded. Soft footfalls from the clearing heralded a sharp whisper from Lucy Harper. "Skye? Are you there? Where did you get to?"

Fargo saw her out of the corner of his eye. She had not stayed under the prairie schooner as he had told her. He wanted to twist his head and shout for her to get back under the wagon but it might mean taking a bullet at the expense of her folly.

"Answer me, will you? I'm worried sick."

Fargo decided to take the chance. But as he opened his mouth, an indigo patch of what appeared to be vegetation separated from the rest and resolved into the vague outline of the killer. Once again his rifle was trained on Lucy Harper. Fargo rotated on the ball of his left boot to squeeze off a shot but the killer spotted him and spun, and two shots boomed in swift succession.

Fargo swore he heard lead buzz past. He returned fire, four swift shots of his own, and the figure disappeared. Whether he had scored or the killer had merely gone to ground, Fargo's couldn't say. Bellowing to Lucy, "Get back to the wagon!" he flung himself down.

Again the night exploded with gunfire. The killer was still very much alive and came uncannily close to ending the fight then and there.

Rolling to the right, Fargo fired at the puffs of gunsmoke. A bullet smacked into a tree behind him; another dug a furrow in the earth at his elbow. He banged off two more shots, not really expecting to have any effect. But suddenly the underbrush crackled noisily to a hunched, fleeing form.

Fargo gave chase. Heedless of low limbs and tree stumps and random boulders, he flew to the northwest as if the wings of Mercury were on his ankles. He must not let the killer get away or whoever it was might try again another day.

"Skye!" Lucy bawled.

Fargo hoped she had the presence of mind to do as he had said. He could not wage the fight and protect her at the same time. A glimpse of the bushwhacker spurred him to greater speed, but as fast as he was, he was not able to gain.

Up ahead a larger shape materialized out of the night, a four-legged shape that stamped a hoof and whinnied. The killer reached it and swung lithely into the saddle. A flick of the reins and a slap of the killer's legs, and the horse raced to the northwest.

Fargo wedged the Henry's stock to his shoulder. He yearned to shoot, to bring the rider crashing down, but a stand of pines enveloped both man and animal, and any hope he had was shattered.

Swearing under his breath, Fargo lowered the Henry and listened to the gradually receding hoof-beats.

Lucy was not under the wagon when Fargo came to the clearing. She was in the open, wringing her hands.

Fargo did not mince words. "You don't listen worth a damn."

"I couldn't help myself," Lucy said. "I was worried about you. You can't fault me for that."

"Yes, I can," Fargo said harshly. "Your mistake could have got both of us shot. And I'm not hankering to be dead."

"I didn't mean—" Lucy said, and stopped.

Fargo strode past her to the fire. The stew was bubbling, and the aroma reminded him of how famished he was. "We'll eat. Then you can turn in."

"What about you?"

"Our friend could come back later. If he does, I'll be ready for him," Fargo said grimly.

"I was looking forward to the two of us—" Again Lucy stopped. Much more softly, she said, "I am sorry I didn't listen to you."

They ate the stew in silence. Fargo kept an eye on the Ovaro, which he had neglected to do before. But the pinto did not prick its ears or otherwise show alarm. He felt safe enough to treat himself to a second helping. As he was soaking up the last of the broth with a piece of bread, Lucy Harper cleared her throat.

"Who else could it have been but Max Perkins? I can't believe he would do something like that."

"He's fond of you, remember."

"But not fond enough to kill over me," Lucy insisted. "I know him. For all his faults, for all his gruff ways, he prides himself on making it to Oregon without losing an emigrant. Does that sound like someone who would murder from ambush?"

"There's no telling what a person will do." Fargo told her about the figure aiming a rifle in her direction.

"That settles it, then. It had to be someone else. Max Perkins would never harm me."

"Jealousy makes people do strange things," Fargo mentioned, "things they would never do when they are in their right mind."

"You don't understand. There is nothing between Max and me. We've never kissed. Never embraced. Never did anything like that. The friendliest I've been is to smile at him. He has no reason to be jealous."

"If you say so." But Fargo had known men to be jealous over women with no excuse other than the men liked them and they did not want another man to breathe the same air.

"You'll see. I intend to confront Mr. Perkins when we reach Fort Hall. If he lies, I will sense it, and there will be hell to pay."

Fargo did not deem it very wise of her but he did not say anything, for now. Taking his rifle, but leaving his saddle and bedroll by the fire, he headed for the trees to the west.

Lucy brought him to a halt with "Must you go so soon?"

"Would you rather we chewed the fat and took bullets in the back?" Fargo rejoined. She had no reply, and soon he was seated with his back to an oak and the Henry across his legs. It would be quite brisk by sunrise, but that was fine; it would help keep him awake.

Showing remarkable poise, Lucy went about her chores as if nothing out of the ordinary had occurred. She washed the pot and stored it and the tripod in the wagon; then she sat up mending a dress by firelight until shortly before midnight.

Several times Fargo caught her staring wistfully at him. When she finally turned in, he had to resist an urge to go over to the wagon and ask if she wanted company. It did not help that she lit a lantern, casting her shadow on the canvas, and then proceeded to shed her dress and slip into a nightgown.

Fargo smiled to himself. She had to know he could see her shadow. Any other time, the invitation would have sent him hastening across the clearing to her side. But not this night. Not with their lives at stake.

If Fargo thought the minutes crawled by earlier, they were snails now. He sat perfectly still for as long as he could, then changed position. The lantern had long since gone out, so he had the night, and the woods, to himself.

The Ovaro and the team animals were dozing. Fargo very much wanted to do the same but he yawned and shook his head back and forth to dispel spreading cobwebs of weariness.

Midnight came and went.

To keep awake Fargo thought about several ladies he had known on more than friendly terms. When his eyelids became leaden, he thought instead about the letter in his pocket. It had been sent by means of army channels, which showed that the civilian who sent it had influence with the military. In his mind's eye he once again read the contents:

Mr. Fargo,
My son has gone missing. I am offering ten thou-
sand dollars for his safe return. I have been as-
sured you are one of the best trackers in the

country, and that there is no one better for the job. Are you interested? If so, I await you at Fort Hall until the twelfth of next month.

Respectfully,
BENJAMIN ZARED

Short and to the point, and signed with a flourish. Fargo recollected hearing of Zared. Something about him being one of the wealthiest men in New York. Or was it New Jersey? Money made in freighting, if Fargo's memory served.

Fargo was glad to help out. But he had to wonder why Benjamin Zared had gone to the extraordinary trouble of sending for him when it would have been so much easier, and quicker, to find a tracker at Fort Hall or any of other settlements. To send all the way to Denver, when every minute the son was missing added to the probability he would never be found, struck Fargo as strange.

The reward was substantial. Ten thousand dollars was more than Fargo earned in a year. Hell, it was more than he earned in five years from scouting and the like.

Fargo had been to Fort Hall plenty of times. Everyone who took the Oregon Trail ended up stopping there to stock up on provisions. It was the last settlement before the Willamette Valley, and Portland.

A sound intruded on Fargo's reflection. The Ovaro had nickered. Instantly he was fully awake and fingering the Henry.

Something moved in the brush twenty yards or so to the northwest. Something bigger than a rabbit and noisier than a deer. It couldn't be the killer. The last time, the man had made no more noise than a Sioux or a Cheyenne warrior.

But it was damn sure someone, or *something*.

Fargo slowly stood and tucked the Henry to his side. Few wild animals blundered about at night like a boar in a china shop, not with so many predators abroad.

There was one animal, though, that did rove about at night with impunity. It had no natural enemies. Its size alone was proof against attack. Lord of all it surveyed, it was the only creature alive that need not fear other animals. Its might and ferocity were such that everything else fled at the sight or scent of it.

The crackling grew louder.

Fargo had his back to the tree and had done nothing to attract the creature's interest, yet it appeared to be making a beeline right for him. Suddenly the Henry did not feel adequate. He would rather have a buffalo gun. Or better yet, a cannon.

The next moment the darkness disgorged a monster. A thousand-pound-plus behemoth with a hump on its front shoulders, legs as stout as redwoods, and four-inch claws that could shred flesh as easily as Fargo's Arkansas toothpick sliced through soft wax.

A monarch of the mountains had come for a drink and found Fargo instead.

The grizzly snorted and growled and reared onto its hind legs.

3

Fargo froze. Any sudden movement might incite an attack, and the giant bear was so close that it would be on him before he could take three steps. He considered scrambling into the tree but he could not possibly climb beyond the brute's reach before it reached him. The smart thing was to wait and see what the grizzly did.

Grizzlies were notoriously unpredictable. Where one might attack without warning, another might flee at the mere scent of a human being.

This one did not flee. It sniffed loudly several times. Its sense of smell was sharp but not its vision, and it was possible the bear had not noticed Fargo yet.

Then the great head dipped and bestial eyes fixed on his, disabusing Fargo of any hope that the grizzly did not realize he was there. A rumbling growl issued from its cavernous maw, and teeth that could crush the thick leg bones of a buffalo glinted palely in the starlight like so many daggers.

Fargo fought an urge to bolt while slowly curling his trigger finger around the Henry's trigger. He did not want to shoot. The bear's brain was sheathed in a skull as thick as an old-time knight's helmet, while its heart and other vital organs were protected by thick layers of fat and muscle. Even at that range, the Henry might not bring it down.

The grizzly tilted its head as if it was not quite sure what to make of him. Again it growled, but not as loudly, and took a shuffling step nearer.

The bear's musky odor was strong in Fargo's nostrils, that sickly sweet sweat smell mixed with its fetid breath and the scent of blood. It had killed recently, unless Fargo missed his guess, and probably eaten what it killed, which meant it might not be hungry. Bears were forever ruled by their stomachs.

Fargo heard a hoof stamp, the Ovaro or one of the mules. The grizzly's massive head swung toward them but it did not charge. After a bit the bear dropped on all fours.

They were almost nose to nostrils when the grizzly halted. So close, the bear's breaths were like blasts from a blacksmith's bellows. So close, Fargo swore he could see a piece of flesh wedged between two of its teeth. So close, imminent death hovered over Fargo like the Reaper waiting to descend.

Then a miracle occurred. The grizzly sniffed again, and its upper lip curled. Suddenly it backed away, swung to the right, and plowed into the vegetation like a bull buffalo. The breaking and rending of limbs and brush continued for quite some time, until at last Fargo was alone with the dark and the trees and, wonder of wonders, alive and unscathed.

Fargo leaned back and smiled. Tension drained from him like water from a sieve. He almost laughed out loud, he was so relieved. But since bears were known to change their minds, he quickly rose and moved to a different tree and climbed to a convenient fork.

It wasn't comfortable but it was safer, and Fargo had a better view of the woods and the clearing. If the grizzly did change its mind, he would spot it well before it reached him.

Hours passed, and the forest was quiet. Along about four Fargo descended and crossed to the dead fire. Rekindling a few hot embers, he soon had flames licking hungrily at his hands as he held them out to warm them.

Dawn was not far off, and while Fargo was tired, he preferred to stay awake. He soon had the coffee left over from the night before on to boil. Undoing his bedroll, he draped a blanket over his shoulders and sat with his back against his saddle. He closed his eyes, intending to rest until the coffee was done, but the next thing he knew, he sat up to find the sun had risen and the new day begun.

Annoyed at himself, Fargo filled his cup. The coffee was too hot for him to drink. He blew on it, tried a tentative sip, and nearly burned his throat. Setting the cup down, he busied himself saddling the Ovaro.

He let Lucy sleep another half an hour, then went to the prairie schooner and rapped on the side. Apparently, in her drowsy state, she mistakenly thought she was still with the wagon train because she mumbled, "I will be out in a minute or two, Mr. Perkins. Please don't start the rest of the wagons without me."

Lucy's embarrassment when she poked her head out was comical. She blinked at Fargo, then at the clearing, and said sheepishly, "Oh my. I plumb forgot. How can that be?"

Fargo had fixed a cup of coffee for her. "Here. But I should warn you. I make coffee strong enough to float a horseshoe."

"Thank you." Lucy fluffed at her hair, then climbed down. "I must look a sight. The thing I dislike most about traveling by wagon is that people see you at your most unflattering."

"Any man would be proud to wake up to someone as pretty as you," Fargo soothed her anxiety.

"You say the nicest things." Lucy sipped, and smiled, and said, "I take it we had no visitors?"

"Only one, and it had four legs." Fargo did not elaborate.

"We wasted a whole night?" Lucy sadly shook her head. "What a shame. I'll never know what I missed."

"We're still breathing," Fargo said, and winked.

Laughing, Lucy sashayed to the fire. "I'll fix breakfast and we can be on our way."

"What's your hurry?" Fargo came up behind her, looped his free arm around her waist, and lightly nuzzled her neck. "We have all day."

"In broad daylight?" Lucy responded. "Besides, I'm a mess. My hair is a tangle and I haven't had a bath in ages. I just wouldn't feel right."

Fargo nodded toward the river. "There's all the water we need. And I've never exactly been shy."

"Go for a swim together?" Lucy's eyes sparkled at the suggestion but her upbringing prompted her to say, "What if someone came along and saw us? I would get a reputation worse than a dance hall dove."

"We'll find a spot where no one can see us," Fargo suggested.

Lucy scanned the river. "It's a tempting notion, I must admit. But I need a little private time to myself before you join me."

"Fine by me." Fargo did not ask why. Long ago he had learned that where women were concerned, private meant exactly that.

"I'll holler when I'm ready." Lucy hurried into the wagon and reappeared holding a towel and lye soap and a brush for her hair.

Fargo made a circuit of the clearing. He saw no sign of Perkins or anyone else, and since they had pulled off the trail, it was unlikely they would be disturbed by anyone happening by. Still, when Lucy called his name, he took the Henry along, and a blanket, besides.

She had gone around the next bend to a pool sheltered by a high bank and dense thickets. Her dress lay over a bush and she was in the river, crouching so the water was up to her neck. "I'm not so sure about this."

"We don't have to if you don't want to." When she did not say anything, Fargo removed his hat and stripped off his buckskin shirt.

"My, oh, my. I never suspected you had all those muscles."

Fargo unhitched his gun belt and placed it beside the Henry. Sitting, he tugged out of his boots, aware she was watching him intently. When he stood and started to peel his pants down, she let out a gasp. "Is something wrong?"

"No. It's just, I mean, well, I don't do this every day. I haven't seen many naked men. You will have to bear with me."

Her mention of "bear" caused Fargo to pause and scour the river. The grizzly was probably long gone, but just in case, he moved the Henry and the Colt closer to the water's edge before he waded in.

Lucy's gaze was glued to his body—or, rather, a part of his body not normally exposed to scrutiny. The pink tip of her tongue rimmed her full red lips and she said in a husky tone, "I can't believe I am doing this."

Fargo stopped when the water rose to just below his waist. The Snake was clear and clean and cold, not fouled with the excess of human habitation as many waterways and streams east of the Rockies. He splashed water on his chest and back. Then, inhaling, he held his breath and tucked at the knees. Goose bumps erupted all over him. He twisted, spied Lucy's pale legs, and launched himself at them underwater. She gave a start when he broke the surface next to her, and drew back with a hand to her throat.

"Oh, my! You scared me."

With glistening drops cascading from his body, Fargo placed his hands on her shoulders. To his mild surprise, she was quaking like a leaf. "If you are this afraid," he began.

"No," Lucy said, and impulsively pressed against him, her face against his chest, her eyes closed. "Be patient. I'm embarrassed, is all."

"You have nothing to be embarrassed about." Fargo

stroked her wet hair and slowly ran his hand down her back.

"That feels nice," Lucy said softly.

Fargo felt her tense as his fingers came to her back side. He let his hand rest there, while with his other hand he cupped her chin and raised her head. "Look at me."

"I'd rather not just yet if you don't mind."

Bending, Fargo pecked her lightly on the forehead, then on the tip of her nose, then on her chin. At each contact she uttered a tiny mew. He began to straighten but suddenly her eyes opened and she mashed her mouth against his, hard as could be. Her fingernails bit into his shoulders. She kissed him with an urgency that was as much panic as it was desire. Pulling back, Fargo grinned. "Whoa, there. Slow down. We have all the time in the world."

"I'm sorry. I'm not any good at this."

"Sure you are." Fargo covered her mouth with his, albeit as softly as a feather, and slowly parted her lips with his tongue. She hesitated for a few seconds. Then her mouth opened and her tongue met his in a velvet swirl accompanied by a deep moan of innermost longing.

Her breasts were cushioned against his chest. As their kiss deepened, Fargo covered one breast and gently squeezed. Her response was to voice a smothered cry and arch her back into a bow. He tweaked her nipple and felt it harden like a tack.

"Ohhhhhh," Lucy said when they broke for breath. "You make my senses swim. Do you know that?"

Fargo switched his hand to her other breast and his mouth to her neck, while he massaged and pinched her bottom. Gradually her body grew warmer, despite the chill water. Groaning, she locked her fingers in his hair and pulled so hard, she threatened to pull some out by the roots.

The effect on Fargo's manhood was to be expected.

He became as rigid as a flagpole. When he pressed his member against her thigh, she drew back as if it were a red-hot branding iron.

Clasping her hands, Fargo started to draw her toward shore and the blanket he had brought, but the moment his pole appeared out of the water, she stopped and stared in rapt fascination, almost as if she had never seen a man's organ before.

Fargo wanted to beat himself with a war club for not seeing the truth sooner. "Maybe this is not such a good notion," he offered so she could back out if she were so inclined.

"It's fine," Lucy said, much too quickly.

"We can do it some other time if you want," Fargo said, knowing full well that if the opportunity passed, she was unlikely to agree later.

"No, no, no," Lucy said, and bestowed a look on him that Fargo could only describe as pleading. "You don't understand. Please. I'm all right. I promise. We can't stop. Not after I've gone so far."

"It always helps when you make up your mind to do something," Fargo said, "to just do it." So saying, he took her hand, and before she could divine his purpose, he enfolded her fingers around his member.

Lucy's eyes grew as wide as walnuts and she turned to stone. "Goodness gracious! What am I supposed to do now?"

Fargo could not reply. A constriction had formed in his throat and he was tingling from head to toe.

"I never," Lucy breathed. Timidly, she moved her hand down a few inches and then back up again. "It's so smooth. Like glass or marble."

It was all Fargo could do to focus. His temples were throbbing. If he was not careful, he would explode prematurely.

"So smooth," Lucy repeated, running her fingertips the length of his manhood. "And look at how the veins stand out! That's a good thing, isn't it?"

It was a very good thing but Fargo was struggling to maintain control and did not answer her.

"I always thought they would be different," Lucy chattered on, "like the haft of a hammer. But yours is like a rake handle. Or a hoe."

To shut her up, Fargo kissed her. Lucy's ardor matched his. It was she who parted his lips with her tongue and delved her tongue deep into his mouth, never once letting go of his member. Fargo let her do as she pleased. It seemed to ease her nervousness.

"You kiss marvelously," Lucy complimented him. Panting for air, she nibbled his shoulder and his chest and ran her tongue across his throat to his left ear, which she nipped. At the same instant, her fingers cupped him, low down.

Fargo came close, so very close. His entire frame shook from his need for release, but gritting his teeth, he held back the deluge.

Now the moccasin was on the other foot—hers. "Are you all right?" Lucy asked. "Is the water too cold for your liking?"

Fargo scooped her into his arms and carried her to shore. He kicked the blanket to unravel it, and when it would not open as he wanted, he lowered her to a patch of grass instead. Not once did her hand leave him.

"Be gentle with me," Lucy whispered.

Although Fargo yearned to take her hard and fast, he stretched out beside her. Her breasts were slick with river water; several drops ringed a nipple. He licked them off, then licked and sucked both her nipples until her globes were heaving and she was rubbing her thigh against his.

"I want you," Lucy moaned.

Her hunger was mutual, but now that Fargo could think again, his body was once again under his full control. He kissed her, not once but a dozen times. His fingers explored every velvet nook and satiny cranny of her voluptuous contours. Her inner thighs were especially sensitive, and when he breathed into her ear, she wriggled and squirmed and dug her nails so deep into his biceps, she drew blood.

"Please," Lucy said, her eyes hooded with raw lust.

Fargo eased her onto her back and stretched a leg across hers. His palm on her knee, he rubbed slowly upward in small, enticing circles until he was near her core. When he touched her, she gasped and became completely still. He stroked her slit and she came up off the ground as if seeking to take wing. Her arms flew around his neck and she planted smoldering kisses on his face.

His next move was to insert a finger. At this, Lucy cried out, then bit him on the shoulder. She was not gentle; why should he be? Fargo drew his finger almost out, then plunged it up into her.

"Ahhhhhhhh!" Lucy's strawberry lips formed an O. Her eyelashes fluttered like tiny wings. She was nearly beside herself—even more so when Fargo added a second finger and thrust both in as far as they would go.

"More!" Lucy gushed. "I want more!"

Fargo obliged. He kissed, he licked, he rubbed, he stroked. He brought her to the brink and poised her there, her body a fine instrument he had tuned to a fever pitch. Then came the moment when he spread her legs wide and positioned himself on his knees between them. She watched in hungry anticipation as he rubbed his pole up and down on her womanhood, a prelude to inserting his member inch by gradual inch until he was in her to the hilt. Lucy shivered and shook and bit her lower lip, immersed in the delirium of blissful rapture.

Fargo adopted an ages-old rocking rhythm as natural to man as breathing. With his hands on her hips, he stroked with rising urgency until it had the desired effect.

Throwing her head back, Lucy Harper uttered an

inarticulate wail. Her thighs clamped tight, as did her inner walls. In great, throbbing waves of ecstasy, she spurted. The release drained her, and afterward she lay limp and soaked with perspiration. But if she thought they were done, she was mistaken. Fargo began to move his hips again.

"You haven't?" Lucy said in amazement, and another moan was drawn from her throat and borne on the breeze.

Fargo's own release was a long time coming. But at length he lay atop her heaving breasts, as spent as she was. Since he had not had much sleep the night before, he was soon dozing. How long he had slept he could not say, when shouts from the vicinity of the clearing snapped him to immediate wakefulness. He recognized one of the voices. Shaking Lucy, he whispered in her ear, "Get up and get dressed or you will really have something to be embarrassed about."

Sluggishly rising on an elbow, Lucy blinked in the bright sunlight and looked around in mild puzzlement. "What's that?"

More shouts served to enlighten her, and presently they were both fully dressed and hurrying back along the river to the prairie schooner.

There were four of them.

The wagon boss was cupping his hands to his mouth to shout Lucy's name again. Lowering them, he said gruffly, "So there you are, Miss Harper! I was afraid hostiles got their heathen hands on you, which would serve you right, in my opinion."

Lucy stiffened in indignation. "You came all the way back to insult me? Is that why you are here, Mr. Perkins?"

"I came back because I was worried, and some of your fellow emigrants came along." Perkins motioned at the other men.

The oldest of the three, a kind gentleman in homespun, removed a floppy hat and smiled at Lucy. "My

44

missus fretted all night long, Miss Harper. You and her have become good friends, and she was terrified something had happened to you." He glanced at Fargo. "She couldn't understand why you stayed out here all by your lonesome."

"I appreciate Martha's concern, Mr. Gelford," Lucy said. "I certainly did not intend to worry all of you. A wheel broke, is all, and I couldn't reach Fort Hall before nightfall."

"Who is this?" a much younger emigrant asked, bobbing his chin at Fargo.

"A friend," Lucy said, and let it go at that.

Gelford put his hat back on. "We'll escort you on in, if you have no objections, ma'am. My Martha will blister my ears if we don't."

Lucy bestowed a smirk on Max Perkins. "Am I to gather I am still a member of the wagon train?"

"Of course," Perkins responded. "What gave you the idea you weren't? You paid through to Oregon, and by God, that's where I'll guide you unless you quit the train before we get there."

Fargo moved to his saddle. "I reckon I'll be getting along, then."

Lucy turned, her face inscrutable. But in her eyes shone genuine affection. "Whatever you think is best. I want to thank you for your help with the wheel, and looking after me. Maybe we'll run into each other again."

"Maybe," Fargo said. While the emigrants and the wagon boss hitched the team, he saddled the Ovaro. Forking leather, he reined over to where Lucy was talking to Gelford. "It's been a pleasure," he said, touching his hat brim.

"That it has, Mr. Fargo," Lucy said formally, and smiled.

It turned out they were closer to the settlement than Fargo thought. It had grown since his last visit. Around the old Hudson's Bay trading post had sprouted cabins and frame houses and the makings of an eventual town.

The influx of gold-hungry pilgrims accounted for a lot of the growth. Fort Hall was a stopping-off point on their push into the interior. The trading post and a new general store were doing a brisk business.

In a postscript to the letter, Fargo had been advised to ask at the post for Benjamin Zared. He was directed to a nearby boardinghouse. A hitch rail out in front was nearly full.

A sign advertised *Mrs. Rogers's Boardinghouse. Reasonable rates.* Under it had been attached a shingle which read *All rooms have been taken.*

The house was so new it smelled of fresh paint. Several chairs had been placed on a narrow porch, and each was occupied. Fargo was halfway up the path when the three men in the chairs rose and moved to block him from entering. Stopping short, he hooked his thumbs in his gun belt. "Would one of you happen to be Benjamin Zared?"

The three were cut from the same cloth; lean, hard, and cold, dressed in black suits, black hats, and black boots. "We work for Mr. Zared," the foremost said. He had a hooked nose and a thin mouth, and he reeked of arrogance. "I'm Pike Driscoll, his chief bodyguard. Who might you be?"

Fargo told them, and showed the letter.

Driscoll read it and handed it back, then said over a shoulder, "Jim, run up and let Mr. Zared know this one has arrived."

As the underling hastened inside, Fargo asked, "Why does Zared need protecting? Is someone after him?"

A suggestion of a sneer curled Pike Driscoll's mouth. "You have no idea who Mr. Zared is, do you?"

"I've heard he has money," Fargo admitted.

"For your information, Benjamin Zared is one of

the richest men in the whole country," Driscoll boasted. "He has holdings in nearly every state."

"That doesn't explain why he needs men like you."

"Let's just say that Mr. Zared has made a few enemies here and there," Driscoll said. "He's had to step on a few toes, and those who get stepped on don't like it much. So he has men like me to protect him. A lot of men like me. And he pays us really well to see to it he doesn't come to harm."

The bodyguard who had gone in was back shortly. "Mr. Zared will see him, Pike. We can take him right in."

"Thanks, Walker." Driscoll motioned. "You heard the man, buckskin. Let's not keep Mr. Zared waiting."

The man's tone grated on Fargo like fingernails on a chalkboard. "I'll make you a deal," he said. "If you don't call me buckskin, I won't call you dumb as a stump."

"My apologies," Driscoll said with a sneer. "I didn't realize you had such a sensitive nature."

Fargo started up the steps to the porch but stopped when Driscoll thrust out a hand.

"Not so fast. First we take your hardware."

"No."

"You can't go in to see Mr. Zared heeled," Driscoll said. "No one can. It's a rule he made."

"Then I won't see him." After his clash with the rifleman the night before, Fargo was not about to go anywhere in Fort Hall unarmed. He had not caught anyone shadowing him since he arrived, but that did not mean the killer wasn't watching him at that very moment. The street was filled with people.

"Yes, you will," Pike Driscoll insisted.

Fargo turned to go but the bodyguard came down the steps and gripped him by the sleeve.

"Didn't you hear me, buckskin? Either you walk in or we carry you in. Which will it be?"

4

Skye Fargo was only willing to abide so much. "You don't leave a man much choice," he remarked.

Pike Driscoll came to the edge of the porch. "It's nothing personal. It's my job. Mr. Zared wants to see you, so in you go." He beckoned impatiently. "Let's have that six-gun."

"If you insist." Fargo made a show of slowly gripping it and easing it from his holster. "Here you go."

Driscoll smirked and bent lower. "I knew you could be reasonable."

"Reasonable as hell," Fargo said. In a streak he slammed the barrel against the bodyguard's temple.

Caught off guard, Pike Driscoll was knocked against the rail. His legs splayed from under him and he melted onto his side.

The other two men in black were a shade late in reacting. Both clawed for revolvers under their jackets but froze at the click of the Colt's hammer.

"I wouldn't," Fargo cautioned. He carefully relieved both of their artillery and tossed the weapons into a flower bed.

"Driscoll will have your hide for this, mister," one predicted.

"Let him try," Fargo said. He commanded them to pick Driscoll up and carry their unconscious burden indoors. A narrow hall brought them to a sitting room. On a settee sat a white-haired gentleman with bushy side whiskers. He wore an immaculately tailored navy frock coat with a striped vest and striped trousers. Across from him in a chair perched an attractive brunette, about thirty or so, in a floral silk dress. They were talking in hushed, earnest tones. At the sight of the bodyguards they fell silent, and the white-haired man demanded, "What is the meaning of this? What happened to Driscoll?"

Fargo was behind the bodyguards, unseen. Now he strode past them, the Colt level at his waist.

Unruffled, the white-haired man looked him up and down. "Well, isn't this interesting."

The woman put a hand to her throat and nearly came out of her chair. "My word! What is going on here?"

Twirling the Colt into his holster, Fargo responded, "Some people don't know how to take no for an answer."

"You must be Skye Fargo," the white-haired gentleman said.

"And you must be Benjamin Zared." Fargo shifted so no one could slink up on him unnoticed from the hall. "I came a long way at your request, and I don't take kindly to the reception."

Zared addressed the bodyguard named Walker. "Jim, please be so kind as to explain." Zared listened, then sighed and spread his hands apologetically toward Fargo. "My sincere regrets over how you were treated. In my defense, Mr. Driscoll was only doing what I pay him to do, namely, safeguard my person from those who would harm me. Long ago I gave a standing order that no one is to be admitted into my presence armed."

A groan from Driscoll signaled his return to consciousness. Snorting like a mad boar, he shook off the men holding him and turned toward Fargo. "Damn you! You had no call to do that! You're a dead man—do you hear me?" His face was contorted in fury and his hand was poised to flash under his jacket.

Fargo was sure the bodyguard would draw on him until Benjamin Zarek said softly, "Mr. Driscoll, that will be quite enough."

Pike Driscoll deflated like a punctured waterskin and snapped to attention, as if he were a soldier on a parade ground.

"Sir?"

"I must ask you to forgo your natural impulse. Mr. Fargo is here at my request, remember? If you must assign blame for the misunderstanding, blame me. I should have instructed you to admit him without disarming him."

"Whatever you say, sir," Driscoll said. "He took me by surprise. It won't happen again."

"The three of you may leave," Zared dismissed the boydguards. "My daughter and I desire some time alone with my guest."

Fargo glanced at the woman. She did bear a certain resemblance to Zared, especially around the eyes and in the shape of her face. She also filled out the smart dress she wore almost as nicely as Lucy Harper had filled out hers.

Benjamin Zared rose to offer his hand. "Let us try this again, shall we? I am delighted you came." He indicated his daughter. "This is Edrea. She will be my liaison with you and the rest on this venture. If there is anything you need, anything at all, you only have to ask her."

Fargo was more interested in his host's other comment. "That's twice you've mentioned 'the rest.' I take it I'm not the only one you sent for?"

"Have a seat and I'll enlighten you." Zared waited, and after Fargo was comfortable, he sank back down on the settee. "To answer your question, no, you are not the only one. I trust you won't hold it against me, but with my son's life at stake, half measures were not called for."

"About your son—" Fargo began.

Zared held up a hand. "Please indulge me. Rather than repeat myself to each of you, I would rather assemble everyone here in, say, an hour, and present my proposition then."

"The others don't know any more than you do," Edrea Zared interjected. "One of them arrived nearly a week ago but the rest only in the past few days."

"Their timing has been most fortuitous," Benjamin Zared said. "Perhaps it is an omen things are finally going my way." He paused. "What can one more hour hurt, after all those you spent traveling?"

"In the meantime," Edrea said, "we have a room reserved for you on the second floor. Would you like me to show it to you?" She rose without awaiting a reply and stepped to the hallway. "This way, please."

Fargo followed her up a flight of stairs. On the landing were two more men in black, lounging against the wall. When they saw Edrea, they straightened. Both bowed their chins as she passed.

"You have them well trained," Fargo observed.

"Power and wealth demand a degree of respect, don't you think?"

"I wouldn't know," Fargo said. "I've never been the one and never had the other."

"I, on the other hand, have never known any other life. My father was rich when I was born and he has only become richer. I pray that when my times comes, I can do as well as he has in increasing the family's fortune."

"You must be worried sick about your brother."

An innocent comment on Fargo's part, yet Edrea Zared nearly broke stride. "Of course I'm worried. But I am also mad. Between you and me, he had no business going off into the mountains. Thanks to him, my father and I have been put to a lot of bother."

Fargo thought it strange she was more mad than

upset, but sisters and brothers were often at one another's throats. "Do you really think he is still alive after all this time?"

"Who can say? My father does, and that's what counts." Edrea stopped next to a door. "Here we are." A key was in the latch. She turned it and held the door open for him to enter.

As boardinghouses went, the room was nicely furnished. Fargo patted the quilt on the bed and noticed the washbasin was full. "I've seen worse."

"I am happy you are pleased," Edrea said without a shred of genuine sincerity. "Now if you will excuse me, I have preparations to make." She smiled and backed out, closing the door after her.

Fargo stripped and shook his buckskins out the window to rid them of the dust they had accumulated. His beard needed a trim but his razor was in his saddlebags and he did not feel like fetching it. Instead, he dressed and lay on his back on the bed with his hands behind his head. He would use the time to rest.

A light rap on his door dictated otherwise. Fargo thought maybe Edrea had forgotten to tell him something but it was someone else entirely. "Well, I'll be damned!" he declared. "Don't tell me they offered you the job, too?"

The man who entered was not nearly as tall or as broad across the shoulders as Fargo, but in other respects they were much alike; the man wore buckskins, he had a dark beard, his skin had been bronzed by countless hours under the burning sun, and he carried himself much like a panther. He was not armed. "As I live and breathe!" he exclaimed, breaking into a smile. "They'll let anyone in here."

"Kip Weaver," Fargo said.

"It's been a while, hoss."

The fraternity of frontier scouts was a small one, the number of those who were exceptional even smaller. Kip Weaver was widely considered as good as Fargo. A Pennsylvania farm boy, he came west with his parents, who were massacred by the Sioux. An old frontiersman by the name of Brent Hollings took Weaver under his wing and molded the youngster into a scout. Later Hollings gave up the ghost, dying with his boots off in a house of ill repute when his heart gave out. Ever since, Kip Weaver had done the old scout proud.

"Who else is here?" Fargo asked.

"You're the first I've seen, only because I happened to spot you coming down the hall with the lovely Miss Zared." Kip folded his arms and leaned against the wall. "They've kept me pretty much in the dark, and I can't say as I like it."

"Weren't you working for the army the last we met?" Fargo recollected. That had been at Fort Laramie over a year ago.

"The soldier boys will just have to get by without me for a spell." Weaver grinned. "It isn't every day I have a chance at ten thousand dollars."

"I never knew you cared that much for money," Fargo said, only partly in jest.

"Anyone who doesn't is a fool," Kip declared hotly. Then a smile split his sun-bronzed face. "What say we find a saloon and treat ourselves to some coffin varnish? On me?"

"Didn't they tell you? Benjamin Zared wants us to meet with him in about forty minutes," Fargo mentioned.

"That's forty minutes we could spend drinking." Kip grinned, then became serious. "Between you and me, hoss, I can't say I've been all that impressed with Zared and his crew."

"People say he is as rich as Midas."

"And bossy, too. He always wants everyone at his beck and call. I had better things to do than sit around twiddling my thumbs waiting for him to explain things."

"Maybe we can have that drink after," Fargo suggested.

"I'd like that. Lord knows, I could use one. I've tried to swear off while I've been here but it hasn't been easy. A man gets used to his creature comforts." Weaver chuckled and winked.

If his friend had one failing, Fargo recalled, it was that Kip Weaver was much too fond of whiskey. Fargo liked to drink as much as the next man, but for Weaver, drinking had become a religion. Nearly every night, Kip could be found in a saloon, drinking himself into a near-stupor. Fargo hated to admit it, but Weaver was one of the few persons on the face of the earth who could drink him under the table, and still go on guzzling.

"We'll do it up right later," Kip said eagerly. "Turn this settlement upside down and give them something to remember us by, eh?"

"Still the same old Kip," Fargo remarked.

"You almost make it sound like that's a bad thing," Weaver said good-naturedly. He clapped Fargo on the shoulder. "Hellfire and tarnation, it's grand to see you again! Gossip has it you nearly lost your hide more than a few times since we shared a bottle last."

"I've heard the same about you."

Weaver moved to a chair and straddled it. "The damn Piegans nearly had my hair a few months back. Shot my horse out from under me with an arrow, then ran me ragged for pretty near a week. The war party just wouldn't give up. I had to use every trick I know, and then some, to shake them off my scent."

The Piegans, as Fargo was aware, had been generally unfriendly since the days of Lewis and Clark. Lewis and some companions had caught several Piegan warriors trying to steal their guns and powder, and in the ensuing struggle, one Piegan was stabbed to death and another was shot. As a result, the Piegans were always on the lookout for white intruders in their territory, and woe to the white man who fell into their vengeful clutches. They never forgot a grudge.

"At one point I had gone so long without food and water," Weaver was saying, "that I was as weak as a newborn kitten, and near delirious. They surrounded me in a patch of woods." He gave a little shudder at the recollection. "I crawled inside a log to hide. There I was, helpless, with those bloodthirsty devils all around me, poking their red noses into every bush and thicket. I thought for sure they would find me, and I'd end my days burned at the stake, or maybe tied down over an ant hill, or skinned alive and left for the buzzards and the coyotes."

Fargo grunted. The same fate hung over the head of each scout like a guillotine's blade about to fall. He had come close to experiencing them on more than one occasion.

"I tell you, hoss, it sure put the fear of the Almighty in me," Kip Weaver said. "I could have cried, I was so scared."

Fargo laughed at that. Weaver was one of the most fearless men he knew.

"I'm serious. When I realized they had gone on by the log without finding me, I laid there whimpering like a baby, I was so happy."

"We all have close shaves," Fargo said.

"Some are closer than others. But hell, that's the life we've chosen, isn't it? We have to take the good with the deadly, the close shaves with the spectacular sunsets."

"The important thing is you're still breathing."

"And I aim to go on doing so for a good many years yet," Weaver declared. "I'd like to end my days whittling in a rocking chair."

Fargo never gave much thought to how he would end his days. When it came, it came, and there was nothing he could do about it.

"I never used to think about dying much"—Weaver

would not let it drop—"but I do now practically all the time. Pitiful, huh?"

"A scare will do that."

"Good old Skye," Weaver said. "How you have lasted so long with that sympathetic nature of yours is a mystery."

"How's that?" Fargo asked.

"The habit you have of always putting yourself in other people's moccasins. You're hard as gristle on the outside but inside you're mush, and if you're not real careful, one day the mush will do you in."

"Thanks heaps," Fargo said, and they both laughed.

"Damn, it's good to see you!" Weaver reiterated. "We have a lot of catching up to do."

Which was exactly how they spent the next half hour. Fargo related his recent escapades, and Kip Weaver recounted some of his. They were so engrossed in their talk that when a knock came on the door, Fargo was surprised at how much time had gone by.

It was Edrea Zared. "So here you are, Mr. Weaver. I was just at your room and you weren't there."

"It's hard to be in two places at once, ma'am," Weaver teased her.

"I trust the two of you can find your way to the sitting room. My father expects you in five minutes. Be punctual."

As Edrea walked off, Kip Weave smirked and said quietly, "There's one rose that has never been plucked, I warrant. Comes from having ice in her veins."

"There could be more to her than she lets on," Fargo said.

Weaver chuckled. "When it comes to females, you're worse than a bull elk in rut." Laughing, he clapped Fargo on the back.

The two bodyguards were still on the landing. Downstairs, in the hall, stood Pike Driscoll and Walker. Driscoll glared at Fargo but Fargo ignored him.

Extra chairs had been brought to the sitting room. Benjamin Zared had the settee to himself, his arms spread out across the back, sitting tall and straight and looking for all the world like a foreign potentate about to hold a royal audience. His daughter was in a chair to his left, facing the rest, a sheath of papers on her lap.

Of the three others present, Fargo recognized one, a tall, morose man in a buckskin jacket and brown pants, distinguished by the fact that where his nose should be there was an oval leather patch. His name was James Smith but he was more commonly known as No-Nose Smith, thanks to a run-in with hostiles. A tomahawk had taken off his nose and part of his cheek, leaving him scarred emotionally as well as physically. For where before James Smith had been an easygoing, likable rogue who spent all his idle hours in the company of willing doves, after his mutilation, Smith became grim and taciturn and avoided human contact except as it was required in his capacity as a scout.

Now Smith nodded at Fargo and Kip Weaver, all they could expect from him by way of a greeting even though they had known him since before the mishap.

The other two were strangers. Right away Fargo saw that they were related; their features were identical. The same sandy hair, the same pointed chins, the same pouty mouths and green eyes, the same wealth of freckles. They had to be brother and sister. Both were in their twenties, Fargo judged. The man wore a green shirt and britches and a coonskin cap like the cap once favored by the famous bear hunter and hero of the Alamo, Davy Crockett. His sister wore identical clothes, but instead of a coonskin cap, she wore a cap made of fox fur complete with the head and tail still attached.

"Come in, come in, gentlemen," Benjamin Zared urged, pointing at two empty chairs. After they sat, he cleared his throat and looked at each of them in turn. "First, let me thank each of you for answering my letter. I sent out other notices but only you five had the courtesy to show up."

"Shucks, Mr. Zared," the man in the coonskin cap said with a distinct Southern drawl, "courtesy had nothin' to do with it. Silky and me hanker after that fortune you're offerin'."

"Honesty. I like that," Benjamin Zared said. "Before we go any further, I should introduce everyone for the benefit of those who might not have met."

The brother and sister were Billy Bob and Silky Mae Pickett. They hailed from South Carolina. They always smiled, the two of them, as if life were a source of great humor. When Silky Mae was introduced, she smiled at Fargo and gave him the sort of scrutiny he was more accustomed to getting from ladies on city street corners late at night.

"So you're Fargo? We've heard about you. Folks say you're Daniel Boone, Kit Carson and Jim Bridger all rolled into one." Silky Mae had pearly-white teeth she showed constantly. "I doubt you have heard of us, but down south we have somethin' of a reputation."

"The two of you?" Kip Weaver said.

Silky Mae flashed him a tight smile. "Why, yes, Mr. Weaver, the two of us. Or is it that you think a woman can't track and shoot as good as a man?"

Billy Bob Pickett snickered. "You best be careful, Mr. Weaver. My sister doesn't like it none when her gender is belittled. She can hold her own against any man, and I should know."

"No offense meant, ma'am," Kip Weaver assured her. "It's just that we don't meet many females in our profession."

"No offense taken," Silky Mae said, but her tone gave Fargo the impression that she was less than pleased. "And yes, most women would rather spend their lives chained to a stove or a washtub. Not me. I like my freedom too much to ever shackle myself with a husband." She shifted her attention to Fargo. "I hear tell you're the same way. They say you've bedded more fillies than there are blades of grass on the prairie."

"Behave, sis," Billy Bob chided her.

"I'm only repeatin' what I've heard," Silky Mae said with feigned innocence. "If Mr. Fargo takes exception, he's welcome to put me in my place."

Before Fargo could respond, Benjamin Zared leaned forward on the settee. "If you don't mind, and even if you do, can we restrict ourselves to the issue at hand? I didn't ask you to come all this way to listen to accounts of amorous adventures. You're here because I am in dire straits and need the help of the most skilled trackers money can buy."

"Your son went missing, your letter said." This from No-Nose Smith.

Benjamin Zared nodded. "None of you have ever been a parent, so you cannot possibly appreciate how deeply the loss of a child hurts. It is a heartache beyond all understanding."

"You think your son is dead?" Kip Weaver asked. "Then what do you need us for?"

"I don't know whether Gideon is or he isn't," Zared said. "If he isn't, my joy will know no bounds. If he is, then I want you to find his remains and bring them back to me." His face clouded. "And if he was slain by hostiles, find out which tribe and I will wipe them out—every last buck, squaw, and nit."

Grief made a person say things they otherwise wouldn't. Fargo was willing to excuse his host's comment on that basis. But something told him it was no idle threat, and exterminating a tribe was something he would never stand for.

Zared happened to be looking at him, and something in Fargo's expression must have given his thoughts away because the distraught father quickly said, "I don't mean that literally, of course. It's emotion talking. If my son has been killed, it's only natural I would want those responsible to pay."

"I sure would if he were my boy," Billy Bob Pickett said.

"You can wipe out all the redskins you want, Mr. Zared," his sister chimed in. "We're hill folk. Where we come from, people live by the feud, and have for hundreds of years. We've lost kin to other clans and made them pay. We wouldn't begrudge you doin' the same. No, sir."

"I would," Fargo said.

The Picketts regarded him with amusement, and Billy Bob said, "You're an Injun lover—is that it? You would let a pack of red heathens get away with spillin' white blood?"

"We don't know what happened to him yet."

Silky Mae nodded. "That's true. But I must say you are a powerful disappointment. Any white man who would side with redskins ain't much of a man at all."

5

"That will be quite enough," Benjamin Zared said. "Petty squabbles are pointless. It's my boy we must concentrate on."

No-Nose Smith stirred. "Suppose you tell us more about him, and how he came to go missing."

"Gladly," Benjamin said, and bowed his white mane in sorrow. "Part of the blame is mine. I didn't take him seriously enough. I assumed he would be content to follow in my footsteps but that wasn't good enough for Gideon. He always had to do things his way."

"Gideon?" Silky Mae repeated. "That's a pretty name. I like it."

Benjamin Zared either did not hear her or chose to overlook her comment. "As all of you are no doubt aware, I am quite wealthy. I inherited a small fortune, then built it up until I'm richer than most people ever dream of being."

"Lucky you," Billy Bob interrupted.

"Luck had nothing to do with it, boy," Benjamin said curtly. "I worked damn hard to get where I am. Eighteen hours a day, seven days a week. Sweat and savvy, that's my secret."

"Was your son a hard worker, too?" Kip Weaver inquired.

Benjamin's head lifted. "It would please me immensely if you would refrain from referring to Gideon in the past tense. Until we can prove beyond a shadow of a doubt that he's gone, I will continue to think of him as alive."

Silky Mae said sarcastically, "Your boy wasn't content bein' rich? What was wrong with him? Was he addlepated?"

"He wanted to be his own man, earn his own wealth," Zared said. "He needed to prove to himself that he could stand on his own two feet."

"Which he did by traipsin' off into the wilds?" Billy Bob thought it hilarious, and his sister joined in his mirth.

"I'll thank you to keep personal comments about my son to yourselves," Benjamin said sternly. "I grant you he made a mistake but I won't sit here and hear him insulted. Understand me?"

"Sure, old man, sure," Billy Bob Pickett responded. "For ten thousand dollars we can be as quiet as mice."

Edrea had listened to enough. "You will refer to my father as Mr. Zared, not 'old man,' or I will have our bodyguards escort you from the settlement with instructions to shoot you on sight if you ever come anywhere near us."

Silky Mae bristled. "Now you just hold on there, missy! We don't take kindly to threats."

"*Enough!*" Benjamin Zared came off the settee with his big fists clenched. "Keep civil tongues in your heads, you and your brother, or you will answer to me." He practically shouted, and on hearing him, in rushed Pike Driscoll and Walker with their hands under their black jackets.

"Is there a problem, sir?" Driscoll asked.

"Nothing I can't handle."

From the way Zared said it, Fargo didn't doubt for a second that he would make a formidable enemy. Something to keep in mind, he told himself.

"Very well." Driscoll was disappointed. "But if we can be of any help, you only have to call us."

"Do you think I don't know that?" Benjamin Zared

snapped. Composing himself with an effort, he sat back down. Edrea reached over to pat his hand, and he smiled and squeezed her fingers. "Now, then, where was I? Oh, yes." He focused on No-Nose Smith. "My son heard about the gold finds on Orofino Creek and became convinced that if others could strike it rich, so could he. Against my express wishes, he decided to penetrate deeper into the mountains than anyone has ever gone before. I tried to talk him out of it. I pointed out the many dangers but he refused to heed. The young, Mr. Smith, always think they know better than their elders."

"He went alone?" Smith asked.

"No. I wanted him to take nine or ten bodyguards along but he would not hear of it. Gideon and his best friend, Asa Chaviv, left Fort Hall nearly two months ago, and that was the last anyone has seen of them."

"Don't forget Tabor," Edrea said.

"Who?" from Silky Mae Pickett.

Benjamin appeared annoyed by his daughter's mention of the name. "Tabor Garnet, my son's betrothed."

Fargo was stunned, and he was not the only one.

"Wait a minute," Kip Weaver said. "A woman has gone missing, too? And you didn't think to mention her until just now?"

"I would have gotten around to it."

A strained silence descended, broken when Edrea Zared nervously coughed and said, "Please don't misconstrue. My father is concerned for Miss Garnet's welfare, too. And that of Mr. Chaviv. They both visited our home many times, and my brother planned to eventually take Miss Garnet for his wife."

"So we have three greenhorns to find, not just one," No-Nose Smith said. "This changes things."

"It changes nothing," Benjamin Zared disagreed. "The ten thousand goes to whoever finds my son alive. It's that simple."

Kip Weaver's brow furrowed. "What if we only find Miss Garnet? Or that Chaviv fella?"

"I repeat," Benjamin said. "The ten thousand dollar reward pertains specifically and exclusively to my son."

The implication troubled Fargo. Essentially, Zared was saying that he did not give a damn about the other two. Fargo mentioned as much.

"Why do you people persist in putting words in my mouth?" Zared took exception. "If you find my son's companions I will be as pleased as can be, but it is not the same as finding my son."

Edrea came to her father's defense. "No, it is not. Honestly, gentlemen, and you, too, Miss Pickett. You make it sound as if it is wrong for a grieving father to yearn to learn the fate of his only son. Of course he cares about Tabor and Asa, but they are not his children. What purpose would it serve for my father to offer a reward for them when their own families are not offering one? Try to look at this logically and you will realize my father is not an ogre."

Silky Mae Pickett shrugged. "It makes no difference to me, sweetie. Ten thousand is still more money than I've seen in my lifetime, and I'll do whatever it takes to get my hands on it."

Fargo was bothered by something else. "Do you want us to work together or separate?"

Benjamin Zared leaned back. "My business enterprises have taught me that the secret to success is competition. Were I to offer a lump sum to all of you, it would lessen your incentive. You are to work alone. The first one to find my son gets the ten thousand. Everyone else goes home empty-handed."

"Hold your horses." Billy Bob came out of his chair. "My sister and me always work as a pair. *Always*," he stressed. "We wouldn't split up for the Almighty. We sure as blazes won't split up for you."

"He's right," Silky Mae confirmed. "We do it together or we don't do it at all."

"Suit yourselves," Benjamin said. "You may head back to South Carolina whenever you wish. I still have the other three."

No-Nose Smith also rose. "No, you don't. This is loco, mister. Anyone missing for two months in this neck of the country is a pile of bleached bones by now. You're asking the impossible."

"I agree," Kip Weaver said. "We're trackers, not miracleworkers. I won't waste my time on a wild-goose chase."

"Sorry, Zared," Fargo said, "but they're right. I'd like to help you find out what happened to your son but you're going about it all wrong." He started toward the hall with the others but a plaintive cry from Benjamin Zared brought them to a stop.

"*Please!* Don't go! You don't realize how much it means to me." Zared's eyes were misting and his big frame shook from the intensity of his emotions. Collecting himself, he motioned at the chairs. "I beg you. Sit back down. If I have offended you, I apologize."

Billy Bob Pickett shrugged. "I reckon it won't hurt to listen some more." He and his sister returned to their seats.

No-Nose Smith stayed by the door. "I'll hear you out but I'm not making any promises."

"Me either," Kip Weaver said.

Fargo reclaimed his chair and folded his arms across his chest. He had come this far; he might as well see it through.

"Very well, then," Benjamin Zared said. "If the Picketts want to work together, I have no objections. In fact, you can work with one another as you please. I will pay each of you five thousand dollars whether you find my son or his mortal remains, with an extra five thousand to whoever actually does." Zared paused. "What do you say? It's as fair as I can make it."

"Five thousand is a nice amount," Silky Mae said. "Ten thousand is even better."

Edrea Zared was not happy by the unfolding events. "You sure are a greedy one."

"At least I ain't stingy with what money I have," Silky Mae rebutted. "Your pa is one of the richest jaspers around. His pride and joy disappears, and all he offers is a measly five grand? If it were my boy, I'd pay any amount."

"That's easy to say when you don't have any," Edrea said testily.

"Now, now," Benjamin said. "She has a point, daughter. Five thousand does sound stingy, doesn't it? Very well. I will pay each of you five thousand dollars for your participation, and an extra twenty to whoever finds my son." He smiled at Silky Mae Pickett. "Is that to your liking?"

Her eyes lit like candles and she and her brother giggled like kids just given their heart's fondest desire. "I'll say it is! And don't you fret none, Mr. Zared. For that much, Billy Bob and me will turn this whole countryside upside down. You wait and see if we don't."

"Twenty thousand?" Kip Weaver whistled. "That would give me a tidy nest egg for when I'm too old to sit a horse."

"With that much, I could—" No-Nose Smith began, then did not finish his remark. "Count me in, Mr. Zared. I'll find your son or die trying."

Benjamin Zared smiled. "That's four out of five. How about you, Mr. Fargo? You are conspicuous by your silence."

Fargo could use the money. Poker and doves were costly habits. But he could not shake the feeling that there was more involved than met the eye. "I can't quite make up my mind," he admitted.

"What is there to think about? Twenty thousand dollars is a small fortune, is it not?"

"That it is," Fargo said. And it would buy him a seat at a high-stakes poker game in Saint Louis held each October, where if he won, he stood to pocket half a million dollars. He had long wanted to enter but never had the fee.

"Well?" Edrea Zared prompted. "Don't keep my father in suspense."

"I'll do it," Fargo said.

Relief etched Benjamin Zared's face. "I am grateful. Between the five of you, my son will be found. I'm sure of it." He sat back on the settee. "The next issue, then, is how soon you can depart. Keep in mind I will pay for whatever provisions you require. That includes mounts and packhorses."

"You don't say," Billy Bob said, and winked at his sister. "We can use a couple of pack animals."

No-Nose Smith said, "I can be ready to head out at daybreak."

"Same here," Kip Weaver threw in.

"I take it all of you can?" Benjamin Zared beamed. "Excellent. Edrea will take care of you from here on out. Any questions, talk to her. I have business matters to attend to." Standing, he came to each of them and shook their hands.

Fargo found the tycoon's grip surprisingly strong.

"My highest hopes rest in you," Zared said quietly so none of others would hear. "Every officer I talked to gave you a glowing recommendation. They say you are more at home in the wilds than you are among your own kind."

"I wouldn't go that far." Fargo liked the scenic splendor of the wide-open spaces, true, but saloon doves had a scenic splendor of their own, which he admired just as much.

"In any event, the best of luck to you," Benjamin

said. To them all he said, "Take care out there. I don't want any of you to come to harm."

The warning was justified. As Fargo was aware, the country north of Fort Hall was largely unexplored. The gold seekers streaming in from points east tended to concentrate where there was gold to be found. The rest of the wilderness was unknown and unmapped, and that much more dangerous.

Kip Weaver and No-Nose Smith were waiting for him on the porch.

"We thought you might like to wash the dust of the trail down before we buy our supplies and whatnot," Kip said. "There's a saloon near the trading post that doesn't water down its whiskey and has the friendliest fillies this side of the Divide."

It was a little early for Fargo to indulge, but he said, "Why not?"

"What do you make of Zared?" Kip asked.

"He's accustomed to getting his own way," Fargo said. "Men like that can be dangerous."

"I don't trust him," No-Nose said. "He hides a lot, and men who hide how they feel are as liable to slit your throat as not."

"I agree with both of you," Kip said, "which makes me wonder why in God's name we agreed to his proposition."

"It's the son and his friends," Fargo said. "They deserve to be found."

No-Nose commented, "A man makes his own bed. He should take the lice without complaint. It's the girl I'm thinking of."

Kip grinned and poked Smith's arm. "You always did have a soft spot for the fairer sex, James."

"My ma raised me to treat women special," Smith responded. "I'm not one of those who can bed them and leave them." He gave Fargo a pointed look.

"Now don't start that again," Kip said. "At Fort Laramie you two nearly came to blows, as I recall."

So did Fargo. No-Nose tended to treat all females as queens and did not take it kindly when other men did not show the same respect.

"Women are God's gift to creation," No-Nose said in all seriousness. "They tend us when we're sick. They feed us and mend our clothes and keep us warm on cold nights. Without them life wouldn't be worth living."

Fargo started to tell him how silly that was, but Kip quickly interjected, "You missed your calling, James. You should be a Bible thumper instead of a scout."

"Don't make fun of me."

Kip sighed and rolled his eyes at Fargo. "I swear, James. I like having you for a friend but you can be exasperating at times. I'm as fond of womanhood as the next coon but they have their flaws, the same as men do."

"Name one," No-Nose said.

"I could name fifty," was Kip's rejoinder, and then he said to Fargo, "What do you think of the Picketts? Now there's a pair."

No-Nose smiled. "Silky Mae is pretty."

"Pretty or not, I wouldn't turn my back on either one," Fargo said.

"They are young, is all," No-Nose said. "The young are always high-spirited and selfish."

"Do you defend kittens, too?"

To his credit, No-Nose did not take offense. Instead he said, "Shoot me full of arrows all you want. But I can't help it if my life's ambition isn't to bed every female between the Mississippi River and the Pacific Ocean. As for kids and kittens, I suppose you would have me kick them to amuse myself?"

Kip Weaver laughed and slapped Fargo on the back. "He has you there. Let's call it a draw and get on with our drinking."

At that early hour, the saloon was only half full. Kip claimed a corner table and bellowed for the barkeep to bring a bottle and three glasses. He drained his first glass in a gulp and immediately refilled it. The second glass he drained in two gulps.

Fargo settled for a sip. As his friend filled the glass a third time, he asked, "When did this start?"

"What?"

"You are even more fond of bug juice now than I remember you being," Fargo said. "At the rate you're guzzling, you'll finish the bottle in five minutes."

"So I drink a bit more? So what?" Kip responded. "The risks I take in my job, I'm entitled."

Fargo remembered Weaver's account of nearly being slain. He had known other men changed by near-death, and not for the better. "Do you drink as much on the trail, too?"

Kip froze with the glass halfway to his mouth. "You've become nosier than I recollect. How often I do or don't wet my throat is none of your business."

"I won't partner with a lush," No-Nose said.

"Who asked you to?" Kip snapped. "Call me that again and there will be hell to pay, friend or no friend."

Their heated exchange was nipped short by four men, who had filed into the saloon and moved toward the bar. The foremost glanced at their table, blinked in surprise, then reddened in anger and came toward them.

"Hell," Fargo said under his breath.

Max Perkins halted and planted his feet as if daring Fargo to do something about it. "It's my lucky day."

"I'm not in the mood," Fargo warned him.

Kip had finished his third glass of redeye and was pouring a fourth. "Do you know this sodbuster, hoss?"

"I'm not no dirt farmer!" Perkins objected. "I'm a wagon boss. And I have a grief with your friend, here. It seems he had his way with one of the female passengers on my wagon train."

"Fargo and a woman? I'm plumb shocked," No-Nose Smith said sarcastically.

Kip grinned and waved his glass in the air. "Good for him! A man can't stay a virgin forever!"

"You're either drunk or a fool, and I can't abide either," Max Perkins declared, "just as I won't abide a polecat who trifles with the affections of a woman under my charge."

"Fargo does his share of trifling—that's for sure," Kip said, and tittered. "I stopped counting at five thousand seven hundred and sixty three. I swear, the ladies flock to him like she-bears to honey. And yes, I'm jealous."

"You're babbling," Perkins said, and turned to the three emigrants, none of whom Fargo had seen before. "This is the one I was telling you about. The one Lucy spent the night with."

"You should know," Fargo said. "You spied on us last night, and tried to bushwhack me."

"Are you as drunk as your friend? I wouldn't leave my train in the middle of the night, and I damn sure wouldn't waste lead on a lecher like you when my fists can do what needs doing just as well."

Fargo had a knack for judging human nature, and his intuition told him Perkins was telling the truth. But if it had not been the wagon boss, then who? And more important, why?

"But this time I'm not alone," Perkins was saying. "And these emigrants think even less of what you did than I do."

All three were young and powerfully built, farmers, by their attire, maybe with designs of their own on Lucy Harper.

"You don't want to do this," Fargo said.

"What's to stop us?" Parker growled.

Incredibly, Kip had emptied another glass. "You're not too bright, are you, pilgrim? In case you haven't noticed, my pard isn't alone."

Max Perkins leaned on the table. "Are you and this noseless monstrosity taking Fargo's side?"

"What did you call me?" No-Nose Smith asked.

Ignoring him, Perkins boasted, "All I have to do is go out on the street and give a holler and I'll have ten more men to back us up."

"You'll need them," No-Nose said, and came out of his chair as if fired from a cannon. His fist caught the wagon boss flush on the chin and Perkins staggered back against a table. The bartender yelled, "None of that!" but the emigrants did not listen. They threw themselves at Fargo and his friends.

"Oh, hell," Kip Weaver said, and reversing his grip on the whiskey bottle, smashed it over the head of the brawny farmer who was reaching for him. Bits of glass and a spray of whiskey flew every which way.

For his part, Fargo had hoped to avoid a fight. Now that it had been thrust on him, he had a hankering to stomp the wagon boss into the plank floor. A fist clipped his cheek and he retaliated by sending Perkins sprawling with an uppercut. An emigrant grabbed his arm, and Fargo discouraged him with a jab to the jaw.

Max Perkins had recovered and was barreling back for more.

Springing around the table, Fargo ducked a clumsy punch to the face, then landed one to the pit of Perkins's stomach. The man had learned nothing from their previous dispute. Once again Perkins sought to overcome him by brute strength, never realizing, in his folly, that Fargo was not only faster and more skilled at trading blows, but considerably stronger, as well.

Within seconds, the wagon boss lay sprawled on his back on the floor with Fargo over him, fists clenched, hoping Perkins would try to rise so he could knock him down again.

Fargo had not paid any attention to what was going on around him, a mistake he regretted when he heard the click of a gun hammer, and the hard metal of a gun's muzzle gouged his temple.

6

The bartender was a portly pot bubbling with anger. "When I said none of that, I damn well meant it!" he roared while pressing a scattergun to Fargo's head.

"Tell it to them," Fargo said.

Max Perkins cocked a fist but then did a marvelous imitation of granite when the scattergun was abruptly trained on him.

"So much as twitch and there won't be enough of you left to pick up with tweezers," the bartender exaggerated.

"You don't understand," Perkins protested.

"No, *you* don't savvy, you pigheaded idiot," the bartender cut him off. "There will be no fighting in my saloon. Ever. I don't have money to waste fixing busted chairs and tables and glasses." He stepped back, covering Perkins and the emigrants. "Since these other gents were here first and minding their business, I want you and your three friends to skedaddle, and I don't mean next week."

The wagon boss did not know when to keep his mouth shut. "I resent this shabby treatment."

"You do, do you?" the bartender said, and drove the shotgun's twin barrels into Max Perkins's gut. Perkins doubled over, wheezing in agony, and the portly bartender wagged the scattergun under his nose. "How about that? Was it shabby enough for you?"

Perkins made a few noises reminiscent of a chicken being strangled.

To the emigrants the bartender said, "Take this jackass and make yourselves scarce before I get really mad."

Kip Weaver had sat back down and was carefully brushing pieces of glass from the table. "When you're done removing the riffraff, hoss, how about a new bottle? I'm not nearly booze blind enough."

"You pay for the broken bottle first," the bartender said. "I saw you break it over that fellow's noggin."

"They don't make whiskey bottles like they used to."

The bartender chortled and headed for the bar, the scattergun under an arm. "You sure are a caution, Weaver."

"You know him?" Fargo asked.

"Oh, we're the best of friends. I've favored his establishment every day since I arrived. You could say I've become a fixture." Kip smacked his lips in anticipation and, when the bottle came, immediately opened it and filled a glass. The next moment the glass was empty.

"You've changed."

"Don't we all?" Kip filled a different glass and slid it toward Fargo, then did the same for No-Nose Smith. "To our health, gentlemen!"

"To sobriety," Smith said, and took the barest of sips.

"You're no fun, James," Kip complained. "No fun at all. It's not good to go through life so serious."

No-Nose touched the patch over the cavity in the center of his face. "I have good cause."

"We all have scars. Yours is just more obvious than most." Kip refilled his own glass but for once let it sit there. "Life is too short to let our scars ruin it. Live to the fullest is my new motto, and you would do well to do the same."

"That's the whiskey talking," Fargo said. He could not get over how drastic the change was. Kip Weaver had always been uncommonly fond of liquor, but he had never been *this* fond.   •

"Shows how much you know, pard." Kip picked up his glass but instead of drinking he turned the glass around and around in his hand. "Have you ever been afraid, Skye—so afraid you came near to peeing your pants?"

"We all have moments like that."

"You're too kind by half. I doubt you have ever been truly and really afraid once in your whole life. It's not in you. Not the high and mighty Trailsman."

"Cut that out," Fargo said.

"Why? You know I'm right. So does James. Ask him."

No-Nose fidgeted uncomfortably in his chair. "You shouldn't be talking like this, Kip. We're your friends."

"A man can never have too many of those," Weaver said. "But no matter how many he has, they don't count for much if they're not by his side when he needs them the most. Where were the two of you when those Piegans nearly lifted my hair?"

"Now you're being silly," No-Nose Smith said, and stood up. "I've had enough. Tomorrow at first light I head north. I wish the two of you luck, but I need the full twenty thousand and nothing will stop me from earning it." He touched his hat brim and left.

"Peculiar hombre, that James," Kip said. "Won't cuss, rarely drinks, and treats women like they are special. I hope he grows up someday." Chuckling at his wit, he emptied another glass.

"What about you?" Fargo asked. "Do you want to work together or go it alone?"

Weaver held the bottle in both hands and swirled it as he had the glass a minute ago. "I like you as a brother. But this time I reckon we should split up. To each his own, eh?"

"However you want it." Fargo preferred to search

by himself anyway. By nature he was a lone wolf. Running with a pack was not for him.

"Don't hold it against me," Kip said. "There's no one I respect more than you. But friendship should never stand in the way of filling one's poke."

"Don't you have that backward?"

Kip kissed the bottle and set it back down on the table. "It's nothing personal, hoss. But I've learned my lesson. I'd like to live to a ripe old age, and that twenty thousand is enough to live on the rest of my days." He swayed as if he were drunk but Fargo wasn't fooled. "Consider this a warning. It's every man for himself—or woman, as the case may be. I won't let you or anyone else get between me and the prize."

First Smith, now Weaver. Fargo recollected a quote he had heard somewhere: "The root of all evil is money."

"My God. Which pocket did you pull that one out of? Or did you get religion and not tell me?" Kip chuckled. "Money is also the root of a lot of good." He paused. "More redeye?"

Suddenly Fargo wanted fresh air. "I'll see you at the boardinghouse later." Kip said something but Fargo was not listening.

The sun struck his face full-on and Fargo squinted against the glare. Since he wasn't leaving Fort Hall until morning, he bent his boots toward the hitch rail where he had left the Ovaro. He would put it up at a stable for the night, with orders to feed it oats and brush it down. It was the least he could do, given that they were in for weeks of hard travel over some of the most rugged terrain anywhere.

The stable, though, turned out to be full.

"I'm sorry, sonny," the old man who owned it apologized. "There ain't a stall left. It's all the gold-hungry jackasses passin' through."

"What about the corral out back?" Fargo had noticed it as he came down the street. "Can I put him up there and still have the oats?"

The man was agreeable, and soon Fargo was retracing his steps to the boardinghouse with his bedroll over one shoulder, his saddlebags over the other, and the Henry in hand. Driscoll admitted him without a word and he went up the stairs to his room. As he was reaching for the door, he saw it was open a crack and heard soft sounds from within. He slowly pushed it open.

Silky Mae Pickett was on her hands and knees peering under the bed. Her back was to him and she had not heard him.

"Lose something?" Fargo asked.

"What the hell!" Silky Mae blurted, pushing onto her knees and twisting. "You scared the livin' daylights out of me!"

"If you were looking for me, I doubt I would be under there."

Silky Mae laughed. "That was a good one."

"What are you doing here?" Fargo asked, wondering where her brother had gotten to. He had the impression they were inseparable.

Silky Mae stood and placed her hands on her hips. "Is that any way to greet a gal who compromises her reputation by comin' to your room all by her lonesome?"

"You haven't answered my question." Fargo moved so his back was to the wall and he could watch her and the doorway, both.

"Goodness gracious, you sure are a suspicious cuss," Silky Mae teased. "And here I heard you were right fond of the ladies."

"I've heard the same rumor."

Silky Mae adopted a seductive look and sashayed up to him with an exaggerated sway of her hips. "I hope it's more than that," she said softly, placing a hand on his chest.

Somehow Fargo had not thought of her as the kind to throw herself at men. He did not say anything as she slowly traced a finger to his neck and then around to his ear. "Cat got your tongue, handsome?"

"I'm trying to figure out what you're up to," Fargo confessed.

Silky Mae's jaw muscles twitched. "You're not at all what I expected. Or is it that you don't find me pretty?"

"Any man would," Fargo said. She was no Lucy Harper but she was attractive in her own right. Her eyes had a lively spark to them, and her lips were invitingly shaped. Her bosom was ample but exactly how ample was hard to judge because of the loose-fitting shirt she wore. The same with her legs, thanks to her pants.

"Then it must be something else," Silky Mae said. Frowning, she stepped back and sat on the edge of the bed. "I must say, I'm terribly disappointed."

"What would your brother say if he were to walk in?"

"Billy Bob keeps his big nose out of my personal life, or else. Oh, he's always goin' on and on about how I should act like a lady and always do what's proper." Silky Mae uttered a most unladylike curse. "Easy for him to say. Whenever he has the itch, he visits a saloon or a house of ill repute. But when I get the itch, I'm supposed to ignore it."

"Where is Billy Bob right now?" Fargo asked.

"Out buyin' our supplies and whatnot," Silky Mae replied. "He doesn't like to take me shoppin'. Claims I'm always buyin' things I shouldn't." She swore again. "He doesn't savvy womenfolk at all."

Fargo closed the door and threw the bolt. When he turned, her eyes had widened and she did not appear so sure of herself. "Well, then, suppose I take care of that itch of yours." Stepping to the bed, he set down his effects and reached for her.

78

"Not so fast," Silky Mae said quickly, sliding back. "There's something I'd like to talk about first."

"I'd rather kiss than talk." Fargo gave her a dose of her own medicine. Sitting, he draped his arm across her shoulders and felt her stiffen.

"Land sakes, you're more changeable than the weather. You go from cold to hot in the blink of an eye." Silky Mae laughed but the laugh rang false. "I didn't necessarily mean that we had to do it right this instant."

"Oh?" Fargo said, and before she could think to move away or stop him, he covered her right breast with his hand, and squeezed.

"Oh!" Silky Mae gasped.

Fargo found her nipple and pinched it, none too gently. "This is what you came for, right?"

Trembling, Silky Mae swallowed hard, placed her hand on his, and slowly peeled his fingers from her body. "Not now," she said huskily.

"Give me one good reason," Fargo said, and covered her other breast with his other hand. Again he squeezed, eliciting a low whine, and when her grip slackened, he applied both hands to her nipples, pinching and tweaking them through her shirt.

Silky Mae groaned. She licked her lips, then smacked them, and said more to herself than to him, "This isn't how it was supposed to go. It's not how it was supposed to go at all."

"I wouldn't want to disappoint you," Fargo said. He nuzzled her neck and licked her earlobe.

"Damn you," Silky Mae breathed. "My brother would throw a fit."

Fargo raised his mouth from her ear. "I won't tell him if you don't." He had not intended for it go to this far. He figured he would call her bluff and she would push him away and stomp out in a huff. Instead, she suddenly flung her hands behind his head and pulled him to her as if she were trying to crawl inside his skin. She kissed him hard, almost fiercely, her breaths coming short and fast. He rimmed her lips with his tongue but she did not open her mouth to admit him.

When the kissed ended, Silky Mae sat with her bosom heaving and her cheeks as pink as twin peaches. "My goodness. That was nice."

"It gets nicer," Fargo said, and pressing his body full against hers, he began to ease her onto her back.

"What am I doing?" Silky Mae said. Abruptly sliding out from under him, she stood up. "I'm plumb sorry." Shaking her head, she backed toward the door. "I just can't. Not now."

Fargo sighed and propped his elbow on the bed and his head in his hand. "Whatever you want."

Silky Mae smoothed her shirt. "Lordy, you're slick. You could talk a nun out of her habit." She threw the bolt open but did not open the door. "My head is spinnin' so, I almost forgot why I came."

"It wasn't to seduce me?" Fargo pretended that his feelings were hurt, and frowned.

"As I keep tellin' you, maybe later." Silky Mae adjusted her fox hat. "No, the real reason was to ask you to throw in with Billy Bob and me."

"The three of us?"

"Why not?" Silky Mae rejoined. "You're the best of the bunch, if what folks say is true. My brother and me would rather have you workin' with us than workin' against us."

"You don't mind splitting the reward money three ways?"

"Not at all," Silly Mae said.

Fargo smothered a grin. She was the world's worst liar. She was no more willing to share the money than she was her body. She just wanted him to think she was.

"Splittin' twenty thousand three ways is more money than splittin' ten thousand two ways," Silky Mae went on. "And with you on our side, the three of us are bound to find Zared's boy, or his bones, before anyone else does."

"I wouldn't take Kip Weaver or No-Nose Smith lightly," Fargo advised. "They can track as well as I can."

"You're too modest. But even if that's so, a lot can happen out in the wilderness. Accidents and such."

The veiled threat caused Fargo to sit up. "You better not be saying what I think you're saying. They happen to be friends of mine."

Silky Mae chuckled. "Why, ain't you the saint?" She glanced toward the floor, then said, "Think it over. I've got to go." Turning, she hurried out as if her britches were on fire and she needed water to extinguish the flames. She did think to close the door after her.

"She's a strange one," Fargo said aloud, and he lay on his back with his fingers laced under his head. The situation was becoming too complicated for his liking. Kip and No-Nose were out to get the full twenty thousand no matter what, and now the Picketts were up to something. Exactly what was hard to say. He did not believe for a second that they wanted to work with him.

Then there was Benjamin Zared. A man with his money could hire a hundred people to look for his son if he wanted. Hell, a thousand. But Zared was content to use only the five of them. Granted, they were all skilled trackers, but an army of searchers could cover the territory from end to end a lot faster.

Equally troublesome was the fact Zared did not seem to give a damn about his son's fiancée and friend. And what sort of man was Gideon Zared that he dragged the woman he loved off into the mountains after gold? Didn't Gideon realize how perilous the mountains were?

A soft sound intruded on Fargo's musing. He cocked his head and listened but it was not repeated.

He had provisions to buy but he was in no hurry. He had the rest of the day, and he only needed a few items. On the trail he tended to travel light. Instead of packhorses laden with grub and the like, he lived off the land as much as possible. Some coffee, some jerky or pemmican, a little flour and maybe a little sugar, and he was set.

Again there came a soft sound, a vague rustling that brought Fargo half up with his head tilted. Again he listened intently but again the sound had stopped. He wasn't sure if it came from inside his room or from without, and he was about to rise and check the hall when someone knocked on the door. "Did you forget something?" he asked, thinking it was Silky Mae.

The door opened, framing Edrea Zared, who regarded him quizzically. "Not that I'm aware of, no."

"I thought you were someone else," Fargo said.

"The young lady I saw leaving your room? Frankly, I wouldn't have thought she was quite your type, but then, you never know about a person, do you?"

"Why, Miss Zared, is it me, or are your claws showing?"

Edrea sniffed as if she had detected a rank odor. "Who you spend your time with is of no interest to me, I assure you. But I will say that you would not be her first. My father dug up as much information as he could on all of you, and the adorable Silky Mae, by all accounts, has the morals of a female alley cat in heat."

Fargo grinned. "My, my. Such language."

"You are not nearly as funny as you think you are," Edrea said. "Add your name to her long list. See if I care."

"Is that why you came to see me? To protect my virtue?"

"I'm amazed you can claim you have any, after all the escapades you've had." Edrea paused. "What did that army captain say about your love life? Ah, yes. Now I remember." She paused once more, for effect. "Women are drawn to you like does to a salt lick." She snapped her fingers. "Oh. And my favorite comment, from a colonel of your acquaintance. And I quote, 'Fargo has bedded more women than the entire Seventh Cavalry.'"

"Not quite that many."

"You are much too modest," Edrea countered. "But your good looks and your charm are wasted on me. I'm not going to fall into your arms like Silky Mae apparently already has."

"She had a business proposition."

"I'll bet she did. But all I am interested in is ensuring that my brother and the others are found as quickly as practical, and brought back safe and sound."

"Provided they are still alive," Fargo said.

"Gideon is alive. I know he is. I can feel it. My father belittles my intuition, but as surely as I am standing here, my brother is not dead."

Fargo kept quiet, but the odds against it were high. "I hope you're right." Since she had given him the opening, he asked, "Why is it your father forgot to mention your brother's betrothed?"

"Haven't we already discussed that? He naturally believes that when you find Gideon, you will find Tabor and Asa."

"There's something you're not telling me," Fargo said.

Edrea Zared blinked, then laughed as if the suggestion were ridiculous. "Don't be absurd. We told you everything you need to know. Everything of importance."

"Why are you here?" Fargo asked testily. He resented being lied to.

"My father neglected to mention one aspect of the

hunt. He would like each of you to take a few body-guards along. In your case, Pike Driscoll and two others."

Fargo would not have been more surprised if she asked to go herself. "Out of the question."

"Hear me out," Edrea said. "My father wants to be kept informed of your progress. His bodyguards will serve as messengers and relay any important news to us."

"No."

"What harm can it do? They will be under orders not to interfere or hamper you in any way."

"It's still no." Fargo did not trust Driscoll, or any of the bodyguards, as far as he could throw them.

"Give me one good reason."

"I'll give you several." Fargo ticked them off on his fingers. "One, they are greenhorns. Two, the more of us there are, the more noise we make, the more sign we leave, the more likely it is hostiles will discover us. Three, we would need a couple of packhorses, and that would slow us down considerably."

"What is it about you scouts?" Edrea said in annoyance. "Mr. Weaver and Mr. Smith both said the same thing. They refused, too. I haven't talked to the Pick-etts yet but they will probably be just as stubborn."

"If you want the job done right, you have to let us do it as we see fit," Fargo recommended.

"And if my father insists?"

"He can hire someone to replace me."

"We don't want that." Edrea frowned. "Very well. I will inform him. He won't like it but he will respect your wishes." She went to leave. "Remember, if there is anything else you require, anything at all, you only have to ask." She pulled the door after her.

It struck Fargo that she had given in much too eas-ily. Shrugging, he decided to go buy his supplies. About to stand, he heard the strange sound he had heard earlier. This time he was able to pinpoint where it came from—somewhere on the floor.

Lying flat on his stomach, Fargo checked every square inch but saw nothing to account for it. Removing his hat, he slid over the side of the bed and lowered his head until he could see under it. Fargo's blood changed to ice in his veins and he held himself stock-still.

Not two inches away, partially coiled, was the last thing in the world that should have been in his room—a large rattlesnake.

7

It was not unheard of in the deserts of the southwest for a man to wake up with a rattlesnake under his blankets. Like all reptiles, rattlers were cold-blooded, and in the chill of the night, the warmth a human body gave off was to a rattler's liking. Nor was it unheard of for settlers to find that a rattlesnake had strayed into their cabin or house after a door was carelessly left open.

But it *was* unheard of for a rattler to find its way into a hotel in the middle of a bustling settlement. Even more improbable that one should somehow reach the second floor unnoticed by the hotel's patrons.

So Fargo could be forgiven the momentary shock that gripped him. Had he thrown himself aside the instant he set eyes on it, the snake would not have had time to strike. But he hung there over the side of the bed, riveted in disbelief, as the rattler reared until its head brushed the bottom of the bed. Out darted its forked red tongue, the tip nearly touching Fargo's face.

They were eye to eye, just as Fargo had been eye to eye with the grizzly by the river. But where grizzlies were unpredictable and might flee or attack as bestial whim moved them, rattlesnakes were as predictable as they were deadly. When they felt threatened, they lashed out, sinking their venomous fangs into whatever threatened them. Movement usually triggered an attack. Any movement at all.

Fargo froze, refusing to so much as blink, as the rattlesnake's tongue flicked out a second time. The brown blotches that ran down its back, each edged by black, pegged it as a common Western rattler. Some grew to be over five feet in length and as thick around as a man's forearm. This one looked to be only three to four feet long, but that did not make its venom any less lethal.

Its mouth opened again, and the snake hissed. Fargo saw its fangs, saw drops of venom glisten on the tips. He fought an instinctive urge to scramble away. He was fast, but he was not faster than a striking rattler when the rattler was so close.

As he hung there, every nerve tingling, an image seared into Fargo's mind—the image he had witnessed when he opened his door: Silky Mae Pickett on her hands and knees on the floor by the bed. Fury coursed through him, but he willed himself to stay calm.

The rattlesnake lowered its broad triangular head to the floor and began to slither from under the bed. To do so, it had to pass directly under him.

Fargo's skin prickled as he watched the snake's scales slide by. He thought he felt his hair brush the snake's back, and he braced for the brittle rattling that gave the viper its name. But the serpent continued to slowly crawl.

Suddenly the bed seemed to move. With a start, Fargo realized his weight was causing the quilt to slide toward the floor—directly on top of the rattler. He loosened his grip slightly and the quilt stopped sliding—but for how long?

Fully half of the snake was still under the bed. Band after scaly band crept past Fargo's face with awful slowness.

Again the quilt moved. Not much, but enough to

send Fargo's blood rushing. He could definitely feel his hair brush the rattler's back but the rattler did not appear to care.

Then the snake's tail slid into view, and Fargo could not quite credit his senses. Rattlesnakes always had rattles—horny segments that, when shaken, produced the distinctive buzz that was the bane of every horseman. A snake as big as the one under the bed should have big rattles to match its size. But this snake had none. Its rattles were missing.

They had been chopped off so the snake would not make any noise before it struck.

Hardly had this registered than the quilt shifted again. Fargo's weight and gravity conspired to pitch him headfirst to the floor. Twisting as he fell, Fargo thrust the quilt at the rattler. He felt something strike the underside of the quilt near his right hand, and again near his head. Then he was in a crouch and in the clear, and a quick bound carried him onto the bed.

Hissing loudly, the rattlesnake thrashed wildly about, its coils outlined under the quilt.

Fargo drew his Colt, then thought better of it. Walls and floors were notoriously thin. The slug might go all the way through and hit someone below.

The right edge of the quilt bulged, and the rattler poked its head out.

Fargo launched himself into the air. He brought his knees up close to his chest; then, at the apex of his spring, he drove both legs straight down and locked them. Like twin sledges, the heels of his boots slammed down on the top of the rattler's head, splintering its thin skull and smashing the skull to a pulp.

By rights the snake was dead. But Fargo had seen where a rattler with its head half blown off had coiled and struck again and again, just as headless chickens sometimes flapped their wings and ran madly about. So instead of stepping off the snake, he sprang back onto the bed.

He need not have bothered. The rattler was as limp as a wet cloth, and as lifeless as the bed itself.

Picking the snake up by the severed end, Fargo spread the quilt and wrapped it inside. Then he went out into the hall. A pair of Zared's bodyguards were at the landing, as usual. They gave him puzzled looks as he approached with the quilt tucked under his left arm.

"Which room are the Picketts in?"

"The third down on the left, sir," said the taller of the two. "But you just missed them. They left a couple of minutes ago."

"I'm obliged," Fargo said. He tried their door. Instead of one bed there were two. A hairbrush on a pillow gave away which was Silky Mae's. He moved her pillow, unwrapped the quilt, and placed the dead rattler where her pillow had been. Then he put the pillow on top of the snake, careful not to disturb the hairbrush. Stepping back, he nodded. She would not suspect a thing.

Fargo took the quilt back to his room and threw it in a corner. At the thought of how close he had come to being bitten, his fury resurfaced. He needed to get out, to do something. Accordingly, he was soon crossing the lobby toward the entrance. He happened to glance out a window, and who should he see standing on the porch but the Picketts, talking to Pike Driscoll.

Billy Bob and Silky Mae had their backs to the door and did not hear Fargo quietly open and close it. Stepping lightly so his spurs would not jingle, Fargo was behind them in two long strides. Driscoll saw him but did not guess his intent as, smiling, Fargo tapped Billy Bob Pickett on the shoulder.

The Southerner started to turn, saying, "What is it?"

His right fist balled at his side, Fargo said, "I have something for you." On "have," he drove his fist into the pit of Billy Bob's stomach and had the satisfaction of doubling him in half. Billy Bob clutched his gut and tried to backpedal but Fargo was not about to let him. He landed a solid blow to the cheek, which crumpled Billy Bob's legs.

"Leave him be!" Silky Mae screeched, and flung herself at Fargo, her fingernails hooked to slash.

Catching hold of her wrists, Fargo shoved. He only meant to push her back but she tripped over her brother and fell.

"What in hell do you think you're doing?" Pike Driscoll roared, and came to their aid by drawing his revolver and swinging it at Fargo's temple, trying to do to Fargo as Fargo had done to him in the sitting room earlier.

Ducking, Fargo slipped in close and planted his knee where it hurt a man the most. Pike Driscoll cried out and covered himself. Billy Bob was dribbling saliva down his chin. Only Silky Mae was in any condition to fight back, and she did.

Fargo nearly lost an eye to her raking fingernails. He rarely ever struck a woman, but after the rattlesnake he was in no mood to go easy on her. He backhanded her full across the mouth, knocking her against the rail. Shocked, she put a hand to her face, then snarled like a feral cat and clawed for a knife at her hip.

"Enough!"

Benjamin Zared's bellow could probably be heard from one end of Fort Hall to the other. He was in the doorway, livid with anger. "What in God's name is going on?" He strode toward them. "Why are you fighting amongst yourselves?"

Behind him trailed Edrea.

"Didn't you hear me?" Benjamin said when no on answered him. "What is the meaning of this outburst?"

"Ask the Picketts," Fargo said.

"Well?" Benjamin addressed Silky Mae. "Why is there blood on your lip, young lady? What brought this on?"

"I have no idea," Silky Mae said, moving to help her brother stand. "We were standin' here, mindin' our own business, and he attacked us without warnin'."

"I'll vouch for them, sir," Pike Driscoll said, his eyes twin barbs of hatred directed at Fargo. "They were talking to me when this bastard marched out and started swinging away. I tried to help them, but—"

"I must say, Mr. Driscoll, I am severely disappointed in your performance," Benjamin Zared said. "Once again you have proven unequal to the occasion. Should there be a third such incident, your employment is in jeopardy."

"Yes, sir," Driscoll said, and if looks could slay, Fargo would be dead on the spot.

"Now then," Benjamin turned. "What brought this on, Mr. Fargo? I was led to believe you are an even-tempered, reasonable man. But your actions since your arrival prove differently."

"The Picketts tried to kill me."

Silky Mae and Billy Bob nearly shouted in unison, "We did not!" and Silky Mae added, "Why in blazes would we want you dead? After we offered to have you throw in with us?"

"You did what?" Edrea said.

"I paid Mr. Fargo here a visit and we talked it over some," Silky Mae said. "And a little bit more than talk."

Billy Bob's head snapped up. "What?"

"Forget that," Benjamin Zared said. "I'm trying to understand why violence was resorted to."

"The Picketts know," Fargo said, and made for the steps. He would not justify himself. The Picketts would only deny it. It would be their word against his,

91

and prove nothing. There was the dead snake, but he would rather it stayed where it was than show it to the Zareds.

Pike Driscoll took a step after him. "Hold on there, mister. Mr. Zared isn't done with you."

"Yes, he is." Fargo did not glance back, and no one tried to stop him. He went straight to the general store for the items he needed and, after buying them, checked on the stallion at the stable. He was in no hurry to return to the boardinghouse, and spent the rest of the afternoon walking around the settlement, thinking about all that had happened and whether he should take part in the hunt for Gideon Zared or light a shuck for less dangerous climes.

Common sense said there was nothing to be gained by sticking around. Sure, he could use the money, but money was not everything. He did not know Gideon Zared personally and was under no obligation to try to find him.

But it rankled Fargo to turn tail, which was essentially what he would be doing. He had never turned tail in his life.

Then there was the girl to think of, Gideon Zared's betrothed, Tabor Garnet. If she was still alive, if she had been taken captive by hostiles, if he could track her down, he might be able to bring her back to civilization. If, if, if, Fargo thought. The odds were long, but while there was any hope at all, he should try.

Fargo had an affliction, as he liked to think of it, common to many men. He could never refuse a damsel in distress, a habit that had brought him no end of trouble. But he could no more deny the urge than he could deny the need to eat or sleep.

Toward evening Fargo strayed into a bustling restaurant. Or so the sign out front advertised. Long plank tables were crammed with hungry, gold-crazed Easterners about to push off into the mountains, confident they would soon strike it rich. The truth was that over 90 percent would not find so much as a grain of the precious ore, and scores would lose their lives.

Fargo had steak and potatoes and washed it down with piping hot black coffee. He was about done when he noticed two buckskin-clad figures rise from end of a far table: Kip Weaver and No-Nose Smith. They had not seen him. Weaver was talking and gesturing, and Smith was shaking his head.

Quickly paying, Fargo followed them. Their argument became heated. He could not hear what they were saying, but at one point, Kip grabbed No-Nose by the arm and No-Nose slapped his hand away. Finally they came to a corner and stopped. Kip said something that made No-Nose clench his fists. Then Kip Weaver spun and stormed off in the direction of the boardinghouse.

Fargo caught up with Smith, who glanced at him but did not say anything. "What was that all about?"

"I'd rather not say."

"This is off to a bad start, James. Kip has become money-hungry, and the Picketts tried to kill me earlier."

No-Nose slowed. "Are they still alive?"

"So far."

"You must be getting soft. I can remember when anyone who tried to rub you out was turned into maggot fodder two seconds after they did it." Smith grinned, then sobered. "But I agree. It's a bad start. We're all at each other's throats."

"I'm not out to harm you," Fargo assured him.

"That's comforting to know," No-Nose said. "I'm not out to harm you, either, Skye. But I need that twenty thousand—need it more than I have ever needed anything in all my born days."

"You sound like Kip."

"Maybe. But he's not after the same thing I am. He wants the twenty thousand so he can give up being a scout. He wants to move to Florida or some such place

93

and live out his days without having to worry about being scalped or killed." No-Nose smiled at a pair of women they were passing and the women veered aside as if he were a leper. "I can't blame him for that."

"It's no excuse for turning on your friends," Fargo siad.

"I'm not turning on anyone. I need to go it alone and earn the full twenty grand so I can live a normal life again." No-Nose sighed. "You have no notion of what it's like. You saw those gals just now? I go through that a dozen times a day. I'm a freak. An outcast. No one wants anything to do with me because I'm so damn hideous."

"That's not true," Fargo said, when he knew full well it was.

"Thanks, but I'm not a simpleton. Hell, when I look in the mirror, even *I* think I'm hideous."

"There's more to a person than how they look."

"Easy for you to say, when you're about the most handsome galoot who ever pulled on britches. Women flock to you like geese to corn."

"You're exaggerating," Fargo said.

"Not by much and you damn well know it."

They came to a store with a glass window, and No-Nose Smith halted and indicated their reflections. "Look there. You, just as good-looking as can be. Me, a monster who gives people nightmares."

"You're too hard on yourself," Fargo said. "You'll do to ride the river with, and that's what counts."

No-Nose gestured at the flow of passersby. "Not where these folks are concerned All they care about is how a person looks. A man can be the worst scum alive but if he has a nice face he is treated better than I am."

Fargo had nothing to say to that.

"I'm tired of being a monster, Skye. Tired of folks staring. Tired of how women won't let me anywhere near them."

"There are always fallen doves," Fargo mentioned.

"I never paid for it before I was mutilated. I damn well refuse to pay for it now," No-Nose said. "I did try once, though. I went to Madam Marcy's in Denver. You know, the place with the red walls and red furniture and all the women wear red."

"A fine establishment." Fargo grinned.

"I thought so, too, after hearing how the customers are treated like kings. So about six months after I lost my nose, I went there one night. Yes, I was a fool. But it had been so long since I had been with a woman, I was going out of my mind. Ever had that feeling?"

"Once or twice."

"Madam Marcy was sweet as could be. She offered me the pick of her girls," Smith related, his tone softening. "There was this one. Pearl, her name was. I don't think it was her real name but that's not important. She was so pretty, she took your breath away. Golden hair, emerald eyes, and lips like ripe berries. I wanted her so much, I was scared."

"What happened?" Fargo asked, although he could guess.

"Things went swell until she took me up to a little red room to get down to business," No-Nose said. "She tried hard. I'll give her that. But when she kissed me, she couldn't keep from shaking. So she closed her eyes, claimed the light was bothering them, even though the lamp was turned down low."

"Maybe you shouldn't tell me the rest."

"Why not? I've gone this far." No-Nose touched the patch over the cavity where his nose had been. "We were kissing and hugging and things were going well until somehow or other Pearl bumped my patch and it slid off. You should have seen the look on her face. The terror. She couldn't help herself. She screamed."

Fargo imagined the scene, and again had nothing to say.

"It brought Madam Marcy. She was mad as a wet

hen at Pearl but I wouldn't stand for Pearl being yelled at or slapped. It wasn't her fault, I said, and to prove it, I took off the patch right there in front of Madam Marcy." No-Nose chuckled. "You will never guess what she did."

"She screamed?"

"Louder than Pearl. Oh, she apologized over and over and offered me any of the other girls I wanted but I wasn't interested. I was dead inside, if that makes sense, and I've been dead inside ever since."

Fargo had not expected the other scout to reveal so much. "I'm sorry to hear that," he said for want of anything else.

"I don't need your pity. I hate pity. I feel even less of a man when people pity me." No-Nose touched the patch again. "You just have no idea what it's like."

They were walking again, and stares were fixed on Smith's ruined face.

"I want to be normal. I want my life back. I want to be able to hold a woman and not have her be sick to her stomach. That's why I need the twenty thousand. That's why I aim to claim it no matter what."

"I've lost your trail."

Smith was quiet a while. Then he said, "There's a gent over in France. A doctor, a surgeon who can work miracles, they say. He has operated on dozens of freaks like me and made them whole again."

Fargo did not see how even the best surgeon in the world could repair the damage done to Smith, but then, soldiers were sometimes fitted with artificial legs and arms.

"I don't know all the particulars about how he works his miracles. But my sister wrote to him, and he answered her that he could give me a new nose, and while it won't be the same as having my own, I'll be able to walk down a street without having people gawk. He gave her his word on that."

"Is he coming to America to operate on you?"

"I have to go to him. I have to go to Paris and the fancy institute he works at, and he'll operate there. He says I'll need to stay at least six months, and there might be more than one operation." Smith paused. "He says it will cost me fifteen thousand dollars."

Fargo whistled softly. That was more than most people earned in ten years. "Why so much?"

"He's the best there is at what he does, this Monsieur Gaston. It takes a lot of skill, and I guess he figures if folks want to be fixed that bad, they'll pay his price."

"Fifteen thousand," Fargo repeated in amazement.

"So now you know why I must find Gideon Zared. Why it must be me and no one else." No-Nose stopped and looked at Fargo. "I have a favor to ask."

"Don't," Fargo said.

"Drop out. Tell Zared you're not interested. Leave it to me and Kip and those brats."

"I can't."

"After I've bared my soul to you? After I've explained? Damn it. This means everything to me, and I won't let you or anyone else stand in my way."

"Is that what Kip and you were talking about a while ago?"

"He wants me to be his partner and split the money fifty-fifty. But half of twenty is ten and ten is not enough for the operation. So I told him no."

"Did you tell him about the operation?"

"He wouldn't care. He needs the money himself. But I figured you would be different. I figured you would help me by not taking part in the search. Kip is good but he's not as good as me, and those Southerners don't impress me much. You're the one who stands the best chance of finding Gideon. So I'm asking you. No, I'm begging you. Please. For my sake. Step down."

"I have a better idea," Fargo said. "We'll work together. If we find Gideon, you keep all the money."

"That's wouldn't be right," No-Nose said. "I'm not much to look at but I have my pride."

So did Fargo. But there was more to it. A lot more. "I'm sorry, James. But I have to see it through."

"And I took you for a friend," Smith said in disgust. "Fine. If that's how you want it, I'll tell you the same thing I told Kip. From here on out, it's every coon for himself. Get in my way and I'll bury you."

8

Fargo had every intention of going to bed early so he could get an early start. But after half an hour of tossing and turning, he tugged on his boots, strapped on his Colt, and ventured from the boardinghouse for a taste of Fort Hall's night life.

Instead of two bodyguards on the upstairs landing, there were four. Benjamin Zared did not want a repeat of the incident on the front porch.

Fargo saw no one else on his way out. According to Edrea, her father had taken every room in the house, even though his party only filled half, paying the landlady double for the privilege.

For once Driscoll was not on the porch. Walker was, and he nodded as Fargo went by.

The night sky was clear, the air brisk. Stars sparkled like celestial gems. Tinny piano music and the drone of voices was punctuated by laughter and an occasional lusty oath.

Fort Hall sure had changed, Fargo mused, but whether the change was permanent or not depended on how long the gold rush lasted.

It had been Fargo's experience that most mining camps and towns did not last long. Dozens sprouted in the Rockies each year. Only two or three were still there a year later. The majority were abandoned when the gold played out, and they fell into ruin, mute testimonials to human greed.

Gold was a magnet. It drew the foolhardy in droves.

Men who had never used a spade or spent more than a few days in the wild believed they could wrest a fortune from the ground. That thousands tried and failed did not deter those who poured in after them. Each one believed he would do better. Each one believed he was luckier than the rest. In their eyes, the Almighty played favorites, and they were the Chosen.

They were like horses with blinders on. They only saw what they wanted to see. So what if countless gold seekers died from hunger or thirst? So what if scores fell to the arrows and lances of Indians who did not like having their territories invaded? So what if savage beasts claimed dozens more? It would not happen to *them*.

Fargo was of the opinion that life was a roll of the dice, and the best anyone could do was not make stupid mistakes that would end the game that much sooner.

Now, deep in thought, Fargo did not realize someone was blocking his path until he nearly blundered into them. Glancing up, he dropped his hand to the Colt but he did not draw.

"Hello there." Lucy Harper smiled. "Fancy running into you again." She wore a calico dress, which tastefully accented her charms.

"Where did you come from?" Fargo was annoyed at himself for his lapse of attention. The Picketts, as Silky Mae had told Zared, lived by the feud, to say nothing of the bushwhacker.

"Is that any way to greet someone who—" Lucy caught herself and lowered her voice. "Someone special?" She anxiously added, "I am special, aren't I?"

"As special as anyone can be," Fargo said.

"What have you been up to?" Lucy wondered.

Fargo explained that he was leaving in the morning, and why, and as he finished, she clasped his left hand in both of hers.

"Then you have the rest of the night to yourself?

So do I. The wagon train doesn't leave for a couple of days yet. We're camped a little ways to the west in a meadow all the trains use." Lucy ran a finger across his knuckles. "We could go to my wagon if you like."

"What about Perkins?" Fargo had enough problems without the wagon boss trying to stomp him into the ground again.

Lucy misunderstood. "He hasn't pestered me since the other day. Mr. Gelford had a lot to do with it. Gelford told his wife how Perkins was treating me, and she and some of the other ladies warned him to quit it. And here I thought they didn't like me." Lucy fluffed at her hair. "Well, if not my wagon, then where?"

Fargo's room at the boardinghouse held little appeal. The walls were too thin, and there were too many ears.

"We can always walk to the river," Lucy suggested.

"Too many people go there for water." Fargo had a better notion. "Are you hungry? I already ate but I'll buy you supper."

"No need." Lucy stepped so close to him, her bosom feathered his chest. "I'm hungry for something other than food."

So was Fargo. The shapely suggestion of her velvet thighs under her dress reminded him of the bliss of the night before. Since he could not sleep, he might as well enjoy himself. "I know a spot," he said, and with her hand in his, he led her north by a circuitous route, always watching behind them in case they were followed.

"I've heard of Benjamin Zared," Lucy remarked. "They say he likes to have his own way, and woe to anyone who stands up to him. You'll be careful, won't you?"

"Always," Fargo said.

"I read in a newspaper about his son, Gideon, when he became engaged. A nice boy, apparently. Not at all like his father. Smart as a whip, the newspaper claimed."

Anyone who would drag his fiancée off after gold was not all that smart, in Fargo's estimation. He checked behind them again. He did not notice anyone following them, and he was about to face front when a dark form detached itself from shadows down the narrow street.

"Walk faster," Fargo said, and pulled her after-him as he hurried to the next junction and turned right. As soon as they were out of sight of the stalker, he darted between a cabin and an outhouse and hunkered behind the latter.

"What are you doing?" Lucy asked. "It stinks here. Surely you don't expect us to—"

Fargo flicked a hand across her mouth. "We're being followed."

"Any idea who it is?" Lucy whispered when he removed his palm.

"We're about to find out."

The man shadowing them did not keep them waiting. Within seconds he appeared, looking right and left, plainly afraid he had lost them.

Fargo let him go by. Since their stalker had not pulled a pistol, neither did he. Rising, he asked the man in black, "Looking for someone?"

Jim Walker spun and immediately flung his arms out from his sides. "Don't shoot! I'm not out to harm you."

"Prove it," Fargo said.

"I'm under orders from Mr. Zared," Walker revealed. "He wants to be kept informed of where you go and who you see."

"Does he, now?" Fargo was tempted to pistol-whip the bodyguard, but the man was only doing as he had been told.

"Yes, sir. Whenever any of you leave the boardinghouse, one of us is to follow and report back to Mr.

Driscoll. We've been doing it since we got here, but you're the only one who has caught on."

"Zared can do whatever he wants with the others, but not me," Fargo said. "Understood? Go tell him that."

"He'll be awful mad you caught me," Walker said. "He might even fire me, and I have a wife and family."

"That's between you and him."

"Please," Walker said. "I like my job. Zared pays really well. Can't we work something out?"

"I'm listening."

"How about if I don't follow you but tell Mr. Zared I did? I'll make up a report about where you went and what you did, and he will never know. This way I get to keep my job."

Fargo mulled it over. Walker seemed honest enough, but he had been led to believe Zared's bodyguards were loyal to Zared and him alone. "I don't know."

"Why not do him the favor?" Lucy interjected. "What can it hurt?"

"Thank you, ma'am," Walker said.

Although part of him was convinced he was making a mistake, Fargo said, "All right. Off you go. But if I catch you following me again—"

"You won't, as God is my witness!" Walker beamed and backed away, saying happily, "Thank you, thank you. Both of you." He was swallowed by the darkness.

Lucy squeezed Fargo's arm. "That was awful nice of you."

"It was awful stupid of me," Fargo disagreed, and continued north. Soon they left the settlement behind. As he recalled, not far off was a certain spot he had been to once years ago, when Fort Hall was just a trading post. It was a low rise sprinkled with large boulders.

"You can trust him," Lucy declared. "I am sure of it."

103

As a personal rule, Fargo never trusted people until they proved they were worthy. He was not like Lucy, who overflowed with trust—trust in the Almighty that she would make it to Oregon on her own; trust that she would be spared the ravages of starvation and hostiles; trust in the good natures of her fellow emigrants. She wore her trust like a shield. But her trust had not stopped Perkins from lusting after her, or her wagon from breaking down. Life had a way of disabusing folks of their illusions.

"It's a pretty night," Lucy commented, snuggling close. "All it needs is a full moon and it would be perfect."

Fargo was thankful for the moon's absence. The less light, the less chance of anyone or anything spotting them.

"You're not very talkative, but that's all right. Most men aren't. Me, I like to talk, to socialize. It is what I miss most. There's not much time for it when the wagon train is on the go." Lucy rested her cheek on his shoulder. "When I reach Oregon, I'll attend every church social and dance I can."

"Maybe find yourself a husband." Fargo glanced behind them but Walker had been as good as his word.

"Eventually," Lucy said, "but I'm in no rush, unlike a lot of girls I've known, who couldn't wait to be hitched. A lot of my friends were married by sixteen or seventeen, but not me. I like my freedom too much, I reckon."

"That makes two of us," Fargo said.

"You're a man. It is easier for you. When a man stays single and gallivants around, people don't mind one bit. But if a woman does it, they whisper behind her back. They accuse her of all manner of shenanigans." Lucy rubbed his palm. "People can be so cruel."

"You're learning."

"My grandmother used to say I was too nice for my

own good, but I don't see how a person can ever be too nice, do you?"

"You're asking the wrong person," Fargo said. "I never turn the other cheek."

"You let that man go, didn't you? You're not as mean as you pretend. Deep down you are a kitten."

She was as wrong as wrong could be but Fargo did not debate the point. Let her think what she wanted.

"Did I tell you Perkins came by my wagon this morning?" Lucy said. "He apologized for the misunderstanding, as he called it, and said if I ever had need of him, all I had to do was give a holler." Lucy laughed. "As if I would ever let him anywhere near me."

They were winding through trees. Fargo was alert for signs of life but all he spotted was a doe that slunk quietly off.

Lucy had turned into a regular chatterbox. "Do you ever wonder why things are the way they are? Why is it that we can't all get along and live in peace? I mean, look at the Indians. Some of the emigrants hate them for no other reason than their skin is red and ours is white. That's not right. Me, I judge people by who they are, not their skin color. What do you think?"

"I think you talk too damn much." Halting, Fargo embraced her and bent his mouth to her throat. Her skin was warm. When he licked her neck, she shivered.

"Goodness gracious, how I like what you do to me," Lucy cooed. "There has never been anyone who twists my insides into knots like you do."

"You're talking again," Fargo said. To silence her, he kissed her and let the kiss linger. She was much more brazen than the last time. Her tongue rimmed his gums, then met his, all the while her hands molded his shoulders.

When Fargo reluctantly broke the kiss, Lucy was breathing heavily. She was quick to arouse, and not the least bit ashamed of her hunger.

"I haven't stopped thinking about us. About how wonderful it was. About how much I would like to do it again."

So would Fargo. Once more he headed north, moving faster. An owl hooted to the east. To the west a coyote yipped.

"I love to listen to the animals at night, don't you?" Lucy asked. "Sometimes I hear screams and howls I can't identify. Once a cry sounded exactly like a woman. One of the men told me it was a cougar. Do cougars do that? Scream like women?"

Fargo kissed her again. His right hand roamed to her back side.

"My, you're naughty," Lucy giggled. "My father would shoot anyone who did what you are doing."

"I would shoot back," Fargo said, bearing to the northwest. Hardly had he taken ten steps than the trees ended and before them reared the rise. He climbed to a flat-topped boulder as big around as a bed and patted the top.

"Up you go."

"You want us to climb up there?"

"We can see anyone coming from a long way off." Fargo laced his hands together and bent low. "I'll give you a hand."

"Under a tree would do just as well," Lucy said, but she placed her right foot in his palms and her left hand on his shoulder. "Nice and slow, if you please. I'm not a mountain goat."

A surge of Fargo's shoulders, and it was done. Lucy sat atop the boulder, her legs dangling over the edge, giggling to herself.

"Mercy me, you're strong! The way you handled Mr. Perkins, I wouldn't doubt you are one of the strongest men I have ever met."

Taking a step back, Fargo crouched, then launched himself upward. He hooked his forearms and elbows over the rim, then swung his legs up.

"You make it look easy," Lucy said.

Rising, Fargo slid his hands under her arms and brought her to her feet. The boulder was roughly circular, about ten feet across, more than enough room for a starlit frolic.

Lucy gazed toward Fort Hall. "You're right. We can see a long ways from here but no one can see us."

Fargo pulled her to him and hungrily applied his mouth to hers. His hands rose to her breasts. They were as full and ripe as before. When he pinched both her nipples at the same time, she uttered a moan from deep down inside of her and dug her fingernails into his biceps.

Fargo kissed her chin, her ear, her eyebrow. He ran a hand through her lustrous silken hair. Her body grew warmer with each passing second. When he cupped her bottom, she ground herself against him. The friction caused his manhood to rise and bulge.

"Is something stirring down there?" Lucy grinned. "I wonder what it could be."

"Let's find out." Grasping her right wrist, Fargo lowered her hand to his member. At the contact she gasped and her eyes grew wide.

"Oh! My heart is hammering! I can't hear myself think." But that did not stop Lucy from lightly running her hand up and down. "Dear Lord, you excite me!" she breathed into his ear.

It was mutual. Fargo kneaded her bottom, stroked her thighs, dallied at her breasts, all a prelude to taking her in his arms and carefully lowering her to the boulder. The smooth stone surface was nearly as flat as a kitchen table, and as uncomfortably hard.

Fargo cupped Lucy's face and sucked on her strawberry lips. Her bosom, so full and soft, cushioned his chest. Her thighs closed about his right leg like a vise, and her nails sank into the back of his neck.

"Have you wanted me as much as I have wanted you?" she asked.

"No more talking," Fargo said between kisses. Too much would spoil things. It would dampen his ardor, like throwing a bucket of water on a fire. Fortunately, Lucy applied her lips to his neck, licking around and around until she came to his ear. Inhaling his earlobe, she nipped it ever so gently with her teeth.

Fargo, meanwhile, was prying at her dress and undoing buttons. It took a while to gain access to her hidden charms. At last her globes popped free, the nipples like erect twin nails, her breasts so wonderfully inviting that he gave each his undivided attention for minutes on end.

Lucy shivered and *oooohhh*ed and *aaahhhhh*ed. Her hips rose rhythmically in anticipation. Her thighs were twin ovens, but they were nothing to the heat that came from her core.

Enough of her dress and undergarments were undone that Fargo could trace his tongue from her bosom across her belly to above the junction of her legs. He nuzzled her crinkly short hairs and her bottom gave a little jump.

At that point most men would have been so absorbed in what they were doing that their senses would have been dulled. But not Fargo. He had learned to always keep a small part of himself aloof from lovemaking. To always be alert for sounds that might indicate the presence of enemies or prowling beasts. So it was that, as he nuzzled her, he heard the soft crackle of underbrush in the woods they had passed through to reach the boulder.

Instantly, Fargo was on an elbow, his neck craned. Lucy opened her mouth but he covered it with his left hand and whispered, "Not a peep. I heard something."

It might be a deer. Or a raccoon. Or any of the many other creatures that roamed the wilds after the sun went down. Or it could the two-legged creature known as man, up to no good.

Fargo wondered if maybe Walker had gone back on

his word and followed them. But no, he was sure no one had. A minute went by and he was beginning to think it was safe when the pad of stealthy footfalls rose from near the very boulder they were lying on.

Lucy tensed under him. Her hand gripped his arm in panic.

Motioning for her to stay still, Fargo slowly eased off her and crawled to the edge. Removing his hat, he drew his Colt. The footfalls had stopped but he did not see anyone.

Warily, Fargo leaned far enough out to spot two forms a dozen feet away. Dappled by pale starlight and shadows, they raised their muzzles and sniffed a few times. Grinning, Fargo almost said, "Boo!"

The coyotes had caught their scent but were unsure where they were. The pair, probably a male and female, padded past the boulder and were soon lost to view.

Fargo holstered his revolver and slid next to Lucy.

"What was it?" she whispered.

Unbuckling his gun belt, Fargo told her. Setting it aside but within quick reach, he stretched out next to her and pecked her on the tip of her nose. "Now where were we?"

"You've forgotten already?" Lucy teased. "I better remind you."

The kiss she bestowed was as hot as lava. Her left hand found his member. Her right molded his chest and hips and thighs. Lucy Harper was not one of those women who lay like lifeless logs; she enjoyed stimulating him as much as he enjoyed arousing her.

Their mouths fused. Fargo delved his tongue into hers, then let her delve hers into his. She tasted deliciously sweet, like hard molasses candy. He pulled on her right nipple, pulled on her left. She seemed to particularly like it when he pinched them, so he pinched both and she thrust her hips against him in urgent passionate need.

Fargo had held off touching her womanhood on purpose. Now he slowly slid his hand between her hot thighs and covered her moist slit. She moaned and closed her legs so his hand was trapped there. As delicately as if his finger were a feather, he ran it along her slit to her tiny knob. She was wet for him, so very wet, and her knob had to be throbbing.

The slightest touch, and Lucy came up off the boulder, clinging to him as if she were trying to stop him from running off. But Fargo was not going anywhere. For long minutes he caressed her. For her part, Lucy fondled him while keeping her mouth glued to his.

Eventually the moment came when Fargo penetrated her with his middle finger. Her slick inner walls rippled to his touch. When he inserted a second finger, she groaned so loudly it was a wonder they didn't hear her in the settlement.

No new sounds came out of the darkness. Fargo felt it safe to part her thighs and kneel between them. He started to undo his pants but Lucy was so eager, she swatted his hands away and unveiled his pole herself. Gripping it, she pumped him.

Then and there, Fargo nearly lost control. Gritting his teeth, he willed himself not to explode. She had hold of the tip and was guiding it to where she yearned for it to be. Warmth and wetness enveloped him, and he was sheathed in her scabbard. He held still and she did the same as waves of pleasure washed over them.

"I could do this forever and ever," Lucy whispered.

She was not the only one, Fargo thought, as he gripped her hips. He looked into her eyes and smiled, and she licked her lips and nodded.

Then it was in and out, in and out, her legs locked at the small of his back. Fargo's knees scraped on the rock. The night blurred, as it always did, and for a brief span there were the two of them and only the two of them, adrift in the ultimate bliss the human body could know. Eventually they coasted to a stop and were still.

Fargo rolled off her onto his side. He was in no hurry to head back. The peace and quiet were a welcome change. But it was only temporary. Tomorrow he must set off into the savage heart of the mountains, and it was entirely possible he would not make it out alive.

9

Before first light, Fargo was up and dressed and about to leave the boardinghouse when out of the sitting room stepped Benjamin Zared. The face under the white mane of hair was haggard.

"So you're the first to leave? I can't thank you enough for going after my son. He means everything to me." Zared offered his hand. "The best of luck."

"Thanks." Fargo was not disposed to chat. He had to get to the stable. "If they are alive, I'll bring them back."

" 'They'?" Benjamin said, and caught himself. "Oh. Tabor and Asa, too. Why, of course. I'll be waiting to welcome them with open arms." He glanced up the stairs. "Watch your back out there. The Picketts are madder than ever at you over something that happened last night."

"What would that be?"

"Someone put a dead rattlesnake in Silky Mae's bed. She had turned in and was almost asleep when she slid her hand under her pillow and touched it." Benjamin grinned. "You should have heard her shriek. They blamed you but I pointed out you had been gone almost all day so you could not have been the culprit."

Fargo wondered if Zared suspected the truth. "Thanks for the warning." Not that he needed one. The others had made it clear that it was every tracker for him- or herself. He went to leave but Zared was not finished.

"How long do you estimate the search will take?"

"There's no way of telling," Fargo said. He would hunt for a month, and if he had not turned up a trace of Gideon by then, he would bow out.

"I don't mean to press you," Benjamin said, "but the sooner we find him, the better for my peace of mind. I have been worried sick, Mr. Fargo. I can't eat. I can't sleep. I can't hardly function."

"I'll do what I can," Fargo promised, which was the most he could do.

"I have every confidence one of you will succeed. When I need something done, I always hire the best."

Again Fargo made for the door. This time he had his hand on the latch when Zared said his name.

"In case I haven't made myself clear, don't let anyone or anything stand in your way. Do whatever it takes to find my son. If you need help, whether it be supplies or some of my men to back you, get word to me." Benjamin paused. "I expect to be in Kellogg in a couple of weeks. You can reach me there."

Fargo hid his surprise. Founded as a mission nearly twenty years ago, Kellogg was a small community well to the north. "Exactly how far into the mountains do you think your son went?"

Benjamin shrugged. "Who can say?"

A vague feeling gnawed at Fargo like a beaver on a tree—a feeling that Zared was not being entirely honest with him. "Kellogg it is," he said, and went out.

Fort Hall was still asleep. Only a few other early risers were up and about. A dog barked at Fargo from the yard of a frame house but ran off when Fargo threw a stone at it.

Before a golden glow suffused the eastern horizon, Fargo was in the saddle and a mile from the settlement. His plan was to cut across to the Big Lost River and follow it up into the Lost River Range. Once there, he would travel from gold camp to gold camp, seeking word of Gideon Zared's party.

Fargo was relieved to be away from the settlement. Civilization had its allures, but give him the untamed wilds any day. The towering peaks, the virgin forest, the rushing streams and clear high-country lakes were a tonic to his soul. He soon settled into a routine: up at dawn, coffee and whatever was left over from supper for breakfast, ride until noon and rest for half an hour, then push on until near twilight, when he would camp and take the Henry and shoot something for supper. Some nights he had rabbit, other nights squirrel. Ten days out from Fort Hall he shot a buck, salted strips of meat, and hung them over a makeshift rack. His saddlebags bulged with jerked venison when he rode on.

Everywhere Fargo stopped, it was the same. At every saloon and every establishment that sold dry goods and victuals, he stopped and asked about Gideon Zared. Everywhere it was the same: No one recollected seeing Gideon's party.

In due course Fargo was deep in the Salmon River Mountains. Here and there gold camps had sprung up. Most were lucky to boast a hundred inhabitants, whose dwellings consisted largely of tents and lean-tos. At each camp he made the rounds of places where Gideon Zared might have stopped. At each one he was given the same answer.

Beyond the Salmon River Mountains, to the north, were the Clearwater Mountains. The Bitterroot Range bordered both to the east. Thousands of square miles, much of it unexplored, and Gideon Zared somewhere in that vast maze. To say it was like looking for a needle in a haystack was an understatement.

Still, Fargo persisted. He reasoned that Gideon might have taken any one of a dozen routes from Fort Hall.

Then, one evening, as Fargo was resting by his campfire after a long day in the saddle, it occurred to him that, with his fiancée along, Gideon would probably take the easiest route. From Fort Hall to Fort Boise would be Fargo's guess, and from there, north to Lewiston.

From Lewiston, Gideon either went on north into the remote Coeur d'Alene Mountains, or east to Kellogg and then into the distant Bitterroots.

Fargo tried to think like the younger Zared. The Bitterroots were a lot farther than the Coeur d'Alenes, and closer to Blackfoot territory. To a young man with a woman to look after, the Coeur d'Alenes were a much safer proposition.

So it was on to Lewiston.

Day blended into day, night into night. Fargo came to a stream that had no name, and a small gold camp. A dozen tents and one dugout were clustered near where the prospectors panned and dredged. Across the side of the largest of the tents, in crude letters, was *SALOON*. Only two people were inside. Everyone else was off panning or at their digs.

The proprietor was an older gent with gray hair. He brought over a bottle and a glass and filled the glass to the brim. "Anything else, mister?"

"Leave the bottle." Fargo had no intention of getting drunk but one glass would not suffice. He paid, and as the proprietor turned to go, he said, "I don't suppose you saw any sign of two young men and a woman about three months ago?"

The man snickered. "How in hell am I supposed to remember that far back? Hell, I can barely recollect what I had for breakfast yesterday." Chortling, he took a couple of steps, and stopped. "Although—"

"Yes?" Fargo prodded.

"Females are as scarce as hen's teeth in these parts. Married men won't bring their wives for fear of the savages. So it's an event when a filly shows up."

Fargo leaned forward expectantly. "You remember them, then?"

"There was this girl," the proprietor said. "A pretty snip of a thing, as friendly as could be. I think two young fellas were with her."

"You think?"

"I was interested in her, not them. She wanted milk and was sad when I didn't have any. But what could I do? Cows are even scarcer than females."

"Did she say her name?"

"Now that I think about it, yes, she did, but I have no idea what it was."

"Could it have been Tabor? Tabor Garnet?"

The man nodded. "Could have been. It could also have been Martha Washington or the Queen of Sheba for all I know. I told you I don't recollect what it was."

"What *do* you remember?"

The man's brow puckered and he gnawed on his lower lip. "It's been so long. But I seem to recall as how they wanted to know how far it was to Canada."

"Canada?" Fargo repeated in surprise.

The man nodded. "Yep. That's what it was. I remember more now. When they came in, I was plumb flabbergasted. Women are scarce enough, but to have one walk into a saloon"—he smiled at the memory—"and such a cute little filly. Anyway, all they wanted was something to eat, and when I brought it, the girl asked if I knew how long it would take them to get to Canada."

Fargo was perplexed and it must have shown.

"I asked what in the world they wanted to go to Canada for, and one of the boys nudged her. Then she smiled real sweetly and told me she was just curious, is all." The man looked at him. "Anything else, stranger?"

"No, thanks." Fargo sat back and took a sip of whiskey. As it burned a pleasant path to his stomach, he tried to reason out how Canada figured into the situation. Why look for gold north of the border when there was plenty to be found south of it? It made no sense.

Suddenly Fargo was aware that the other customer had risen and come over beside him. Shifting in his chair, he placed his right hand on his Colt.

"No need for that, friend," said a middle-aged man in a derby. He had watery eyes and a red nose and a nervous tic to his mouth. "I couldn't help but overhear about the girl and her friends."

"What about them?"

"Well, I talked to them for a bit. My name is Harvey Wilcox. I'm a whiskey drummer. I sell it to the saloons in all the gold camps." Wilcox nodded at an empty chair. "Mind if I sit?"

Fargo pushed the chair from the table with his boot. "Be my guest."

Wilcox removed his derby and set it on the table. "Thank you. I don't suppose you could treat me to a drink? I lost all my money in a poker game last night."

"You can't drink your own stock?" Fargo asked.

"I sold the last I had with me to Dempsey there," Wilcox said with a nod at the proprietor, "and the mangy buzzard won't let me have any on credit."

"Another glass," Fargo called to Dempsey. To Wilcox he said, "but you better not be lying about talking to the girl."

"Oh, no, sir, I would never do a thing like that," Wilcox assured him. "I can prove it, too. My memory is better than Dempsey's. Her name was Tabor."

"You heard me tell him that," Fargo said.

"True. But you didn't tell him that the names of the boys she was with. Gideon and Asa."

Fargo's suspicions evaporated, and he bent across the table. "What did you talk to them about?"

"I happened to be here on my last trip up, and when they came in, it was about the middle of day. Like now, there weren't many at the tables. After they ate, the three of them came over and she asked me the same thing they had asked old Dempsey. How far is it to Canada? I told them I wasn't sure but I reckoned they could make it to the border in three weeks or thereabouts."

More mystified than ever, Fargo downed some whiskey.

"They were upset at that," Wilcox related. "The one boy, Gideon, was fit to be tied. He thought they were a lot closer."

"What does Canada matter?" Fargo asked aloud, more to himself than to the drummer.

"They didn't say," Wilcox answered, "but I can tell you one more thing for certain sure." He paused. "They were scared, those three—powerful scared."

"Of what?"

"They didn't say but I could tell. A drummer has to learn to read people if he's to make a sale, and I read them as scared out of their wits. It was little things, like how they kept glancing at the tent flap, and how whenever they heard someone ride by, the boys would put their hands on their rifles."

Fargo had to admit the drummer was an observant cuss. "Did they say anything else? Anything at all?"

"Not to me, no. But after they asked about Canada, they went back to their table and whispered among themselves. I couldn't hear much but I overheard enough to know that they were arguing over where they should go from here. That one boy, Gideon, was all for pushing for Canada. But the girl and the other boy weren't so sure. The girl mentioned New York a couple of times."

"I am obliged for the information."

"There's more," Wilcox said. "One thing I did hear clear as could be was when the Gideon boy told the others that they were as good as dead if they were caught. His exact words."

Fargo drained his glass in two gulps. "I don't suppose you heard them say where they were going from here?"

"As a matter of fact, I did. The girl wanted to go to Lewiston. To be among people for a while, she said."

Dempsey was walking toward them with the glass. "I don't like you mooching off my other customers," he complained to Wilcox.

"It's all right," Fargo came to the drummer's defense. "He's earned it." He filled Wilcox's glass himself, and mentioned, "Gideon's father has hired me to find them."

"You, too?"

Fargo leaped to the obvious conclusion. "Someone else has been asking after them?"

The drummer nodded. "Two days ago another man came through. Tough-looking bastard, with a patch over his nose. Never gave his name. I was outside when he rode up, and I was the first person he asked. He never even dismounted. I told him what I knew, and off he went, riding hell for leather."

Fargo had assumed that he had outdistanced the others but he was wrong. No-Nose Smith was now ahead of him, and that much closer to finding the younger Zared and his companions.

"They sure were a nice bunch, those kids," Wilcox was saying. "Polite, too. Called me sir, and all three thanked me."

Fargo was thinking of Smith, and Canada, and what Gideon Zared had to be afraid of.

"If you ask me, they had no business being in these mountains. It was as plain as that red bandanna of yours that they are city folk, and city folk don't last long out here."

"You're city-bred," Fargo said.

"True. Very true. But I know my limits. I stick to the main trails when I make my rounds of the camps,

119

and I always ride with others for protection." Wilcox smiled. "I hope for their sake you find them before they get themselves killed."

Since the sun would set in less than half an hour, Fargo decided to push on early in the morning. He shared half of the bottle with the drummer and, when he was ready to leave, slid what was left toward him. "The rest is yours."

Wilcox's face lit up and he smacked his lips in anticipation. "I'm grateful. Yes, indeed. You are a peach of a human being."

"Don't overdo it." Fargo exited the tent and forked leather. He followed the stream past the claims and into the next expanse of verdant forest. Twilight had descended when he stripped the Ovaro and bedded down for the night.

As he lay propped on his saddle, listening to the crackle of the fire, Fargo racked his brain for an explanation as to what Gideon Zared and the other two were up to. If they really were making for Canada, they were biting off more than they could chew. To survive in the country north of Lewiston was a challenge for seasoned frontiersmen. For greenhorns it was certain death.

The warmth, the crackling, and the peaceful night combined to lull Fargo into dozing. He drifted on a tide of chaotic dreams for he knew not how long. Then, in the blink of an eye, he was fully awake and not sure why. The answer came when the Ovaro whinnied. Easing onto his side, he saw the pinto standing with its ears pricked, staring intently into the forest to the north.

It could be anything: another grizzly, a black bear, a mountain lion, wolves, coyotes, even two-legged predators. Indians, though, rarely roved abroad at night. It was white men who were fond of striking from ambush in the cover of darkness.

The Ovaro continued to stare. Fargo waited for some

sign—a grunt or a snarl or a cough, anything. He laid his hand on the Henry, which he always kept beside him when he slept.

Finally, a sound. But it was not the kind Fargo expected. It was the muted ratchet of a rifle lever being slowly worked so as to feed a round into the rifle's chamber. Instantly, Fargo flung himself backward and rolled toward cover.

A rifle cracked, once, twice, three times. Fargo heard the slugs thud into the ground. He had his blanket to thank. It had clung to his shoulders and was flapping as he rolled, confusing the bushwhacker's aim.

Then he was in the undergrowth, scrambling on his belly until he was safe behind a pine. The firing had stopped.

Twisting, Fargo scanned the clearing. All he saw was the Ovaro. He turned to crawl to the west when a thought jarred him to his marrow. *The Ovaro!* He could not say why, but he had a vivid and certain conviction that the bushwhacker might decide to shoot the pinto.

Fargo tried telling himself that was silly. Indians never shot horses; they would much rather steal them. A white man might shoot one, but only if he did not have a horse of his own. *Or,* Fargo thought, *if he had reason to want to strand someone afoot.*

Fargo's body seemed to move of its own volition. He was up and barreling through the brush, bearing east, not west. Then he abruptly cut toward the clearing near where the Ovaro stood. He broke from cover on the fly and was at the stallion in a twinkling.

A sharp tug, and the picket pin was out and Fargo was swinging onto the Ovaro's broad bare back. He slapped his heels against its sides and the pinto bolted toward the woods. Simultaneously, lead sizzled the air above Fargo's head.

The bushwhacker had time to get off only one shot

before the Ovaro plunged in among the trees. Fargo quickly reined to the left in a wide loop that would bring him up on his attacker from the east. He was not foolish enough to ride into a blazing muzzle, so when he had gone halfway around the clearing, he reined the Ovaro to a stop.

Before Fargo could alight, hoofbeats resounded. The bushwhacker was lighting a shuck. Fargo started to give chase but reined the Ovaro up. It was too risky to go after the man at night. The killer might stop and wait for him to blunder into a hail of lead.

Fargo reined into the clearing. This made twice now someone had tried to ambush him out of the darkness— someone who had trailed him all the way from Fort Hall. Who wanted him dead that badly? He pondered that question until midnight but could not answer it. One thing was for sure, though: Whoever it was, he was bound to try again.

From then on out, he must be extra wary, Fargo resolved.

The fire had burned low but was not quite out. Fargo did not rekindle it. He gathered up his saddle, blankets, and bedroll and moved everything into the trees. He spread out his blankets, picketed the pinto, and prepared to catch some sleep.

Slumber proved elusive. The attempt on his life had Fargo's mind racing faster than the pinto. He tossed and turned until almost three a.m. and was up shortly past five. He chose to forgo his usual coffee. Saddling up, he roved through the woods to the north and, after a while, found what he was looking for: hoofprints. He was not surprised to find the horse had been shod.

Fargo followed the tracks and soon established the killer was heading northwest, toward Lewiston. He also established that the rider had not stopped for the night but had ridden the whole night through, and by now was miles and hours ahead.

"I'll find you, whoever you are," Fargo vowed aloud. And when he did, there would be a reckoning.

Lewiston was days away. Fargo was content to stick to the tracks until he reached it, but the second day after the attempt on his life, as he was winding up a switchback, he came to a spot where the bushwhacker had stopped. Fargo figured it was to rest his mount, but the man had inexplicably broken into a gallop until he came to the crest, and from there headed east at a trot.

To Fargo it was strange behavior. He had assumed the man was heading for Lewiston. Presently the trees thinned, and the forest gave way to terrain so rocky, the killer's horse left few prints.

Suddenly Fargo understood. The man had not stopped on the switchback to rest his horse. No, the killer had stopped to check his back trail, possibly with a spy glass, and had discovered he was being pursued. Now the killer was trying to lose him.

Drawing rein, Fargo leaned on his saddle horn. Tracking the bushwhacker now might take days, time he could not afford to waste. As much as it galled him, he had to let the man go.

On to Lewiston. Since the killer was now behind him, Fargo made it a point to repeatedly check his back trail. He did not see anyone or hear anything but he had a feeling he was being followed, a feeling that grew stronger as the day wore on.

Fargo made a cold camp next to a small spring and hid the Ovaro in a thicket. Pemmican sufficed for his supper. On edge from the previous attempt on his life, he did not fall asleep until well after midnight. He tossed and turned a lot.

Dawn found him traveling. By midmorning he reached a pass that would take him into the next valley. That high up, he could see for miles. He couldn't miss spotting gray tendrils of smoke to the southeast.

"So," Fargo said to himself, and dismounted. Taking the Henry, he descended a short distance on foot and sat on a log to wait.

It was over an hour before hoofbeats rose dully from below.

Fargo moved behind a fir and steadied the Henry's barrel against the trunk. The hoofbeats grew louder. There were more than there should have been if it was only one rider.

More minutes went by, and Fargo's patience was rewarded. Into view, riding in single file, climbed three men dressed alike, in black hats, black jackets, black pants, black boots: three of Benjamin Zared's bodyguards, the last leading a packhorse.

In the lead was none other than Pike Driscoll.

10

The three bodyguards were typical of most whites. They paid no attention to the surrounding woods. Slouched in fatigue, they climbed until they were almost in the shadow of the fir tree Fargo was behind. He chose that moment to growl, "That's far enough."

Pike Driscoll drew sharp rein. He swooped a hand to his jacket but turned to stone when he saw the Henry trained on his chest. "You!" he blurted.

The others made no move for their guns. They showed no great surprise, nor any fear.

"It better be good," Fargo said, moving out from under the fir.

"What?" Pike Driscoll asked.

"The reason you are following me. The reason you tried to blow out my wick last night."

"Someone took a shot at you?" Driscoll's surprise was not feigned. "It sure wasn't me. It wasn't any of us. Hell, Mr. Zared would have us gutted and quartered if we laid so much as a finger on you. He's counting on you to find his boy."

"Then why are you following me?"

"Mr. Zared doesn't like to leave anything to chance," Driscoll said. "He sent some of us after each of you to stay close and be of help if need be."

Fargo frowned. It sounded like something Benjamin Zared would do. But he did not like it. He did not like it one bit, and he told Driscoll as much.

"I'm only doing my job. Me, I could care less if you

ran into trouble—say, a war party out for your scalp. But Mr. Zared wants you alive and healthy until his boy is found, so here I am."

"Have you seen any sign of any of the others? Weaver? Smith? The Picketts?"

"We sure haven't. But then, we left Fort Hall before they did. We had to, in order to catch up to you." Driscoll gestured. "Are you fixing to shoot me or can I move?"

Lowering the Henry, Fargo asked, "Where is Zared right this moment?"

"On his way to Kellogg, if he's not there already," Driscoll answered. "I was fixing to send word to him once we reached Lewiston. And before you ask, I talked to that whiskey peddler at the last camp. He told me where you were heading."

Fighting his anger, Fargo reclaimed the Ovaro and swung into the saddle. As he shoved the Henry into the scabbard, the three bodyguards came up.

"Look, Trailsman," Driscoll said. "I don't like you and you don't like me. But that shouldn't keep us from getting along until this is over. What do you say we bury the hatchet and go on to Lewiston together?"

Fargo could think of nothing he would like less, but he heard himself say, "I reckon we might as well."

Driscoll brought his mount up alongside the Ovaro as they entered the pass. "If it makes you feel any better, I like being here even less than you like it. I told Mr. Zared that none of you needed a nursemaid, but Mr. Zared does as he damn well pleases and it pleased him to have us follow you."

It occurred to Fargo that maybe he could benefit from their unwanted company. "It must be hard working for a man like Zared."

"You have no idea," Driscoll said. "Not that he's mean-tempered or anything, but we don't dare buck him. We do as he wants when he wants. No questions asked."

"Does he treat his son the same way?"

"He's no more bossy than most parents, I guess. They have their spats, if that's what you're getting at. The boy is a chip off the old block. He always wants to do things his way, and his father be hanged."

"Do you like him much?"

"Gideon? He's all right. He always treated me decent enough. Although he did get mad at me a few times over his father having us keep an eye on him."

Fargo digested that a bit. "Zared had you spy on his own son?"

"Mr. Zared keeps a close watch on everybody he has an interest in," Driscoll explained. "That includes his boy. Especially after Gideon took up with Tabor Garnet. Mr. Zared was worried she might be after Gideon for his money."

"Zared told me his son came into these mountains after gold. That doesn't sound like Gideon had much money of his own."

"No, but the boy stands to inherit a fortune when Mr. Zared dies, which has Edrea mad as a wet hen."

Fargo was learning more by the minute. "Gideon will inherit more than she does?"

Driscoll laughed. "Almost all of the family's money goes to him. You see, Mr. Zared and his daughter aren't on the best of terms—something to do with her blaming him for her mother's death. So when Mr. Zared passes on, she'll get one hundred thousand dollars and her brother gets millions."

They wended down the mountain. Fargo waited a while, then asked, "Do you have any idea why Gideon would want to go to Canada?" He was watching Driscoll from under his hat brim, and the chief bodyguard's reaction was revealing: Driscoll recoiled as if he had been slapped.

"Where did you hear a thing like that?"

"From the same drummer you talked to."

Pike Driscoll pretended to be interested in a cloud

formation, then replied, "The drummer must have been mistaken. There's no reason for the boy to want to go that far north."

Fargo would bet his last dollar that the bodyguard was lying, but he did not let on. "It's bad enough Gideon dragged his fiancée up here."

"Don't tell Mr. Zared I said this, but his son isn't the smartest person I've ever met. The boy never thinks things through. He's always going off half-cocked."

"Strange he would prospect for gold when he stands to inherit millions," Fargo remarked.

"Boys his age are always doing stupid stuff" was Driscoll's opinion; then he added, "But we all pay for our mistakes sooner or later, don't we?"

"Sooner or later," Fargo agreed. After that Driscoll drifted back to his friends. By late afternoon they were thousands of feet lower and still had a ways to go to reach the bottom.

On a flat bench Fargo drew rein and rose in the stirrups to survey the land ahead. When he happened to glance down, there, next to the Ovaro, were more of the shod tracks he had followed that morning. The killer was still bound for Lewiston, and somehow had gotten ahead of him again.

It was close to five o'clock and Fargo was giving thought to where they should stop for the night when Pike Driscoll trotted up.

"We were wondering if you would care to ride all night? That way we would reach Lewiston by noon or so."

"My horse is tired and so am I," Fargo said.

"So are ours. But another day of hard riding won't kill them."

Yet another sign of an amateur, Fargo reflected, was a man who did not take proper care of his horse. "You can do what you want but I'm making camp."

"Aren't you fed up with sleeping on the hard ground? I know I am. Give me a soft bed any day."

A meadow spread before them. Coming to a halt, Fargo wearily swung down. He ignored the looks Driscoll and the other two men in black cast in his direction, and loosened the Ovaro's cinch. He was reaching up to take hold of the saddle when three shots crackled from across the meadow, from high on the slope on the far side.

Instinctively, Fargo dropped into a crouch and spun while sweeping the Colt clear of his holster. Driscoll and the other two bodyguards did the same but they were slower. For tense moments they waited for more shots or an outcry but there was only the sigh of the wind in the woodland canopy.

"What do you think that was?" one of the men in black asked.

"A rifle," Driscoll said.

"No. I mean, who do you think was shooting, and why?"

"How in hell would I know, Baker?" Driscoll snapped. Slowly rising, he slid a short-barreled Smith & Wesson under his black jacket.

"Should we have a look?" the third bodyguard asked.

"Use your head, Hodges," Driscoll responded. "We're not poking our noses into something that might not concern us."

"Maybe it does concern us," Baker said. "Maybe it was some of our own men in trouble."

"None of the others are within miles of us," Driscoll told him.

Fargo was not so sure. He had a hunch it was one of the other scouts who had taken a shot at him the previous night, and if Weaver, Smith or the Picketts were in the area, then the bodyguards assigned to follow them would be, too, although he had seen no sign of them so far.

Driscoll was staring at him. "You don't agree?"

Briefly, Fargo related the latest attempt on his life, and the shod horse he had tracked for a while.

"Damn it all," Driscoll grumbled. "Maybe we should go have a look." He motioned at Baker and Hodges. "Mount up. We'll leave the packhorse here, but one of you hobble him."

Fargo had no interest in accompanying them. Even if other bodyguards were involved, it was of no consequence to him. Except that whoever had tried to kill him might also be up on that mountain. "I'll go along."

"I'd rather you didn't," Driscoll said. "My job is to keep you alive until Zared's son is found."

"I'm going."

No more shots shattered the stillness, but Fargo shucked the Henry from its scabbard anyway and fed a cartridge into the chamber. With the stock resting on his right thigh, he spurred the Ovaro into the trees.

The bodyguards had their pistols out. At a command from Pike Driscoll, they spread out. Driscoll would rise in the stirrups every twenty or thirty feet to scour the vegetation.

"We'll never find anyone in this tangle," Baker said.

The undergrowth was dense. Deadfalls slowed their progress even more. Wildlife, Fargo noted, was absent, but that could be because the sun was about to set and the animals that came out during the day were retreating into their dens and burrows before night fell and the meat-eaters claimed the land.

"I hate these mountains," Hodges remarked. "I can't wait until we're back east where we belong."

"Hush, you simpleton," Driscoll ordered.

Fargo was slightly in the lead. They had climbed a considerable distance and he was thinking of turning back when he spied a saddled horse off through the trees. Drawing rein, he pointed.

Driscoll and the other pair stopped, and Driscoll

motioned for Baker to swing right and Hodges to swing left. Driscoll kneed his mount past the Ovaro. "Stay put," he directed.

"Like hell." Fargo could take care of himself. Every nerve jangling, he kneed the pinto on.

The riderless horse spotted them but did not run off. Soon they saw a second, and a third. The reins of all three were dangling, and from the sweat that glistened on their bodies, they had been ridden hard to get to where they were.

"Do you see that?" Pike Driscoll whispered.

Fargo had. A large red stain on one of the saddles, blood so fresh drops were falling to the grass.

"That's not good," Driscoll stated the obvious.

Baker and Hodges were converging. It was the latter who stiffened and pointed and exclaimed much too loudly, "There, Pike! Look there!"

A black-clad leg with a black boot attached lay amid high weeds. Fargo reached it a second after Pike Driscoll did and stayed on the Ovaro while Driscoll swung down and and rolled the body over.

"It's Sam Varnes. He was assigned to follow No-Nose Smith."

A slug had caught the late Mr. Varnes squarely between the eyes and blown out the back of his skull.

"Who would do this?" Baker asked. "Smith?"

"Look for more bodies," Driscoll said.

They found them. One was sprawled on his face, the lower half of which had been mangled by lead. The third had been shot in the chest, and was alive. The man groaned feebly when Driscoll rolled him over.

"Lattimer? Lattimer? Can you hear me?" the chief bodyguard asked, shaking the stricken man.

Lattimer's eyelids fluttered.

"Speak to me, damn it!" Driscoll fumed, and shook harder.

Hodges protested. "That's no way to treat a dying man."

Driscoll ignored him and smacked Lattimer across the cheek. Lattimer's eyes snapped open but they were glazed and unfocused. "Who did this to you?" Driscoll asked.

Lattimer's lips moved but nothing came out.

"Damn it," Driscoll fumed. "I need to know who did this." He smacked Lattimer a lot harder.

Hodges looked away, but looked back again when Lattimer croaked, "P-P-Pike? Is that you?"

"Of course it's me," Driscoll confirmed. "Varnes and Bryce are dead. Who shot you? Was it James Smith?"

"N-n-never saw," Lattimer stuttered. "Lost No-Nose days ago . . . on our way to L-L-Lewiston." And with that, he exhaled loudly, and died.

Spewing curses, Driscoll stood. "Search for sign! But be careful. Whoever did this might still be around."

"Shouldn't we bury them first?" Hodges asked.

Pike Driscoll, never the most patient of men, lost what little he possessed. "You do what I damn well tell you to do when I damn well tell you to do it!"

Fargo helped. He wanted to know who was responsible as much as Driscoll did. He had not gone far when he came on hoofprints made by a horse with shod hooves—made, in fact, by the same horse as before. The tracks led off to the northwest.

Driscoll and the others trotted over at his holler. Pike, in a vengeful frame of mine, declared, "It had to be No-Nose Smith! When we catch up to him, he is as good as dead."

"But why?" Baker wanted to know. "It makes no sense."

"To us it doesn't but he must have his reasons," Driscoll said. He shifted in his saddle. "How about you, Fargo? Any idea why your friend has turned into a murderer?"

Fargo was at a loss. Even though No-Nose had

made it plain he wanted the money at any cost, killing the bodyguards served no purpose. "We don't know it is him."

"Maybe you won't accept the truth. But Lattimer was assigned to follow him, and now Lattimer and those others are dead. That's good enough for me."

"Do we go after him?" Baker asked.

The sun was almost gone. The shadows had lengthened and darkness would soon descend.

"Not until morning," Pike Driscoll said. "We don't want to wind up like Lattimer, do we?"

They hastily buried the bodies after Driscoll went through every pocket and put everything into his saddlebags. One item proved of interest, a small leatherbound journal belonging to Lattimer, the kind commonly used for diaries and journals. Driscoll slipped it into his jacket, saying, "We'll look at this after we're done."

A rope was tied to the riderless mounts and Hodges was given the task of handling the string.

They had barely started for the meadow when night fell. Fargo picked his way with care. Horses that blundered into deadfalls often suffered broken legs and had to be put out of their misery, and he was not about to let that happen to the Ovaro.

It took two hours. The packhorse was still there. As the bodyguards went about the business of setting up camp, Fargo stripped his saddle off the Ovaro.

Baker started a fire, and coffee was put on to brew.

Pike Driscoll produced the journal. "I never knew Lattimer kept this," he said, flipping pages. "Looks like he started it four years ago, soon after Mr. Zared hired him. A lot of stuff is about his wife." He read a short entry, " 'September second, 1859. I wish I did not have to work such long hours. I miss Katherine so. I rarely get to see her.' " Driscoll stopped and snickered. "How silly can a man be?"

"Get to the end," Fargo said.

Pike flipped more pages, running a finger from top to bottom. "These are about New York. And the trip west." He stopped flipping, and grinned. "Here's one you will like, Fargo." He read it out loud, " 'The last scout has arrived. The most famous of the bunch. People call him the Trailsman. They say he knows the West better than anyone alive.' "

"The last entries are the ones we want."

"What's the matter? Don't you like folks fawning over you?" Driscoll laughed and turned more pages and suddenly sobered. "Here we go." He read an entry, then shared it aloud. " 'I am to follow No-Nose Smith. Varnes and Bryce are under me. Good men. I only hope we don't let Mr. Zared down. I am not much use in the wild.' "

Hodges piped up with, "Say, is there anything in there about me?"

Pike Driscoll looked at him over the top of the journal. "Were you born an idiot or do you work at it?"

"Ahh, Pike."

"It's Mr. Driscoll to you from now on." Driscoll bent his nose to the page. " 'Four days out of Fort Hall. We are staying well back as Mr. Zared wanted. Smith is heading northwest at a fast pace.' " He flipped a couple of pages, scanning them as he went. " 'Ten days now. Never so sore in my life. Not used to so much riding.' "

"He isn't the only one," Hodges said.

Driscoll ran a finger down another page. " 'Twelve days out. Have passed through two gold camps. Smith did not stop. Pushing faster than ever.' " He paused. " 'Day fourteen. Last night our packhorse was spooked by something in the woods. Woke us up about one in the morning. Might have been an animal but we heard nothing, saw nothing.' " He paused again. " 'Day fifteen. Again awoken in the middle of the night by packhorse whinnying and stomping.' "

"Why only the packhorse?" Baker asked.

Hodges snapped his fingers. "Say! Where is their pack animal? It wasn't with the rest."

Fargo had been wondering the same thing. There had been no other hoofprints leading away from the dead bodyguards.

"That's right," Driscoll said, and resumed reading. " 'Day sixteen. What is going on? Last night the pack-horse woke us again. This morning we found it dead. Its throat was slit from end to end. What would do this? Indians? Why didn't they harm us or steal the other horses?' " Driscoll glanced up. "Would Indians do a thing like that?"

"No," Fargo said simply. As to why only the pack animal was slain, it could be it had the sharpest senses, and whoever was in the woods wanted it out of the way.

" 'Day seventeen. I am worried. Whatever killed our packhorse is stalking us. I have not said anything to Varnes and Bryce but I am sure. It must be Indians. Or maybe just one.' "

"I wish we had run into them sooner," Baker said. "They might still be alive."

"Or we would all be dead," Hodges amended.

Driscoll was reading again. " 'Last night the oddest thing. About midnight we heard a strange laugh. It almost did not sound human. None of us slept much. On edge.' " Driscoll swore.

"What in hell?" From Baker. "Did he say a laugh?"

" 'We have lost Smith's trail. How, I do not know. I have been most diligent. But I am so tired. So very tired. Last night more laughter from the woods. We took torches and searched but no one was there. Bryce thinks it is a specter. He and Varnes want to turn back. I refused.' "

A burning limb in the fire abruptly made a popping noise, and Baker and Hodges both jumped.

"Try not to wet your pants, boys," Driscoll mocked them, and turned to the last page. " 'Our horses are

135

worn-out. Us, too. I thought I saw someone in the trees this morning. A glimpse of a face. It was there and it was gone. Could not tell if it was white or red. An hour later someone threw a rock at us.' "

"A what?" Hodges said.

"Pay attention." Driscoll reread the passage. " 'An hour later someone threw a rock at us. It hit Varnes and he was nearly unhorsed. We ride with our guns in our hands. I plan to make it to Lewiston. If Smith is not there, will go on to Kellogg.' " Driscoll closed the journal. "That was the last entry."

"We should head for Kellogg ourselves and report to Mr. Zared," Baker suggested.

"Our job is to follow Fargo," Driscoll reminded him. "Where he goes, I go, and where I go, you two go."

"I don't want to end up like Lattimer."

"We won't," Driscoll declared. "I don't scare easy, and the same tricks won't work with me."

"They would work with me," Hodges said.

Pike Driscoll turned to Fargo. "How about you? You've been awful quiet. What do you think we should do?"

"Push on to Lewiston," Fargo answered. What else was there? Searching for the killer would be pointless. The man could be anywhere.

"Whoever murdered Lattimer is miles away by now," Driscoll assured the men under him. "You can rest easy."

As if to prove him wrong, a sound wafted from out of the night, from high up on the mountain where they had found the bodies. A shrill, piercing laugh unlike any laugh Fargo ever heard. A laugh spawned from depraved depths. A laugh that prickled the short hairs at Fargo's nape.

"He's still out there!" Baker breathed. "And he'll be coming for us next."

11

The bodyguards did not get a wink of sleep all night. Fargo did not get much himself. Several times he drifted off only to wake up with a start at a noise from out of the depths of the forest. Once it was a clacking sound, like two rocks being struck together. The next time it was the sharp crack of a limb being broken. The last, shortly before sunrise, was when several of the horses nickered and acted as they would if a mountain lion were on the prowl.

Fargo's instincts told him they were being watched. He tried to pass it off as nerves but he had learned over the years never to take such feelings lightly. Sometimes they meant the difference between an early grave and ending his days in bed with a big grin on his face.

Pike Driscoll was surlier than usual this morning. He barked at Hodges and Baker to get the horses and pack animals ready, then came over to where Fargo was saddling the Ovaro.

"I've been thinking. What do you guess the odds are that Smith will try to wipe us out like he did Lattimer and those others?"

"I can't predict," Fargo said, "but it wouldn't do to sleep in the saddle until we reach Lewiston."

Driscoll's scowl deepened. "That's what I figured." He gazed at the dense timber across the meadow. "I wish I knew what this was all about."

So did Fargo. No-Nose Smith had always been sensible and dependable, a scout who did his job well and never caused anyone trouble. For him to turn into a cold-blooded murderer was preposterous. Yet stranger things had happened, and Fargo reminded himself that Smith had already promised to bury him if he stood between Smith and the twenty thousand.

Driscoll divided the extra horses between Baker and Hodges. Pike wanted his own hands free to shoot. He took it on himself to ride at the rear so he could protect his two companions.

Fargo did not like the man but he could still respect Driscoll for his devotion to his duty, and for his courage. He assumed the lead, the Henry once again resting on his thigh, his thumb curled around the hammer, his finger on the trigger.

Everything seemed normal enough. Sparrows chirped and flitted about in the brush. A robin warbled undisturbed. A woodpecker assaulted a dying fir. A squirrel scampered along leafy boughs. Reassuring signs, but it could be the killer wanted them to think that. It could be the killer had lain in hiding all night so the woodland creatures would not suspect he was there.

The graves had not been disturbed. Nor did Fargo come across any tracks other than those from the evening before.

It was a long, difficult climb to the crest. In addition to deadfalls, the slope was broken by ravines and drop-offs. Thick firs and pines covered most of the rest, and for a long spell Fargo rode in murky shadow, the clomp of the Ovaro's heavy hooves dulled by a carpet of needles.

They had emerged from the woods and were crossing a grassy glade when it dawned on Fargo that the birds and animals had gone quiet. Ahead were more trees, an impenetrable wall that could conceal a herd of elk—or an assassin.

Fargo could not say what prompted him to tuck the

Henry's stock to his side. He twisted to see if the others were staying alert, and the instant he did, a rifle blasted.

Baker had a hand to his mouth and was stifling a yawn. The heavy-caliber slug cored his hand from back to front, blowing two fingers off, and drilled his mouth dead center. It exploded out the base of his skull in a gory spray of hair, bone and blood. Baker probably never knew what happened. He was dead in the saddle. His lifeless eyes shut, he oozed from his horse like so much burned rawhide.

Fargo was in motion before the body came to rest. Reining to the right, he heard Pike Driscoll shout at Hodges to take cover.

Another shot boomed. Hodges's mount whinnied and pitched forward. It had been the target, not Hodges. He threw himself from the saddle and rolled up into a crouch. Having dropped his rifle, he went for the pistol under his jacket.

A third shot cracked, and an invisible hammer smashed into Hodges and lifted him off his feet. He landed on his back and instantly tried to rise but he had lost control of his body. Convulsing violently, he screamed, "No! No! I don't want to die! I don't want to die!" And then he did.

Fargo made it to the timber ahead of Pike Driscoll, who was fifty feet to Fargo's left. The packhorse and the extra horses had bolted and were fleeing in pure fright down the mountain.

The firing had stopped.

So did Fargo. He sat completely still, waiting for the shooter to move and give himself away. Evidently Driscoll was doing the same because the woods were as quiet as a ghost town.

Something ate at the back of Fargo's mind, a vague unease that troubled him although he could not say why. He tried to shut it out and concentrate on spotting the killer before the killer spotted him. But suddenly he was jolted as if by a physical blow; the bushwhacker had deliberately spared him.

It couldn't be, and yet the more Fargo thought about it, the more sure he became. He had been in front of Baker and Hodges. He had been a better target. But the killer shot them instead of him.

Why? The question seared Fargo like a burning brand. Why let him live? Was it because Smith, if that was who it was, had once been his friend? Was that why the two bodyguards lay out in the grass, nothing but empty husks, and he still breathed the crisp, clear mountain air?

From Fargo's left, where Driscoll was hidden, there was the snap of a dry twig. Instantly the killer fired two shots, one after the other.

Fargo saw him—or, rather, a silhouette that could be a man crouched low. He took a gamble. He aimed and squeezed off a shot.

The silhouette either fell or flattened.

On the chance the killer had seen the Henry's muzzle flash, Fargo spurred the Ovaro a dozen yards deeper into the forest, then drew rein. He did not want to leave the Ovaro. One horse had already been shot, and there was nothing to stop the killer from making it two. But so long as he stayed in the saddle, he could not fight effectively. Worse, he was a wooden duck in a blind, asking to be picked off.

Swinging his leg over the saddle horn, Fargo slid down. He winced when the saddle creaked, and braced for the gunshot sure to follow. But the silence of the woodland was unbroken.

Quickly, Fargo wrapped the reins around a limb, crouched, and cat-footed toward where he had seen the silhouette. Maybe the man was dead. That would account for why he had not shot back. Fargo came to a lightning-charred stump, and hunkered. He was close enough that if a body were there, he should see it. But there was none.

Fargo raked his gaze across every shadow, every nook, but the man had vanished. No-Nose Smith was living up to his reputation—if it was Smith. All Fargo had to go on was Pike Driscoll's suspicion that it was.

Driscoll! Fargo looked in the vicinity of where the bodyguard should be but Driscoll was either not there or well concealed.

The three of them were playing cat and mouse, and who was to say which was which?

Then, well up on the mountain, hooves drummed, only to be drowned out by mocking laughter.

Fargo slowly uncoiled. Apparently the killer was not ready to end it once and for all. The cat and mouse would continue. "Next time, damn your hide," he vowed.

A thicket parted and out stepped Pike Driscoll. "Is the bastard gone—really and truly gone?"

"For the time being," Fargo said.

A string of oaths blistered the air. "That son of a bitch killed two more of my men! If it's the last thing I do, I will see him dead as dead can be."

"Not if I see him first," Fargo said. "But we need to figure out who it is."

"What's to figure out?" Driscoll snapped. "It has to be No-Nose Smith. That's who Lattimer and his men were assigned to follow. Smith murdered them, then waited up here for us." He stopped and thoughtfully regarded Fargo. "Strange, though. Now that I think about it, how is it that he didn't shoot you?"

"You would have to ask him."

"There you were, in the lead, as easy to drop as anyone could wish, yet he shot my men instead." Driscoll grew angry as he talked. "Smith and you are friends, aren't you? Close friends?"

"We are pards, yes," Fargo admitted.

"So he treats you special. Is that how it goes? Or is there more to it?"

"I don't follow you."

"Sure you do. Maybe the two of you are working together. Maybe you led us into his gun sights."

"That's ridiculous," Fargo said.

"Is it? You buckskin types tend to stick together. How do I know this isn't some scheme the two of you cooked up?"

"A scheme to do what?" To Fargo it was a hare-brained notion. "What do I stand to gain?"

"How should I know?" Driscoll growled. "Maybe him and you want all of Mr. Zared's bodyguards dead."

Fargo started to turn away, saying, "What purpose would that serve?"

Suddenly Pike Driscoll grabbed Fargo's arm and spun him around. "Look at me when I'm talking to you."

"Don't," Fargo said.

"Or what? You'll pistol-whip me again? I would like to have you try." Driscoll's knuckles were white where they gripped his rifle. "Lord, how I would like to have you try."

"We'll talk about this later."

"We'll talk about it *now*!" Driscoll had worked himself into a near rage. "I want to know why Smith didn't shoot you! What are you two up to? Is it your way of somehow getting more money from Mr. Zared?"

Fargo was simmering. The only reason he let the chief bodyguard ramble on was because he understood why Driscoll felt as he did.

"With all of us out of the way, you scouts could force him to hand over as much money as you want."

"You're loco," Fargo said.

"Like hell. It makes sense to me." Driscoll was working it out as he went along, or thought he was.

"How does it go? You eliminate all of us? Then you refuse to turn Gideon over to his father until Mr. Zared has paid whatever amount you want?"

"Gideon might not even be alive."

"How much are you after? A million dollars? Two million? Three?" Pike Driscoll took a step back. "That's it, isn't it? Wait until I tell Mr. Zared what you vultures are up to."

"You're a jackass," Fargo said.

"Call me all the names you want. But I'm right. And you know I'm right, which is why you're going to drop your hardware and hike your hands in the air."

"Like hell."

They were only five feet apart, their rifles at their waists although not pointed at each other. Driscoll was as eager as a rabid wolf to strike, but their past two clashes had made him wary.

"I won't do anything to you. You have my word. All I want is to take you to Mr. Zared. We'll let him sort this out."

"I'll go with you to Zared but I won't hand over my guns," Fargo said. He hoped Driscoll would come to his senses but the vicious glint in the other's eyes did not bode well.

For tense moments they locked stares. Then Pike Driscoll abruptly shrugged and smiled. "Fair enough. That's what we'll do then. I'll take you to Mr. Zared."

Fargo had not been born five minutes ago. He was being duped into letting down his guard. But he played along, saying, "Zared is in Kellogg by now. We should still stop at Lewiston first and find out if Smith or the others have been there."

"Of course we should," Pike Driscoll agreed much too readily. "Gather up the horses and I'll see to the bodies."

"After you," Fargo said. Under no circumstances was he turning his back on the other.

"However you want it."

143

Fargo tried to think of an argument that would persuade Driscoll he was not in cahoots with No-Nose Smith. But how did he convince someone whose mind was made up and as closed as a steel bear trap? He followed Driscoll to Hodges and Baker and together they placed the bodies side by side. Since they did not have a shovel, Driscoll had to make do with a sharpened branch. While he dug, Fargo collected the Ovaro and the horses that had strayed off.

So far Driscoll was behaving, but Fargo sensed he was biding his time. Fargo stayed on the pinto.

Presently, Pike Driscoll wiped his sweaty brow with a sleeve and commented, "I could use a hand here." He had dug a shallow six-foot hole but it was not deep enough yet to keep the bodies safe from scavengers.

Reluctantly, Fargo dismounted. If he didn't help, it would take hours, and he wanted to be on his way. "Give me a minute." There were plenty of downed tree limbs to choose from. He selected one that was particulary stout and long enough that he could dig without bending over. Using the toothpick, he sharpened one end and was ready.

Pike Driscoll was hard at work. He had set his rifle aside and did not look up as Fargo bent his back to the second grave.

The ground was hard. Digging required a lot of effort. Fargo fell into a rhythm; he would jab the tip of the limb into the soil, apply his full weight, and flip a clod over. In this way he soon had a six-foot furrow of dirt exposed. He thought of James Smith, and the lengths some people would go to when they wanted something badly enough. But what purpose did it serve to kill Zared's bodyguards? The only answer he could think of was the one he had scoffed at—namely, that Smith intended to somehow squeeze more money from Benjamin Zared.

But that still did not answer the question of why

Smith had spared him. Yes, they were friends, but Smith would not want witnesses.

There had to be more to it, a lot more, but Fargo knew too little to hazard a hunch as to what. The only one with the answers was Smith. Catching him was the key.

More sod yielded to Fargo's branch. Even at that altitude the temperature rose into the nineties in the summer, and he was soon sweating as profusely as Pike Driscoll. Fargo glanced at him from time to time. Driscoll was making good progress. A few more minutes and the first grave would be done.

Some roots resisted Fargo's attempt to loosen them. He bent his knees for extra leverage and speared the branch into the earth as far as it would go. It was then, as he moved the branch from side to side to force it deeper, that the click of the bodyguard's rifle made him want to beat his head against a tree for being so unforgivably careless.

"I will only say this once: Do exactly as I tell you and you will live a while yet."

"I'll ask you again not to do this."

Pike Driscoll laughed. "On second thought, you've lived long enough."

Some people never learned, Fargo reflected. They thought they had the right to do as they pleased, and everyone else be damned. They liked to boss others around, and make life miserable for those they did not like. Pike Driscoll was a living example. His position as head bodyguard to one of the richest men in America was a perfect fit for his bossy nature, and accounted for their previous run-ins. But this was different. Driscoll had made up his mind Fargo was to blame for the deaths of five of his men, and in Driscoll's eyes, he had the right to act as judge, jury, and executioner.

Fargo had tried to avoid trouble. He had no hankering to kill a man who was only doing his job. But there was only so much he could do, only so many times he could go easy on Driscoll before it cost him dearly. Now, with Driscoll's rifle trained on him and Driscoll smirking smugly and about to squeeze the trigger, he tried one final time to avert what could not be averted. "I thought you were taking me to Zared?"

"I'll still take you, all right. Draped over the saddle instead of on it." Driscoll smirked. "Better yet, why go to all that bother? I'll take your effects and your horse and tell Mr. Zared that No-Nose Smith shot you."

"You are no better than whoever killed your men," Fargo stalled while pressing on the branch to gouge it deeper into the earth.

"I've killed when I have had to," Pike said. "Now I have to, or I'm liable to end up like Baker and Hodges." He was smiling and confident since he had the upper hand. "So how do you want it? In the face? Or in the gut?"

"Neither," Fargo said, shifting as he did and flinging loosened earth at Driscoll's swarthy face.

Driscoll ducked, or tried to. The dirt caught him in the eyes. Backpedaling, he frantically tried to clear them. In a twinkling, Fargo pounced. He swung the branch, smashing it against Driscoll's rifle, jarring it from his grasp. Then he swung at Driscoll's head, thinking to knock him out, but Pike ducked and seized the end of the branch. Before Fargo could brace himself and wrest it free, Driscoll howled like a demented wolf and hurled himself at Fargo's legs.

Fargo tried to spring aside but iron hands clamped around his ankles and he was bowled over. He arced the branch at Driscoll's head but it struck Driscoll across the shoulders instead and had no effect. The same could not be said of the punch Driscoll threw at his groin.

Agony exploded below Fargo's belt. Pinpoints of

light sparkled before his eyes. His vision cleared just in time for him to see Pike Driscoll on both knees with a dagger in his hand—a dagger he lanced at Fargo's heart. With a fraction of a second to spare, Fargo thrust the branch between them. The tip of the blade imbedded itself in the wood.

Exerting all his strength, Fargo shoved Driscoll from him. He almost lost fingers when Driscoll slashed at his left hand. Scrambling onto a knee, he drove the sharpened end of the branch at Driscoll's chest but Driscoll swiveled and the branch glanced off his black jacket.

There would be no reasoning with Pike Driscoll now. His features were a mask of bloodlust. He had never possessed much restraint to begin with, and whatever shred he had left had been obliterated in the blazing heat of raw hatred.

The dagger leapt at Fargo's jugular. He avoided it by throwing himself to one side. In doing so, he lost his balance and fell. Since he still had the branch, it was a simple matter to use it as a fulcrum and lever himself back up. But as he rose, Pike Driscoll closed in. One of Driscoll's arms looped around his chest. The other held the glittering dagger, which Driscoll raised to stab.

His arms pinned, Fargo did the only thing he could: He butted Driscoll in the face. The crunch of cartilage elicited a howl of pain. It also drove Pike Driscoll berserk.

In a frenzy, Driscoll sought to plunge the dagger in Fargo's flesh. Fargo countered every blow but he could not keep Driscoll at bay much longer and Driscoll knew it.

The blade nicked Fargo's left ear. He lost several whangs from his buckskins.

Then Pike Driscoll set himself and cocked his right arm. "Say your prayers!" he snarled.

Fargo watched the dagger and only the dagger. It

flashed toward him, and he parried with the branch. Driscoll recovered and went to try again.

Fargo did the last thing Driscoll would expect: He threw the branch at Driscoll's face. Driscoll did what anyone would do. He sidestepped. It bought Fargo the few seconds he needed to bend and dive his hand into his right boot and bring it out holding the Arkansas toothpick.

Now they were evenly matched. Most men would have exercised more caution, but not Pike Driscoll. He flung himself at Fargo as if possessed, more determined than ever to end Fargo's life.

Pivoting, Fargo saved himself from a lightning thrust. He responded in kind, and felt the toothpick bury itself to the hilt in Driscoll's neck.

Pike Driscoll bleated and retreated, pressing his hand to the wound. But the scarlet geyser could not be stopped. A fine mist sprayed between his fingers and red rivulets flowed down his throat.

Dropping his dagger, Driscoll pressed his other hand to his neck. His eyes grew wide with shock. He recognized the inevitable, and cried out, "Not like this!" With each word came copious amounts of blood. He gagged, coughed, and staggered.

Fargo kicked the dagger into the weeds. "I didn't start it," he said, but his words fell on deaf ears.

Driscoll dropped to his knees and blubbered and mewed in panic. He kept saying, "No! No! No!" Each word a wet smack of lips coated with blood. In mute appeal, he looked at Fargo.

"You brought it on yourself. There's nothing I can do."

There was one thing Pike Driscoll could do. His blood-drenched hand vanished under his black jacket and reappeared fumbling with his revolver. "Get you yet!" he blubbered. "Take you with me!"

"Like hell," Fargo said, and palming the Colt, he shot Pike Driscoll in the forehead.

At the *crack*, Driscoll's head snapped back, then slowly lolled forward until his chin rested on his chest. Both arms slumped and the body pitched to the grass, where it twitched for a few seconds

Fargo did not feel a shred of remorse. He had done all he could to avert spilling blood, and then some. It was on Driscoll's shoulders. With a sigh, he replaced the spent cartridge, then wiped the toothpick clean on Driscoll's jacket.

Another grave had to be dug.

It was half an hour before Fargo had Hodges and Baker buried and was rolling Pike Driscoll into the last hole. Pausing, he patted each of Driscoll's pockets. In addition to a comb, a folding knife, and twelve dollars, he found a folded sheet of paper. Curious, Fargo unfolded it. The signature at the bottom identified who had written it.

The letter was from Gideon Zared.

12

It was addressed simply to "Pike," which hinted that Gideon and Driscoll must have been on friendly terms. Fargo folded it back up, slid it into a pocket, and hauled the mortal remains of Pike Driscoll into the grave. He covered the body with several inches of dirt, tamped the dirt down, and added a few rocks and branches to deter coyotes and the like.

For a few moments Fargo stood gazing at the earthen mounds. Six dead men in two days. The killer had a lot to answer for. He turned and went to the horses and added Driscoll's to the string. The extra animals would slow him down but he was only a couple of days out of Lewiston.

The rest of the morning was peaceful. Fargo reached the crest and wound down the north slope. Along about noon he stopped at a stream so the horses could slake their thirst. While they rested, he sat with his back to a pine and unfolded the letter from Gideon Zared to Pike Driscoll.

Before I get to what I am about to say, I must ask you not to show this to my father. If you do, he will be furious. And not just with me.

We have known each other for seven years now. That is a long time. Granted, you are in my father's employ, but we have always been friends. Or at least friendly. Last Christmas I had my sis-

*ter give you a stuffed goose in return for the small
favors you have done. Do you remember?*

*Those favors have meant a lot, Pike. You have
not informed on me to my father when I have
been with Tabor. I hate having to sneak behind
my father's back but he leaves me no choice. You
know how he feels about her. He has forbidden
me to see her, as you are aware. But how can I
not see the woman I care for more than I care
for life itself?*

Fargo stopped reading. The younger Zared sounded
like a love-smitten calf. But what did the father have
against the boy's fiancée?

*I have also slipped you money from time to time.
A fifty here. A hundred there. Money well spent,
since every minute I spend with Tabor is precious.*

*Now I am prepared to pay you more. A lot
more. Five thousand dollars, nearly all I have in
this world. There was a time when my father lavished money on me, but he stopped when I took
up with Tabor.*

*I mention that only to impress on you that if I
had more, I would offer you more. Still, five thousand is nothing to sneeze at. And it is yours, all
yours, if you will do me one last favor. The great-
est favor of all.*

*I intend to run off with her, Pike. To take her
as far and as fast from my father as I possibly
can, never to return.*

*But I constantly have bodyguards with me, and
the others have not been as kindly disposed
toward us as you have. They would tell on me in
an instant.*

Again Fargo stopped reading. Of all the ways to
describe Pike Driscoll, "kindly" was not one of them.

He wondered if Driscoll had duped the boy into thinking he cared about Gideon and Tabor when all Driscoll really cared about was the money Gideon gave him.

I need to meet with Tabor in private several times between now and the end of the month. If you can arrange to be my bodyguard on certain days, I can accomplish this without my father suspecting.

But there is more.

I need several days' head start.

I know my father well. I know how his devious mind works. Once he finds I am missing, he will send his bodyguards out to find me. Eluding them will be difficult unless we work things out so my father does not realize what I am up to until it is too late for him to stop me.

What do you say? Five thousand dollars, and it is all yours with no one the wiser. It is not as if I am asking you to betray my father's trust in anything that might harm him.

I am in love, Pike. I do not mind admitting that. It is love that prompts me to defy my father. It is for love's sake that I am willing to give up all that will be bequeathed to me. If you have ever been in love, then I need say no more. If you have not, or if you think me foolish, I need only mention once more that which will make a tidy nest egg for you.

Five thousand dollars.

Please give me your answer tonight after supper. I could not bear the suspense much longer.

Respectfully

Underneath was Gideon's signature. Fargo reread the letter, then folded it and placed it in his pocket.
A host of new questions needed to be answered.

Had Benjamin Zared lied about his son and the others going after gold? Or was that what Gideon told his father to gain the time he needed to escape? And how was it Benjamin had forbidden Gideon to see Tabor if Gideon and Tabor were engaged? What was true and what were lies? The whole affair was a web of deception.

Not to mention, one of the scouts was on a killing spree. Normally Fargo was more than a match for anyone in the wild. But this time he was up against someone whose skills rivaled his own.

Rising, Fargo stretched and stepped to the Ovaro. As he forked leather, a premonition seized him: a feeling that the dangers he had endured so far were nothing compared to those ahead; a sense that the worst was yet to come.

"I'm getting as bad as an old spinster," Fargo joked to the pinto. But death was no laughing matter, and before the situation was all sorted out, a lot more people might share the fate of Driscoll and the other bodyguards.

That night Fargo kindled a fire in a dry wash where he was out of the wind and out of the sight of unfriendly eyes. He slept with the Henry in the crook of an elbow. Before daylight he pushed on. By ten, clouds covered the sky, harbingers of rain later in the day. Shortly past eleven he came to a grassy tract, and there, made the day before, were tracks left by the killer's mount.

Fargo paralleled them. He hoped to learn more. Maybe the killer would drop something. It was a long shot, but if he could learn who the killer was, he could eliminate the one advantage the killer had.

Another sundown, another night under the stars. Fargo felt safe in making a fire in a clearing but he kept it small. He had shot a squirrel that afternoon and treated himself to squirrel stew and a pot of black coffee.

Fargo liked the wilds at night. He liked listening to the roars, snarls, shrieks, and sundry bestial cries. They were as ordinary to him as the clatter of buckboards and wagons and the clomp of hooves were to city dwellers.

He slept soundly, but lightly, and for once he was up and in a crouch before the Ovaro nickered and stomped a hoof. Draping his blanket over the saddle to lend the impression he was curled under it, he was on his belly at the clearing's edge when a darkling figure materialized on the other side. First one, then another, stalked toward his saddle.

The fire was out so they could not tell he wasn't under the blanket. Nor could he make out more than their shapes and sizes. He centered the Henry on the one on the right and had his finger on the trigger when the man he was about to shoot stopped and addressed his blanket.

"Fargo? Are you awake?"

"It's us. Billy Bob and Silky Mae," said the sister.

Fargo could not have been more taken aback if it were President Lincoln. "Stand where you are," he warned.

The Picketts spun and Silky Mae uttered a nervous laugh. "What are you doin' over yonder? You sure are a tricky critter."

"What do you want?" Fargo demanded. The last he knew, they were ready to skin him alive.

"Is this any way to greet folks?" Billy Bob asked.

"We're not lookin' to hurt you, if that's what you're thinkin'," Silky Mae said. "If we were, we'd have come in quiet-like."

"What do you want?" Fargo repeated.

"To jaw a spell," Billy Bob said. "To set things right. We figured out why you were so mad at us."

"It was the rattler, wasn't it?" Silky Mae asked. "Someone stuck it in your room and you thought it was us."

154

"But it wasn't," Billy Bob took up when his sister paused. "We would never have stuck a dead snake in your room. That's plain childish."

"The snake was alive. Someone left it thinking it would bite me. Didn't you see its tail?" Fargo said.

"It's tail?" from Silky Mae. "It was the head I noticed, crushed to goo like it was."

"Whoever done the deed, it wasn't us," Billy Bob reasserted. "We just wanted you to know."

"And that there are no hard feelin's over what you did," Silky Mae said. "Heck, we would be riled if someone did that to us."

"True enough." Billy Bob nodded. "And we're not the kind to hold a grudge."

"You live by the feud, remember?" Fargo reminded them.

"That's different," Silky Mae said. "A feud is pure hate. It's a life for a life, not a snake for a snake." She laughed merrily.

So did her brother. "Why, we would have to be plumb addlepated to want to kill someone over a dead snake and a little roughhouse."

"And we're not addlepated," Silky Mae said.

Damned if Fargo didn't believe them. But accomplished liars were always believable even when they told the baldest of lies. Still, they had come up on his camp making no effort at stealth. "One of you get the fire going."

"I will." Silky Mae hunkered and poked at the embers. She added kindling and branches and puffed until the kindling caught, all within a span of no more than thirty seconds. She was good, this backwoodswoman. "There," she said as the flames rapidly flared.

Fargo came into the circle of light, lowered the Henry, and noticed they had their pistols but nothing else. "Do you always go around at night without your rifles?"

"We didn't want you shootin' us by mistake," Billy Bob said. "A man sees a couple of varmints comin' toward him in the dark with long guns, he's liable to shoot first and find out who they were after they stop breathin'."

"We're not idiots," Silky Mae said. "Some folks always think we are, us bein' from the South and talkin' like we do and all."

Billy Bob chuckled. "To us, it's the Yankees who talk funny. Why, half of 'em talk like they have marbles in their mouths."

"Especially the Yankees from Boston," Silky Mae said. "You ever heard 'em? Their voice boxes are up in their noses. They talk like this." She pinched her nose and said, "I say, you bounder, you."

Despite himself, Fargo grinned. "How about some coffee?"

"That would be fine," Billy Bob said, "but first we'd like to fetch our horses. I don't cotton to leavin' 'em out there in the dark untended. Who knows what might come along?"

Fargo watched them cross the clearing. The moment they were out of sight, he backed into the shadows, just to be on the safe side. Maybe they were telling the truth, maybe they weren't. It was not worth a bullet from an ambush to find out.

Shortly, though, the Picketts were back, leading their mounts and a pack animal. Fargo gathered up an armful of limbs for the fire and strode into the open. "I reckon I should apologize," he said. "When I found Silky Mae in my room, on her hands and knees by my bed, I figured she was the one who left the snake."

The distaff Pickett squealed as if he had stuck her with a pin. "So that's it! I'd heard somethin' and was tryin' to find what it was when you walked in on me. But I didn't see no snake."

It was possible, Fargo supposed, if the rattler had

been far enough back under the bed. But then, if the Picketts were not to blame, who was?

"What a mix-up," Silky Mae said. "That was real cute of you, leavin' that critter under my pillow."

"It's water over the beaver dam," Billy Bob said. "Let's start fresh like we just met and go from there."

"Fine by me." Silky Mae smiled at Fargo. "I was powerful sad we had a fallin' out. I'd like to get to know you better."

Was it wishful thinking on Fargo's part, or was there a hint of something more than friendliness in her expression and her comment? He squatted, set the Henry down, and opened the coffeepot to see how much was left. Plenty. He placed it on a flat rock to reheat, then sat back with his forearms over his knees. Both the Southerners were staring at him as if he were an exhibit at a county fair. "What?"

"You're about the most famous person we ever met," Billy Bob said, "if you don't count Stephen Douglas when he was stumpin' for president."

"Politicians don't count," Silky Mae said. "They don't hardly amount to a hill of beans, the whole lot of 'em." To Fargo she said, "I suppose you heard about the secession?"

"Who hasn't?" Fargo said. It had been in all the newspapers, and was all most people talked about. South Carolina had seceded from the Union in December of last year and since then other Southern states had done the same.

"All that fuss over negroes," Billy Bob remarked. "There's even been talk of goin' to war."

"Does your family own slaves?" Fargo asked.

"Us?" Silky Mae said, and squealed with mirth. "It takes money to buy slaves, in case you haven't heard, and we can barely afford the clothes on our backs."

"We've always been dirt poor," Billy Bob said, "but that can change if we find Zared's boy."

"I still don't much like workin' for him," Silky Mae

157

said. "Him a damned Yankee, and all. And a snooty Yankee, besides."

"His daughter ain't no better," her brother responded. "I never met a female who put on so many airs. You would think she walks on water, the way she looks down her nose at us."

"I can suffer her airs for twenty thousand dollars," Silky Mae said. "I can suffer all the airs in the world."

Billy Bob leaned back and casually asked, "So have you seen hide or hair of that jasper without a nose or that Weaver fella?"

"No," Fargo said, wishing he'd had a glimpse of the killer.

"Us neither," Silky Mae said. "They lit out of Fort Hall ahead of us and we've been tryin' to catch up ever since."

"Of course, you lit out earlier than everybody," Billy Bob mentioned. "Pretty sneaky, although I can't say as I blame you."

Silky Mae gave Fargo another of her enigmatic smiles. "The early bird gets the worth, brother. He was bein' smart."

"I've never been all that clever," Billy Bob lamented. "Mostly, I chug through life like a steamboat with a busted boiler."

"You do not," Silky Mae said. "You can be as cagey as an old coon when you have to be."

"So can you. And we have to be cagey now, with so much money at stake."

"There are lives at stakes, too." Fargo had never met two people who loved to flap their gums as much as these two. "The boy and his fiancée and his friend."

"We're not forgettin' 'em," Silky Mae said. "But we would be less than honest if we didn't admit to bein' more interested in the money than we are in whether we find them healthy and kickin' or bleached bones."

"They're Yankees," Billy Bob said, as if that were explanation enough.

"It's not like we know 'em," Silky Mae elaborated. "It would be different if they were friends or kin."

Picking up a thin branch, Fargo broke it in half and added the two pieces to the fire. Then he checked the coffee. It would be a while yet.

"You don't gab much, do you?" Silky Mae asked and, before he could answer, added, "But that's all right. I like men who don't bend a gal's ear until it darn near falls off."

Fargo could say the same about women but she might take it personally.

Billy Bob unexpectedly rose. "One of us has to strip the horses, sis. Since you did it last night, it's my turn."

"Bring me my saddlebags and bedroll if you would," Silky Mae requested, and after he moved off, she said quietly to Fargo, "He's not bad as brothers go. Most every gal I ever met has horror tales to tell of brothers who beat 'em or always sassed 'em or wanted to do things brothers and sisters shouldn't do, but Billy Bob has always treated me decent."

"You're an exceptional lady," Fargo commented.

"That's a mighty big word for a mighty ordinary gal. I pull on my britches one leg at a time like everybody else."

"Most women would rather wear dresses and live in town where it's safe and peaceful," Fargo mentioned.

"Was that an insult?" Silky Mae bristled. "So what if I don't wear a dress? I'm every bit as female as any citified priss."

"Sheathe your horns." Fargo smiled. "I admire a woman who can hold her own out here."

"Oh."

"I've only known a few who can," Fargo went on. "I respect them all highly—you included."

A pink tinge crept into Silky Mae's freckled cheeks.

"I'm sorry. Men don't generally say nice things about me unless they are drunk or they want to take my clothes off."

"Well, I'm not drunk," Fargo said.

Silky Mae laughed and slapped her leg. "Why, I do declare, if you're not careful, I'll think you are sparkin' me."

"I'm not looking for a wife," Fargo set her straight.

"And I'm not hankerin' after a husband, so we're even. There's too much of this world I ain't seen, too much I ain't done. A husband would only tie me down, saddle me with kids and such, and I'd never get to see anything."

In that regard they were kindred souls, Fargo mused.

"My brother has promised that once this is over with, we can go on to the Pacific Ocean," Silky Mae said excitedly. "I've been to the Atlantic once, back when I was thirteen, and it gave me goose bumps, all that water movin' like it does, and the waves and all. They say the Pacific is just as big."

"You are in for more goose bumps," Fargo said.

"We might even go on to southern California," Silky Mae waxed enthusiastic. "See some of those old Spanish missions, and lie on the shore in the sun like some do. That would be fun."

Fargo smiled. In many respects, Silky Mae Pickett was a girl in a woman's body—and a nice body, at that: pert and compact but full in all the right places.

"I envy you, travelin' everywhere like you do. No roots to hold you, no ties that bind. Don't get me wrong. I'm fond of my kin. My ma and pa are the best anyone could ask for. Ma is the gentlest soul alive, and she has the patience of a saint. That's what comes of raisin' fourteen kids, I reckon."

Fargo whistled softly. Large families were common, particularly in the South, but fourteen was more than most women would stand for.

"Exactly." Silky Mae grinned. "If I had that many, it would drive me to drink or an early grave, or both."

"Your parents don't mind you coming out here?"

"I'm old enough to do as I please. Besides, my folks raised us to stand on our own two feet, to make up our own minds about things and take the consequences."

Steam was rising from the coffeepot but not enough to suit him, so Fargo slid it nearer the fire.

"That's what life is all about," Silky Mae said. "Consequences. You take this rich kid Gideon. He went off into the mountains after gold and now he's disappeared. It's the consequence of him being as dumb as a stump."

"There is more to it than that."

"Maybe so. But it doesn't excuse what he did. He's a city boy, and city boys are like fish out of water in the woods. I've yet to run into one who can ride a whole day without cryin' about how his legs hurt, or who can butcher a buck or a rabbit without gettin' green at the gills."

"That's hardly fair," Fargo said.

"City folks are different from country folk. They're softer. Weaker. And they do too damn much thinkin'. It comes from livin' more in their heads than in the world around them, if that makes any kind of sense."

Fargo conceded that it did. There was more to this Southern lass than one might suspect.

"Why, you're just full of flattery," Silky Mae teased. "I shouldn't be surprised. From what I've heard and read, you have always have been partial to the ladies." She snickered and winked.

"You shouldn't believe everything you hear or read," Fargo cautioned. "Half of it is lies and the other half exaggerations."

"No one lied about you bein' handsome," Silky Mae said.

Mimicking her, Fargo bantered, "Be careful, or I'm liable to think you're sparking me."

"Maybe I am," Silky Mae said coyly. "Maybe I find you as attractive as everyone says. Maybe, too, I'm doin' more than sparkin'."

"More?" Fargo said.

Silky Mae nodded. "Maybe I'm chatterin' up a storm so as to distract you. Maybe it's a trick to hold your attention while my brother sneaks on around behind you and puts a gun to your back."

Fargo glanced toward the horses. He had completely forgotten about Billy Bob. Suddenly something hard gouged him in the spine.

"No sudden moves, if you please, unless you want to die. In which case I'll be happy to oblige."

Silky Mae giggled.

13

Fargo had to sit there simmering as Silky Mae Pickett rose and cautiously relieved him of the Colt and the Henry. As she plucked the pistol from his holster, she smiled and said into his ear, "No hard feelin's, I hope, you murderin' polecat."

"We found the graves," Billy Bob said. "I dug up one to see who it was, and it was one of those hired guns of Zared's."

"Six of them you killed," Silky Mae said, stepping back and leveling Fargo's own revolver at him, "although the why is a mystery."

Controlling his temper, Fargo asked, "What makes you think I'm to blame?"

Billy Bob came around from behind him. "Play innocent but it won't work. We struck your trail back at the first gold camp you visited. Been doggin' you ever since. Then we came on the graves."

"It wasn't me," Fargo said.

"Liar, liar, britches on fire." Billy Bob looked at his sister. "I still vote we blow out his wick and turn the body over to the first tin star we come across."

"In these parts, there ain't any tins stars," Silky Mae said. "I still say we should hand him over to Mr. Zared and let Zared deal with him."

Her brother considered a bit. "Fine. We'll do it your way. But we truss him up and keep him trussed, and at night one of us is always on guard. Agreed?"

"You're making a mistake," Fargo said. The last

thing he wanted was to be bound and thrown over the Ovaro. Not with the true killer still on the loose. He tensed to spring, but could do nothing so long as they had him covered.

"It won't be the first time," Billy Bob said. "And if we're wrong about you, we'll say we're sorry later." He motioned at his sister. "Fetch a rope."

Silky Mae hurried toward their packhorse.

"I wouldn't try anything," Billy Bob cautioned. "Give me any excuse at all to plug you and I will."

Fargo started to rise but stopped when the Southerner thumbed back the hammer. "Damn it, I didn't shoot those men. They were following No-Nose Smith when they were bushwhacked."

"Sure, sure, and if Smith were here, he would likely as not say they were followin' you."

Silky Mae had a rope in her hand and was hastening back.

"I wish you would listen to me," Fargo said, and as he said "me," he kicked at the fire with his right boot, sending a shower of burning wood and sparks at Billy Bob Pickett's face. Picket threw up an arm to protect his eyes and skipped backward. In a heartbeat Fargo whirled and raced for the undergrowth. A rifle blasted but the lead missed and then he was in among the pines and crouched low.

"Are you all right?" Silky Mae had a hand on her sibling's arm.

"Fine!" Billy Bob snapped, brushing at his cheek. "The varmint damn near set me ablaze! Do you still reckon he's innocent?"

"I don't know." Silky Mae stared at the spot where Fargo had vanished. "My gut says he is but my head says he ain't."

"Your gut or your head?" Billy Bob said. He stomped the ground like an angry bull. "Now we'll both have to stay up all night. We sure as blazes ain't goin' after him in the dark."

"We have his hardware. We should be safe enough."

"He has a lot of Injun savvy, folks say," Billy Bob disagreed. "What's to stop him from makin' a lance or a bow and arrows and pickin' us off Injun fashion?"

As mad as Fargo was, he would not harm them if he could help it. They were only doing what they thought was right. In their eyes, it made perfect sense he was the killer.

"Maybe we should leave him afoot," Billy Bob had gone on. "Take his horse and hightail it to Lewiston. We'll rest up a day or so, then go on to Kellogg. Isn't that where Mr. Zared said he would be?"

Silky Mae nodded. "But what if we're wrong? What if he didn't have anything to do with makin' wolf bait of those gents? Strandin' him is harsh."

"No more harsh than what he'll do to us if he is the one and we give him half a chance," her brother argued.

Fargo had heard enough. Cupping a hand to his mouth and turning away from the clearing so they could not pinpoint where he was, he hollered, "Silky Mae! Billy Bob! I have a proposition for you!"

The Picketts recoiled as if afraid he would rush them. Peering intently into the night, Silky Mae shouted, "We're listenin'!"

"I will go with you to see Zared but I won't do it tied up!"

Billy Bob thought the statement hilarious. When he stopped chortling, he said, "You expect us to take you at your word? After seein' those graves? Why not slit our throats now and be done with it?"

"Billy!" Silky Mae scolded.

"What else do you expect me to say? Would you make a deal with the devil, too, if he promised to behave?"

His sister paid him no heed. "How about if we only tie your wrists? Would that dc?" she yelled.

"No!" Fargo responded. "But you can hold on to my six-gun and my rifle." He always had the Arkansas toothpick should he need a weapon. "How would that be?"

"Can we keep your pants and your boots while we're at it?" Billy Bob mocked him.

Silky Mae put her hands on her hips. "He's tryin' to meet us halfway. The least we can do is agree to his terms."

"*He's* the killer, not us," Billy Bob said. "We give *him* the terms. He doesn't get to give them to *us*."

"Did you hear him?" Silky Mae called out. "I'm sorry. As much as I would like to, I have to abide by his wishes."

"What if I always ride in front of you?" Fargo proposed.

"And what are we supposed to do at night?" Billy Bob demanded. "Even if we take turns watchin' you, sooner or later one of us will make a mistake and we'll become graves seven and eight."

Fargo had to convince them somehow. "At sunset you can take my horse and leave me until morning. I can't track in the dark, so you will be safe." The truth was, though, he could track at night if he had a torch. Or he could find them an easier way: if they were careless and made their fire big enough for him to spy from a distance.

"That's a lot of bother for us to go to!"

Silky Mae glared at Billy Bob, then hollered, "We agree! Come on out! I promise we won't shoot!"

Billy Bob was none too happy. Spinning her around, he snapped, "What in thunderation has gotten into you? *I* didn't agree, and my life is as much at stake as yours."

"We can trust him," Silky Mae insisted.

Fargo chose that moment to rise and walk toward them with his arms out from his sides. Billy Bob promptly pointed a rifle at him and might have fired but for Silky Mae, who grabbed the barrel and shoved it to one side.

"No, darn you!"

Squatting by the fire, Fargo filled his battered tin cup with hot coffee and savored a swallow. Billy Bob had centered the rifle on him again and was rubbing his finger up and down the trigger.

"If you're going to do it, get it over with," Fargo said. "If not, quit pointing that at me. I don't want my head blown off by accident."

"Please," Silky Mae said.

Livid, Billy Bob jerked the rifle down and growled, "You don't know how lucky you are, mister. But hear me and hear me good. Turn on us, and if it's the last thing I ever do, I will see you rot in hell."

On that pleasant note, they drank coffee and waited for the sun to rise. Billy Bob was mad and made no attempt to disguise it from his sister. Silky Mae sat as quiet as a mouse and refused to be baited by his repeated glares.

Fargo was glad when the sky to the east brightened enough for them to head out. He was as good as his word and rode ahead all morning long. At midday they stopped to rest the animals. Billy Bob wanted nothing to do with him but Silky Mae came over to where he sat.

"May I join you?"

"You have to ask?" Fargo smiled and leaned back.

"I just thought you might be upset with me, what with us taking your weapons and all."

"It's your brother who wants to bury me," Fargo reminded her. "I thank you for your trust."

Silky Mae sank down cross-legged and rested her elbows on her knees. "It's a puzzlement. I've never been all that trustin' of folks. There's something about you, something I can't quite figure."

Fargo was amazed she felt that way after how he had treated her back in Fort Hall, and said so.

Touching the cheek he had slapped, Silky Mae grinned. "By rights I should want you fed to the buzzards, shouldn't I? The last man who smacked me was a drunk I bumped into when he came stumblin' out of a tavern in Charleston. I told him I was sorry but he cussed me out and grabbed me by my shirt and slapped me. The next thing I knew, I was standin' over him with blood all over my revolver. I beat him senseless."

"That took grit."

"No more so than you have, I reckon," Silky Mae said. "I refuse to be put upon. It's a quirk I have. So why I don't want you dead, I will never know."

"Lucky me," Fargo said, and lightly patted her leg. He was rewarded with more pink in her cheeks. It confirmed his hunch that it was not trust on her part so much as it was something else.

Silky Mae made a show of gazing over the countryside. "It sure is pretty hereabouts. It's different than South Carolina. The sky seems bigger. And there's so much wilderness. It's makes a body feel powerful small, powerful alone."

"You're not as alone as you think," Fargo remarked, "not with Zared's men trailing you."

"What's that you say?"

Fargo told her about the bodyguards who had followed him and those who had followed Smith. "Odds are, Zared ordered some of his men to follow the two of you, too. You haven't seen any sign of them?"

"No." Silky Mae called to her brother.

Billy Bob took his time coming over, and gruffly demanded what she wanted. After he had heard about the bodyguards, some of the resentment drained out of him and he scratched his chin and said, "You know, there was a couple of times, real late at night, when I could have sworn I saw a campfire way off in the distance."

"I don't like being spied on," Silky Mae said.

"Mr. Zared is just watchin' out after his interests," Billy Bob said. "Nothin' wrong with that."

"If that is all there is to it."

"What else could there be?" Billy Bob faced Fargo. "How about if we wait here for them to catch up to us so you can kill them like you did Pike Driscoll and all those others?"

"Maybe they are already dead," Fargo said. "The real killer has it in for them for some reason."

"Listen to you," Billy Bob scoffed. "Still playin' us for fools. Well, it won't work with me, mister." Suddenly he snapped his fingers and said to his sister, "You know, that's not a bad idea."

"What?"

"Waitin' for Zared's men. There should be three of them, if there were three following him and three followin' Smith. They can help keep an eye on this murderin' coyote."

"I don't know," Silky Mae said.

Billy Bob's anger resurfaced. "Give me one good reason why we shouldn't."

"I don't trust those gents in black. I don't trust Benjamin Zared, either."

"But you trust *him*?" Billy Bob speared a finger at Fargo. "Will you listen to yourself, sis? You're soundin' more and more like a cow-eyed female and less and less like a grown woman."

That was the wrong thing to say. Silky Mae pushed up off the ground like a she-cat ready to rip him apart. "Watch yourself. There are lines you shouldn't cross and that there is one."

"I'll cross any damn lines I want when you put our lives in danger." Billy Bob refused to back down. "You haven't behaved this silly since that time you were twelve and you fell for that boy over to Fiddler Creek."

"Oh, so I'm silly now, am I?" Silky Mae rasped. "I have half a mind to cut loose of you and go my own way."

"What's stoppin' you?" Billy Bob practically shouted. "I bet your friend here would be tickled pink to have you all to himself."

Fargo had been doing some thinking. They were so caught up in their argument that neither noticed when he rose and stepped up close behind Silky Mae and helped himself to her Remington. Cocking it, he stepped past her. "I'll take your pistol as well."

Billy Bob was stupefied.

"Skye! What are you doin'?" Silky Mae was stricken by his apparent betrayal. "You gave your word."

"I warned you," Billy Bob hissed. "I warned you and warned you but you wouldn't listen. Now look. We're both dead."

Stepping far enough back that neither could jump him, Fargo said, "Make yourselves comfortable. It could be a while."

"A while until what?" Billy Bob snarled. "Until you put windows in our noggins? Are you fixin' to toy with us first? Lay a hand on my sister and I'll—"

"You should join a sewing circle," Fargo interrupted. "You could talk rings around the rest of the biddy hens."

Silky Mae started to laugh, and covered her mouth. But her brother was not at all amused.

"I'll come back from the grave to haunt you. I swear I will! You won't have a moment's peace the rest of your days. Our deaths will eat at you until you can't stand it anymore."

Extending the revolver, Fargo said, "Shhhhh."

Billy Bob imitated a clam but his teeth gnashed together and he kept clenching and unclenching his fists.

"Finally a way to shut him up." Fargo stared to the southeast. There was no sign of riders, but then most of the terrain was heavily forested.

Silky Mae was studying him. "I get it now.. You're worried about Zared's men—thinkin' that if they're still alive, you should warn them about what happened to Driscoll and those others."

Fargo spelled it out for her. "The killer might have circled back. He could be out there right this moment, watching us. He killed the bodyguards who were following Smith and those who were following me, so it stands to reason he'll try and do the same to the bodyguards who are following you."

"But why? To what end?"

"We'll ask him when I get my hands on him," Fargo said.

Billy Bob shook his head. "I'm not fallin' for it, mister. You want us to think you're innocent but it won't work."

"If you live to be thirty, it will be a miracle."

The Southerner lapsed into sulking silence but not his sister. Silky Mae looked adoringly at Fargo and said, "Give my brother an hour or so. By then, the fact you haven't shot us should convince even him that you don't want to blow out our wicks."

"Only an hour?"

"Sometimes he acts like he has rocks between his ears but he's a good person at heart," Silky Mae said, then changed the subject. "Since it's not you who killed those men, who then? No-Nose Smith? You know him better than me. Is he capable of somethin' like that?"

"At one time I would have said no," Fargo told her. "But there is something he wants more than anything in the world, and it takes a lot of money. The best answer I can give is maybe."

"What about your other friend, Mr. Weaver?"

"There hasn't been any sign of him since Fort Hall," Fargo mentioned. "But he wants the money, too."

"So the question is, which one of them wants it the most? Unless it's someone else entirely."

Fargo had not thought of that. It could be that neither of the scouts was involved, but that a third party was responsible. But who?

"It sure is a mystery," Silky Mae remarked. "One I can do without. I didn't come all the way from South Carolina to be a target for a bushwhacker. When I get to Kellogg, I'm takin' my five thousand and lightin' a shuck for home."

"I don't blame you."

"You should do the same. These mountains are dangerous enough without havin' a madman runnin' loose."

Fargo doubted very much the killer was insane. Crafty, yes. Ruthless, without a doubt. But there had to be a purpose to the slayings.

An hour drifted by. Silky Mae talked about growing up in South Carolina. How she had always liked doing things boys did more than things girls did. "Huntin' and trappin' and fishin'. That was the life for me. I shot my first rabbit when I was seven, skinned my first muskrat when I was nine. I never wore a dress in my life. My ma would get upset with me sometimes, sayin' as how I should act more like a girl. But my grandma always called me her darlin' little hoyden."

"Where did you learn to track?"

"My grandpa used to take Billy and me down to the creek a lot to read sign. Animals have to drink, too, he'd always say, and to learn what critters were about, we would check where they came to drink. It was a lot of fun. After our grandpa died, Billy and me kept at it."

Fargo could count on two fingers the number of women he had met in his lifetime who liked to do what he did for a living.

"One day when I was sixteen, a cougar took to raidin' farms and hen houses and killin' sheep and chickens and the like. Not one or two at a time like most cougars would do. It would kill every sheep in the pen, every chicken in the coop. Old Man Krebbs

172

lost thirty-two sheep in a single night. Mrs. Baker had eleven of her prized geese ripped to pieces. And the really strange thing is that the cougar didn't eat them. Nary a one. It was bloodlettin' for bloodlettin's sake."

Rare, but not unknown. Wolves and foxes did the same on occasion. Fargo once saw the aftermath of a sheep slaughter attributed to a wolf. Woolly bodies everywhere lying in pools of blood, their throats ravaged but otherwise untouched.

Silky Mae had more. "The people thereabouts wanted an end to it, so they pooled their money to hire a famous hunter from the next county. But Billy Bob and me spoke up. We could kill that cat for them." She paused. "It was our first trackin' job, and we earned ninety dollars. That might not sound like much to you but to us it was glorious."

Her brother had been fidgeting as if he had ants in his drawers, but now he broke his silence to say, "No one else could have tracked that cat. Folks sat up and took notice of us."

Fargo was impressed, too. Next to foxes and bobcats, mountain lions were the hardest animals on the continent to track because they left so few prints. Unlike bears, elk, and deer, which could weigh hundreds of pounds, foxes and bobcats were light, and evidence of their passing was found only in dusty or muddy ground. Cougars were heavier but they were uncannily cautious and had a natural knack for leaving little spoor.

"Before long we were offered another job," Silky Mae was relating. "A black bear that attacked a girl out pickin' berries. Her pa and some friends went after it but couldn't find it, so the pa sent for us. That girl was his only child, and the bear had bitten her cheek clean off. She healed, but she was scarred for life."

"A hundred and fifty dollars her pa paid us," Billy Bob boasted. "And we skinned the bear and made a rug out of the hide."

"That was when we knew we had found our callin'," Silky Mae continued. "Pretty soon people from all over were sendin' for us to track for 'em." She paused.

"How Benjamin Zared heard of us is beyond me. South Carolina is a far piece from his neck of the country."

"There were those stories in the newspaper," Billy Bob said. "The one where we tracked that little boy who was lost and had been missin' for four days. He was barely alive when we found him."

"I remember."

"And there was that account of how we were hired by the sheriff to find a bunch of escaped convicts," Billy Bob bragged to Fargo. "Seven of the worst scum you would ever see busted out of prison. Murderers and rapists and the like. They killed two guards doin' it. Folks locked their doors and shuttered their windows and wouldn't let their kids out to play. Armed men patrolled the roads and streets at night."

"The sheriff must have had a hundred men scourin' the countryside," Silky Mae said. "But they looked for a week and couldn't find hide nor hair of those devils. So he sent for us."

"Five hundred dollars, the state offered," Billy Bob said. "More money than anyone in our family ever had at one time in their whole lives. And we did it! It took us pretty near a month, in the hottest part of the summer, with ticks everywhere, but we tracked those convicts almost clear to Georgia. We were famous. The governor sent his personal thanks. After that, we never lacked for work."

Out of the blue, Silky Mae wanted to know, "Are the Indians in these parts friendly?"

"Some are, some aren't," Fargo said. "Why do you ask?"

"Because there are two of 'em in the woods behind you, and they have arrows nocked to their bowstrings."

14

The Nez Percé were a tolerant people. They had not risen in wrath at the invasion of their territory by thousands of whites. Widely regarded, along with the Shoshones, as one of the friendliest tribes on the frontier, they had been doing their best to get along with the invaders peaceably.

In the past year or so, though, the Nez Percé had begun to rethink their friendliness. They were not stupid. They saw that many whites had despised them for no other reason than the color of their skin. They felt the bitter barbs of bigotry and prejudice. They were treated with contempt by the very people they were letting share their land and rape its resources.

Some of the younger warriors resented it. They bristled at being branded savages and heathens. They wanted to rise up against the invaders, and repay the insults and slurs with lances and arrows.

The tribe's leaders were for peace. The older warriors counseled that since whites were as plentiful as blades of grass on the prairie, the Nez Percé would be unwise to go to war.

For the time being, the friendly faction was winning out. Some Nez Percé even converted to Christianity, thanks to the influence of a growing number of missionaries.

But there had been incidents. A drunken soldier tripped over an old Nez Percé and severely beat him. A prospector tried to force himself on a Nez Percé woman. The young men grumbled and strained at the tribal bit, and their leaders advised them to contain their anger. So far they had.

But in Fargo's estimation there would come a day, a day not long off, when the whites would push the Nez Percé too far. Blood would be spilled on both sides, and the war the tribe had for so long forsworn would take place anyway.

Now, at the mention of the warriors with bows, Billy Bob Pickett pointed and blurted, "Savages! Shoot 'em quick!"

But the pair were not wearing paint. Nor, when Fargo rose and beckoned, did they show any hostility. Only one had an arrow notched to his string, and the arrow was pointed at the ground. Fargo was not fluent in their tongue but he could say, "I greet you as a friend."

The warrior with the arrow smiled. "I greet you same," he said in clipped English. "I am Otter Tail."

"I have pemmican if you are hungry," Fargo said.

Otter Tail seemed fascinated by Silky Mae. "We not stay. We hunt deer. Big buck make food for family."

"Where did you learn the white man's tongue?" Fargo asked, as if he could not guess.

"Reverend Wilcox teach. Teach me white ways. Teach me of white God." Otter Tail touched a small crucifix he wore around his neck.

"Have you seen anything of any other whites near here? A lone white man, maybe, dressed as I am dressed?"

"No. We see gold men at river. We see whites on trail. We see reverend when come to village." Otter Tail tore his gaze from Silky Mae. "See girl like her."

"Was this girl with two men?" Fargo quickly asked. "Men about your age?"

"Yes. We talk. They give jerky. Nice whites. Friendly whites." Otter Tail added, "Girl much pretty."

"Did they mention their names?"

"Girl called"—Otter Tail closed his eyes for fully half a minute, then opened them and smiled—"girl called Pa-bor."

"Could it have been Tabor?"

Again the Nez Percé warrior closed his eyes in intense concentration. "Could be," he admitted.

"Did you learn the names of the men she was with?"

"They not say," Otter Tail replied. "One hold her hand. Sit with her. Walk when she walk. Hearts all same."

Which was the Nez Percé's way of saying Tabor and the young white man were in love. It had to be Gideon, Fargo reflected, and it was a stroke of luck on his part that the younger Zared's party had run into the Nez Percé. "Do you remember much of what was said?"

"Not much, no," Otter Tail said. "Me not savvy their talk. But they afraid. They very afraid."

"Of what?"

"Of men after them. Bad men who scare Ta-bor. She want know trails north. Try get away."

"You saw these bad men with your own eyes?" Fargo quizzed him. "Were they dressed in black?"

"Me see, yes. But they not wear black. Wear many clothes. Have many guns. Have many knives."

Fargo was at a loss. Benjamin Zared had not said anything about anyone being after his son. "How many were there?"

Otter Tail held up all his fingers and thumbs, closed his hands, and held up one finger. "That many."

"What makes you think they were bad men?"

"Me know two from times visit trading post. One be Red Moon. He be—how you say? Breed. That be it. He half-breed. Father white, mother Blackfoot. Much bad medicine, that one."

Among both whites and Indians there was a persistent belief that mixed unions bore tainted fruit. It was

177

not a belief Fargo shared. But half-breeds were universally looked down on and treated as outcasts. "What has he done to be called bad?"

"Red Moon kill Bloods. Red Moon kill Bannocks. Red Moon kill Flatheads. Red Moon kill whites. Red Moon kill everybody."

"Whites? You know this to be true? You saw it with your own eyes?"

Otter Tail was offended. "I speak straight tongue. Me not see but all my people hear."

Hearsay was not the most reliable of sources, but the Nez Percé were not known to be liars. "You said that you recognized two. Who was the other one?"

"Whites call him Otto Pierce."

The name jangled Fargo's memory. Pierce was a hardcase of ill repute, a former trapper and mountain man who had given up furs to live by the gun. Saloon gossip had it that he had robbed half a hundred men and killed half as many more. But there was no proof. No charges had ever been filed against him.

"Which way did Tabor and her friends go from here?" Fargo needed to find out.

Otter Tail pointed to the northwest.

"Toward Lewiston," Silky Mae said. She and her brother had heard the entire exchange. "Gideon and the others would be safe there, wouldn't they?"

Fargo was not so sure. Gideon Zared might think so, and while it was unlikely Pierce or Red Moon would kill him in a settlement, there was nothing to stop them from jumping him and dragging him off into the woods.

"His pa should be told," Billy Bob said.

For once Fargo agreed. But that would take days. They might as well go to Lewiston and see if Gideon was there before they went on to Kellogg. "Thank you for the information," he said to Otter Tail.

Without another word, the young warrior and his

friend left. At the trees Otter Tail paused to look back at Silky Mae. Then they were gone.

"He fancied you, sis," Billy Bob teased her.

"Hush. I did nothin' to encourage him. Besides, he's not the kind of man who attracts me." At that, Silky Mae glanced demurely at Fargo. "I like more mature fellas."

"Since when?" Billy Bob asked, and received a slap on the arm.

The visit by the Nez Percé had so distracted Fargo that he was not paying any attention to the woods to the southeast. So it was that less than a minute after OtterTail and his friend disappeared, a trio of riders materialized out of the greenery and were almost to the clearing before Fargo realized they were there.

"Well, this is a surprise," Jim Walker said. "I had no idea the Picketts and you were partners."

Billy Bob quickly said, "Partners, hell. He's holdin' a gun on us, you Yankee nitwit. Or are you blind as well as dumb?"

Walker drew rein and sighed tiredly. "I'm supposed to protect you with my life, Mr. Pickett. So I would hold that tongue of yours, were I you." He touched his hat brim to Silky Mae. "It's a pleasure to see you again, ma'am. Your brother could learn from your manners." Finally the bodyguard smiled at Fargo. "I'm still in your debt for that favor you did me. Mind telling me what this is all about?"

It took half an hour. Walker and the two men with him were appalled by the deaths of Driscoll and the five others, and Walker asked the crucial question, "Who is killing us off, and why?"

"I wish we knew," Fargo said. "I waited to warn you so you wouldn't end up the same." Fargo twirled the Remington, reversing it so the grips were forward, and handed it to Silky Mae. "I'll have my Colt and my rifle back now."

"Don't give them to him, sis," Billy Bob objected. "I still don't trust him."

"Honestly," she said in annoyance. "There's a nitwit here, all right, but it's not Mr. Walker."

They pushed on toward Lewiston. Fargo roved ahead and to the sides, constantly seeking sign of the killer. But he did not come across any tracks or anything else. Toward sunset he chose a sheltered nook at the base of a bluff for their camp. No one could get at them except from one direction, and one of the bodyguards would always stand watch.

Fargo actually got five hours of good sleep. He offered to help stand guard but Walker said that was their job.

The night passed without an attack. A spectacular dawn found them on the move, and once again Fargo roved to forestall an ambush.

At noon they stopped in a shaded glade. Fargo perched on a boulder that afforded him an unobstructed view of the surrounding forest. He did not look around when someone scrambled up beside him.

"Mind some company?"

"Not if it's a pretty woman."

Silky Mae bowed her head, then slid so close to him, their elbows brushed. There was something different about her; she had brushed her hair and dusted off her clothes and shoes, and several of the top buttons on her shirt, which had been buttoned until now, were unbuttoned, exposing a bit more of her womanly charms.

Fargo pretended not to notice.

Clearing her throat, Silky Mae remarked, "We'll be in Lewiston before too long, won't we?"

"Another couple of hours," Fargo predicted.

"What then? I mean, are you going straight on to Kellogg? And if so, can we travel together?"

"I doubt your brother wants my company." Fargo

could say the same. At that very moment, Billy Bob was across the glade, glaring.

"He's overly protective, is all," Silky Mae defended him.

"I'll think about it," Fargo offered. "I plan to stay in Lewiston a couple of days. My horse needs the rest, and I need to ask around about Gideon and Otto Pierce and Red Moon." Among other things.

"Then we'll stay a couple of days, too."

"Billy Bob won't mind?"

Silky Mae averted her eyes. "I'm a grown woman. I can do as I please. If I want to stay, I'll stay. He can go on without me if he wants. All he cares about is the money, anyway."

"It isn't every day a man stands to make twenty thousand dollars," Fargo commented.

"That doesn't excuse gettin' carried away with greed. He's always been money hungry, but never like this. Never to where it warps his thinkin'." Silky Mae fluffed at her hair. "Will you listen to us? Talkin' about the reward when there is so much else to talk about."

Her inexperience was as plain as it was charming. Fargo gave her the opening she needed by placing his hand on her knee. "I would be honored to treat you to a meal while we are in Lewiston."

"Better yet, how about a drink? I don't often indulge, but in your case, I will."

"I'd like that," Fargo said, and squeezed her leg.

Silky Mae plucked at her shirt, then touched a hand to her forehead. "Is it me, or did it suddenly get hot as Hades?"

As it turned out, they reached Lewiston in an hour and forty minutes. The influx of gold seekers had caused the settlement to swell. It had all the makings of a full-fledged town, including clogged streets and more saloons than a man could shake a stick at.

Among the throng were Irishmen, Scotsmen, Poles, and Chinese.

The stable had a stall for rent at twice the amount Fargo had paid in Fort Hall. A new hotel promised creature comforts, and presently Fargo was back out on the street. Searching for answers promised to be thirsty work, so the first place he stopped was the nearest saloon. He strode in the door, and as his eyes adjusted, who should he see at a corner table but a familiar figure in buckskin.

"Fargo!" Kip Weaver called, and waved. "Over here, hoss! I've got half a bottle left and I don't mind sharing."

The bartender gave Fargo a glass. He selected a chair so his back was to the wall, and clinked the glass against Kip's. "Fill me to the brim."

"What else are pards for?" Weaver laughed as he poured, then drank some whiskey and smacked his lips. "Best bug juice I've had in a while. Must be because an Irishman owns this place. No one knows whiskey like the Irish."

"You're in good spirits," Fargo said.

"Why shouldn't I be? Another couple of weeks and I'll be twenty thousand dollars richer"—Weaver frowned—"provided James doesn't beat me to the Zared brat."

Fargo noticed that Kip did not rate him a threat to his dream. "You've seen him?"

"Seen him. Talked to him. He got in this morning. Half an hour ago he was sitting in the very chair you are."

"Where is he now?"

"I don't know and I don't care. He wasn't all that polite. Told me to bow out before I came to harm. Imagine that!" Weaver emptied his glass in a gulp. "James has changed. He's not the friendly cuss he used to be."

"How long have you been here?" Fargo fished for information.

"Here, as in this saloon? Since ten this morning. Or here, as in Lewiston? I rode in three days ago."

"Have you run into any of Benjamin Zared's bodyguards?" Fargo asked. It stood to reason that Zared had assigned three to follow Weaver as he had all the rest.

"No, but I haven't been looking, either." Kip stroked the bottle. "I've been lubricating my throat. A marvelous pastime, throat lubrication. I recommend it highly."

"You're halfway to drunk," Fargo said.

"Only halfway?" Weaver laughed. "Why, I'm insulted. I'm three-fourths of the way, or better."

"Did Smith say how long he aims to stay in Lewiston?"

Kip Weaver made a clucking sound. "Questions. Questions. Questions. All you do is ask questions. Where is the Fargo I used to know—the one who used to drink and bed the fillies and not be so damn serious all the time?"

"He's more interested in staying alive," Fargo replied. "You should be, too."

"I assure you, staying alive is uppermost in my mind," Weaver said. "How else am I to enjoy spending that twenty thousand?"

"You say I've changed. I could say the same about you," Fargo said. "The Kip Weaver I knew would never get drunk in the middle of a job."

"Shows how much you know," Weaver snickered. "I was always half-drunk. But I hid it really well." He drained his glass. "A man has to be drunk, or crazy, to do what we do for a living. To risk his life day in and day out. To go into country no white man has ever set foot in, never knowing when he'll take an arrow in the back, or be taken alive and tortured." Weaver shuddered. "I saw a scout tortured once. McPherson. The Bloods got hold of him. I tried to sneak into their village to rescue him but there were too many dogs and too many Bloods moving about."

"Taking risks is part of life," Fargo said, but Weaver did not hear him.

"His screams were the worst part. When they carved on him, he would shriek and blubber and beg them not to. And McPherson was a brave man." Kip shuddered again.

"Don't talk about it if it bothers you that much."

"I've relived that day in my head every day. I hear him when I sleep and when I'm awake. I see them cut and chop. I see his guts ooze out." Weaver refilled his glass but was sloppy about it and spilled some. "Is it any wonder I want to give up this life and move to where I don't always have to be watching my back?"

"You've made your point." Fargo finished his own drink and laid a coin on the table.

"The drink is on me, pard," Weaver said. "You're not leaving, are you? Hell, you just got here."

"I have things to do." Fargo did not go into detail.

"Fine. But I'll be here the rest of the day if you want me for anything." Kip patted the bottle. "Me and my other pard, here."

Only then did Fargo appreciate the depths to which his friend had plummeted. He had seen it happen before, seen men lose their nerve and become pale shadows of their former selves. But this was a special shock. He had known Kip for years, ridden with him, faced dangers with him. The Kip Weaver he remembered had been one of the bravest men he ever knew.

On the next corner was a boy of ten or twelve hawking a one-sheet newspaper that called itself the *Lewiston Gazette*. The type was so small that Fargo could barely read it, and half the sheet was advertisements, but Fargo bought a copy anyway. It wasn't the news he was interested in. "How long have you been standing there?"

The boy gave him a strange look. "Since eight this

morning, mister. The paper comes out once a week, and the day it does, here I am, all day long."

"So you must see most everyone who comes into town." From the corner, Fargo could scan the full length of the dusty street in both directions.

"I guess. Why?"

"Did you happen to notice a man in buckskins with a black patch over his nose?" Fargo had to find out if Kip was telling the truth.

The boy scrunched up his face in thought. "Maybe I did, maybe I didn't. For a dollar I might remember for sure."

The urchin's clothes were little better than rags, and he had not had a bath in ages. Fargo fished out a coin and started to hand it to him, but stopped. "No lying. This is important. People's lives are at stake."

"What do you take me for?" the boy indignantly responded. "If I say I saw him, I saw him."

"Then you did?"

"As big as life. I remember it so well because it was only a few minutes after I started selling the paper this morning. The street wasn't crowded yet. And here he came, him with that patch on his face. I wondered what had happened to him that he had to wear it."

Fargo gave the boy the dollar.

"He wasn't very friendly," the boy said. "I hollered if he wanted a newspaper and he didn't even look at me. The last I saw of him, he had reined up down to the general store."

"If you should see him again, it's worth five dollars to you to come to the hotel and let me know or leave word if I'm not there."

The boy positively glowed with excitement. "Five dollars? For that much, I'll get some of my friends and we'll go from one end of this place to the other looking for him."

Fargo had not thought of that. "I like the idea. If you find him, you get the five dollars to split as you see fit. If you don't, I'll give you another dollar for your troubles. Sound fair?"

"Shake on it," the boy said, holding out his hand. "I'm Timmy Williams. I live with my ma over past the blacksmith's. My pa is off looking for gold. He's been gone two months. But he should be back any day now. Then we'll be rich. Or so my ma says."

Fargo told the boy his name, and the number of the room he was in. His next stop was the general store. As he was going in, out came Silky Mae with a bundle clasped to her bosom.

"Just the gent I wanted to see! What time are you comin' for me? Or should I meet you wherever you want to eat?"

Fargo had nearly forgotten his promise of a meal. "Is seven o'clock all right?" When she beamed and nodded, he asked, "Where are you and your brother staying?"

"We're camped in a grove of trees out past the far end of town," Silky Mae disclosed. "Billy Bob refused to rent a room. He called it a frivolous waste of our money."

"You would be safer at the hotel."

"Jim Walker and those others are camped with us," Silky Mae said. "Walker says it's for our mutual protection." She squinted at the sun. "Seven, is it? I better scoot. I have a lot of preparin' to do." Flashing her pearly teeth, she departed.

The store was filled to overflowing. Several women were inspecting bolts of cloth. Four older men were in chairs near a stove that was not lit, puffing on pipes and jawing. The couple who owned the store were kept busy taking orders and answering questions. The husband was helping a lady customer with some yarn when Fargo walked over, his spurs jangling.

"A man with a patch over his nose was in here early this morning. Do you remember him?"

Without looking up, the man said testily, "Mister, I

get a lot of people in here throughout the day. You can't expect me to recall every single one."

Fargo gripped his elbow and applied pressure. "It's important."

Startled, the man turned, and blanched. "Sorry. I didn't mean to be rude. And now that you mention it, yes, I do remember him. How could I not, with that patch? He didn't say much. Just paid for his purchase and left."

"What did he buy?"

"Ammunition. Lots and lots of ammunition. I guess he has a lot of killing to do."

15

Seven o'clock came and went and there was no sign of the distaff Pickett. Fargo was about ready to go find her when something rustled behind him and he was wreathed in the tantalizing fragrance of perfume. Thinking it was a townswoman, he stepped aside, saying, "I'm sorry. I didn't realize I was in your way." Then he stopped, overcome with astonishment.

"Do you like it?" Silky Mae asked.

Fargo could only nod. His vocal cords would not work. It was as if a whole new person stood in front of him. A change as extreme as day from night and night from day.

"It's what was in the bundle I had," Silky Mae mentioned. "The lady at the store said it suits me just fine."

The lady at the store was right. The vivid green dress Silky Mae wore shimmered like grass in bright sunshine. It fit her like her own skin, sculpted so perfectly to her body that every contour was an eyeful. She had done the things women did to their face and hair to lend her an air of elegance Fargo never suspected she possessed.

"What do you think? Do I pass muster?" Silky Mae fidgeted. "I feel damned silly, to tell you the truth. This is the first dress I've worn, and for the life of me, I can't see why they are so danged popular. They're too drafty, for one thing."

"You are beautiful," Fargo said.

"I never took you for a liar," Silky Mae responded. "I'm not stupid. The most I'll ever be is pretty, and then only in a dark room."

Just then a couple of grungy prospectors walked by and could not take their eyes off her. They twisted their necks clear around to keep ogling her, and one nearly tripped over his own boots.

"See?" Fargo said.

"They've been off in the mountains for who knows how long," Silky Mae said. "They're starved for a female, even a homely one like me."

Fargo offered her his elbow. "Shall we?" The desk clerk had told him about a place down the street that served the thickets steaks in the territory.

Holding her head high, Silky Mae let him guide her. "I never did anything like this before, so if I do it wrong, don't hold it against me."

Fargo liked how the dress clung to her legs when she moved, and the enticing swish of the fabric. He happened to glance lower and inwardly smiled. From under the hem poked the scuffed tips of the beat-up old shoes she had worn since he met her. "You spent a lot of money for one meal."

"I wanted it to be special," Silky Mae said. "I wanted it to be perfect."

"Your brother must be happy," Fargo dryly observed.

"Billy Bob and me have had a fallin' out of sorts. He wouldn't stop carpin' about how much I spent, but it's my money. I swear, there are days when he vexes me sorely." Silky Mae brightened and said, "Mr. Walker sure was nice. He said if he was not under orders to watch over us, he would ask me out himself and wrestle you for the right."

The reminder caused Fargo to glance over his shoulder. As he suspected, one of the bodyguards was fifty feet back, pacing them. It was Walker himself. "He's a good man."

"I think so."

Every male in the place admired her as they entered and were ushered to a table. Fargo pulled out her chair and she sat down as gracefully as if she were a lady born.

Silky Mae's lips moved as she read the menu. "Lordy, these meals are pricey. Sixty cents for soup? It's ten cents back home. Duck for a dollar fifty? Why, the best duck in South Carolina doesn't go for but forty cents. And the steak! Land sakes. Who in their right mind would pay three dollars? The blamed cows must be made of gold."

Fargo grinned. "Beef is hard to come by this far north."

"Why not have the venison or the elk meat? They are a lot less expensive."

"Because I want the night to be perfect, too." Fargo was referring to the fact that he was hungry for steak and only steak, but she took it to mean something else entirely.

"You say the sweetest things sometimes. I bet you've swept a lot of girls off their feet."

"A few," Fargo said. He slid his hand into his shirt pocket and produced his surprise. "I got something for you. I had it wrapped."

Silky Mae stared but made no attempt to take it. "Why would you do a thing like that?"

"We're friends, aren't we?" Fargo rejoined. "I saw it in a case at the general store and thought you would like it."

"I've never had a man give me a gift before. It doesn't feel right. Either that, or I'm comin' down with the flu."

"No strings attached," Fargo assured her. "Call it my way of thanking you for trusting me."

"Well, if you put it like that." She opened it slowly, as if afraid of what she might find, then gaped at the contents in wonderment. "They are gorgeous. But you shouldn't have. They must have cost an arm and a leg."

Fargo had spent four whole dollars. Gold, ironically enough, was cheaper than beef. "Try them on."

"I couldn't," Silky Mae said. She carefully held both of the tear-shaped earrings in her palm and ran a finger over them. "These are what all the women are wearin' these days."

"So the man told me." Fargo wagged a finger at her head. "They would look better on you."

"I've never worn earrings." Silky Mae timidly regarded the other diners. "I would look silly tryin' to put 'em on."

"Then I'll do it." Before she could object, Fargo came around the table and took one from her hand.

"Folks will stare."

"Let them. They will think we're lovers."

"Oh, my." Silky Mae's cheeks became their reddest ever. "If my ma could see me now, she would envy me. She used to complain Pa never took her anywhere fancy or bought her doodads." She bent her head to give him access to her earlobe. "How is it you know so much about female stuff?"

"I've seen it done once or twice."

A matron at another table smiled benignly at them, and a younger woman across the way looked jealous.

"I will never forget this night," Silky Mae said softly. For the rest of the meal, she would finger one or the other earring again and again.

Fargo had just sliced off a succulent piece of steak and forked it into his mouth when he caught her gazing at him with more than friendly affection. "There will be other nights, other men."

"What do you take me for?" Silky Mae indignantly demanded.

"The kind of woman who will never be a man's plaything. The kind who knows her own mind." Fargo's verbal molasses had the desired effect.

"Goodness gracious, you give a girl butterflies, even if you are ladling it on uncommonly thick." Silky Mae cupped her chin in her hand. "But ladle all you want. I make no bones about bein' female."

For dessert Fargo treated her to a slice of chocolate cake, which she treated almost as reverently as her new earrings, lingering over every morsel.

"We didn't get much chocolate when I was growin' up," Silky Mae said with her mouth full. "Mostly on Christmas when ma made all sorts of treats." She smiled at him. "Thank you. You made it as perfect as could be."

After she was done, Fargo paid and they left. The night had turned chill. Silky Mae had not brought a shawl and he saw her shiver. Placing an arm around her shoulders, he drew her close to share his body warmth. "We should get you back to your camp."

"Whatever for? I'd much rather walk a spell. That is, if you don't mind."

"I don't mind at all." Fargo had been watching for Walker but had not seen him since they entered the restaurant. If Walker was back there now, it would be hard to spot him. Lewiston was not New Orleans. It didn't have streetlamps on every corner.

"Why do you keep lookin' behind us?"

"Better safe than dead," Fargo said, and grinned. "I'd like to make sure we're not being followed. Are you up to it?"

"Why wouldn't I be?" Silky Mae rejoined, then looked down at herself. "Oh. Don't worry. I can keep up even in this rig."

Fargo walked faster. At the next corner he turned right and increased his pace even more. Beside him, Silky Mae laughed. She liked the excitement. Holding firm to her shoulders, he angled across the street and turned back the way they had come. In a few yards they came to an alley. He turned into it. Almost immediately they were swallowed by a deeper darkness, and unpleasant odors assaulted them. But he kept going.

"How awful," Silky Mae said. "It smells like the hind end of a black bear after it's eaten too many blackberries."

Vague obstacles appeared: empty crates and stacks of timber, piles of refuse and other piles better left unidentified.

Silky Mae pressed close against Fargo. A few times she sounded like she was about to gag but she composed herself. When they came to the next street, she threw back her head and sucked in fresh air in great gulps.

Fargo turned right. He was nearly running. The few people who were abroad gave them no notice. Soon they came to a quiet dirt street lined by cabins and small frame houses.

A large oak loomed. Fargo drew her around to the other side, and stopped. He watched for pursuit but it was soon evident that if Walker had been following them when they left the restaurant, he was not following them now.

"Did we do it?" Silky Mae whispered.

"We're alone," Fargo said.

That they were. Most of the dwellings were dark. Either their occupants had already turned in or were off indulging in the night life Lewiston offered.

Fargo became conscious of her nearness, of her perfume and the soft rustle of her dress as she faced him.

"It sure is a pretty night."

A multitude of stars filled the inky vault overhead. In the distance a wolf howled, a reminder that Lewiston was an island of civilization in a vast sea of savagery.

"It is nice," Fargo agreed. He did not embrace her. He would leave it up to her to make the decision.

"Are you just goin' to stand there?"

"Do you have something else in mind?" Fargo grinned.

"I don't know whether to feel insulted that you don't find me attractive enough or flattered that you treat me like a lady." Silky Mae tilted her head up to him. "But I do know that if you don't kiss me right this moment, I'm liable to bust."

"We wouldn't want that." Fargo opened his arms.

She came into them willingly, even eagerly, her chin raised so her lips were next to his. "A turtle is lightning compared to you," Silky Mae prodded.

"Think so?" Fargo said, and kissed her, lightly at first, the gentlest of contact of his lips to hers. She shivered, but not from the night air, and her arms rose to wrap around his neck. Her breath came in fluttering gasps that turned into a tiny moan when he parted her lips with his tongue and ran the tip of his along her gums. Her tongue met his, and their light kiss turned into a hard and heavy kiss that went on and on.

At last Fargo drew back. Silky Mae placed her cheek on his chest and sighed wistfully.

"That was wonderful. You're only the second man to ever kiss me."

Fargo did not ask who was the first. He ran his right hand down her back. With his other he kneaded a slender shoulder.

"Where can we go that would be private?" Silky Mae asked. "Your room at the hotel?"

That was fine by Fargo, but he had to ask, "What if your brother comes looking for you? That's the first place he'll check."

"Where then? Do you know of another place?"

"What's wrong with right here?"

"Here?" Silky Mae said skeptically, and surveyed the street. "What if someone happens by?"

"I'll shoot them."

Silky Mae laughed and hugged him and pecked him

on the chin. "Here is fine if that is what you want," she said huskily, "but I'll be scared to death of bein' caught. That would spoil it."

"Then the hotel room it is."

Fargo chose a roundabout way, fighting shy of streets where there were a lot of people. He contrived to come up on the hotel from the rear. The back door was not locked. The hinges creaked but the narrow hallway was empty. With Silky Mae glued to his back, he crept to the stairs. The desk clerk was reading at the front desk.

Putting a finger to his lips, Fargo clasped her right hand and crept to the stairs. He had her go ahead of him so he could keep an eye on the desk clerk and the front door. His room was near the end of the hall. He inserted the key and twisted, and the next instant they were inside and secure. He shut and bolted the door.

"Is this private enough for you?"

Silky Mae gazed longingly into his eyes. Even in the near dark, the hunger in them was undeniable. "Yes," she said softly.

"Do you want me to light the lamp?"

"I'd rather you didn't, if you don't mind. I wouldn't be as brave."

Fargo placed his hands on her shoulders and discovered she was trembling again. "What are you afraid of?"

"When you ride a horse for the first time, it can be scary," Silky Mae whispered.

The first time? Fargo mentally repeated. But Edrea had told him that Silky Mae bedded men right and left. "You can back out if you care to."

"Why would you say a thing like that? Don't you want me now, after all we went through to get here?"

"Any man would want you," Fargo said.

"Prove it. Prove a man would find me desirable, that I'm not as ugly as I think I am."

"Why, Silky Mae Pickett," Fargo whispered, cupping her chin, "you are as lovely as any woman I have ever been with."

"I said it before. I'll say it again. You are a terrible liar. But I'll pretend to believe you so it doesn't put a damper on the romance."

"Cut that out," Fargo said. He had to snap her out of her sudden funk. Pulling her to him, he kissed her forehead, then her eyebrows, then the tip of her nose, and finally molded his mouth to hers in a long, languid kiss that brought a groan from her throat. His hands were not idle. With one he molded her pert bottom. With the other, he covered first one breast and then the other and massaged them.

"Ohhhh," Silky Mae cooed when he lowered his mouth to her neck. "You make me all weak inside."

Scooping her into his arms, Fargo carried her to the bed and laid her on her back. He removed his hat and his gun belt and boots and stretched out beside her. She was as rigid as a board, and her throat bobbed when he touched her.

"You need to relax."

"That's easy for you to say. You're not the one with a swarm of butterflies in your belly."

"I know how to get rid of them." Fargo kissed her, the longest kiss yet. Deliberately so, in order that the pleasure would eclipse her anxiety. It worked. She softened and entwined her fingers in his hair.

Just when things were going as they should, sudden footsteps out in the hall caused Silky Mae to stiffen and glance sharply at the door.

"You will spoil it if you are so skittish," Fargo said.

"I thought it was my brother."

"People come and go all the time. It's a hotel, remember? The door is bolted, so if Billy Bob does show up, he'll have to knock. You can hide while I answer it. He'll never know you're here."

"That would be terrible," Silky Mae said. "He would never let me hear the end of it. He expects me to always behave proper, yet he goes off to be with fallen doves all the time." She sighed. "It's not easy bein' put on a pedestal."

"You're not on one now."

Silky Mae burst out laughing. "I'm sure not, am I?" She patted the quilt. "Not unless they make pedestals different than I recollect."

Fargo undid a button, then a second and a third. He kissed her throat and licked her soft skin, tracing a path to her ear. He sucked on her earlobe and rimmed the ear. Sliding his knee between her legs, he rubbed his thigh against hers.

"Lordy, I want you," Silky Mae declared, and lavished a score of scorching kisses on every square inch of his face.

Her dress was almost ready to be pealed off. Sliding a hand inside, Fargo deftly wormed it through her undergarments. Skin made contact with skin, and she gasped. He found a breast. Her nipple was erect. When he pinched it, she squirmed deliciously and gazed at him with eyelids hooded by lust.

"Do that again," Silky Mae husked.

Fargo did, alternating between her globes, pinching and tweaking and caressing until her breasts were heaving and her hips were grinding against him with increasing urgency.

Silky Mae had worked her hands under his buckskin shirt and now she ran them over his stomach and as far up his chest as she could reach. "Take this off," she whispered.

It only took a moment. Removing her dress and underthings took a lot longer. Eventually she lay under him as naked as the day she came into the world. Fargo sorely wished the lamp were lit. Few sights were as exquisite as a beautiful woman naked, and despite her protests to the contrary, Silky Mae was exceedingly attractive. He reached for her but she put her hand on his chest.

"You're not done yet, handsome. You still have clothes on."

"I'll get to it," Fargo said, bending to inhale a nipple.

"You'll do it now," Silky Mae insisted. "We have a sayin' in my neck of the country. You might have heard it once or twice." She paused. "What's good for the goose is good for the gander."

Muttering a comment about stubborn females, Fargo hastily stripped off his pants. "There? Happy now?"

"Am I ever." Silky Mae brazenly placed her hand where many women were too timid to place it without coaxing. "Oh, my. Is this you or a tree?" She stroked him as delicately as a feather. "How does that feel?"

How do you think it feels? Fargo thought. A constriction in his throat threatened to choke off his breath. Her fingers drifted lower, and it was all he could do not to explode.

"I like how you feel," Silky Mae said. "I like how hard you are for me."

"Has anyone ever mentioned that you and your brother talk too much?" Fargo covered her mouth with his. Her tongue and his entwined as her right hand moved in small circles along his thigh.

For what must have been an hour or more, they did all the things men and women do when the need for intimacy cannot be denied. They kissed, they rubbed, they licked, they caressed, their bodies always in motion.

Fargo could not get enough of the smoothness of her legs, the pillowy softness of her breasts, the downy thatch at the junction of her legs. Like a master musician playing a musical instrument, he brought Silky Mae to the pinnacle of desire.

Then came the coupling. Spreading her legs wide, Fargo positioned himself. He rubbed his member along her moist slit and she raised her backside off the bed and hooked her legs behind him.

"Yes! Oh, yes!"

Fargo rubbed her tiny knob. Instantly, Silky Mae bucked like a wild mare and sank her nails into his shoulders. Her nails were not long, as women's nails went, but they were sharp. "Like that, do you?"

Her answer was to take his pole in both hands and insert him in herself, inch by gradual inch, until his manhood was sheathed in her womanly core. They lay still, and Fargo could feel her heart hammering in her chest. Taking hold of her hips, he was about to begin the long climb to release when heavy footfalls echoed from the hallway and came to a stop right outside his room.

"Silky Mae? Are you in there?"

Fargo felt her tense.

"Sis? Do you hear me?" Billy Bob pounded on the door, and when that did not produce results, he tried to open it.

In a panic, Silky Mae tried to push Fargo off but he held her down and whispered in her ear, "Calm down. He can't get in. You're safe as can be."

The door rattled violently, then resounded to the thud of a shoulder thrown against it.

"I'll bust this down if I have to!" Billy Bob fumed. "So help me God, you just see if I don't." Again he hurled himself at the barrier. Again the door held. He might have kept at it until the door gave way but just then the desk clerk's voice intruded.

"What is the meaning of this, sir?"

"I'm lookin' for my sister," Billy Bob explained. "Open this door so I can see if she's in there."

"I will do no such thing. Our guests are welcome to their privacy. And I will thank you not to disturb them further. Please leave."

"Like hell I will," Billy Bob said.

"You can walk out or be thrown out," the desk clerk said. "And if you wake up Mr. Milner, the prospector who is staying four doors down, you will fare a lot worse. He is as big as a moose and as mean as a grizzly, and he does not like being disturbed when he is sleeping off a drunk."

Billy Bob fumed and cursed, but he left.

"Now then"—Fargo grinned at Silly Mae when the footsteps had faded—"where were we?"

16

By noon the next day, Fargo was convinced No-Nose Smith had moved on. He spent most of the morning questioning bartenders and store owners and others, and while a few remembered seeing a man with a nose patch the day before, no one had seen him since. Smith was not staying at the hotel, and had not put his horse up at the stable. Evidently he had whisked into Lewiston, bought ammunition, and whisked out again.

Fargo had a hunch Smith was headed for Kellogg. He was still no closer to figuring out why No-Nose was killing the bodyguards.

After paying his hotel bill, Fargo collected the Ovaro. He was lifting his leg to step into the stirrups when another of his acquaintances came strolling up.

"What's this? You're leaving?" Kip Weaver asked. He had his hat pushed back on his head and was carrying a whiskey bottle a third full.

"We have a job to do, remember?" Fargo climbed on but held the reins still. "Staying here doesn't get it done."

"What can another day or two matter?" Weaver asked. "We'll drink this town dry, like in the old days."

"No, thanks."

Kip Weaver tipped the bottle to his mouth. "I hate to say this, pard, but you're not as much fun as you used to be."

"There is more to life than getting drunk," Fargo said flatly.

"That was unkind, hoss. So what if I'm fond of coffin varnish? I'm not hurting anyone, am I?"

Fargo did not want to overstep himself, but he could not resisting saying, "Just yourself."

"Well, now"—Weaver stood taller and his features hardened—"who are you to take on airs? As I recall, you're not very partial to tea, yourself."

"That's not how I meant it," Fargo said.

"So you claim. But an insult is still an insult." Weaver snorted and tipped the bottle again. "I never took you for the high-and-mighty type. It just goes to show you never known people as well as you think you do."

"If you want to drink yourself to death, go right ahead. But don't blame me for pointing it out."

"I should thank you for bringing my faults to my attention?" Kip scoffed.

"This is pointless," Fargo said, and went to rein the pinto around.

"Hold on, hoss." Weaver gripped the bridle. "I'm not done. You're the one who brought it up, so you should have the decency to hear me out."

"I'm listening."

Weaver shook the whiskey bottle. "Maybe I am too attached to the redeye these days. But I have good cause. I told you how those Piegans nearly lifted my scalp. I've made no secret that my nerve is not what it used to be."

"It happens to all of us."

"Oh, really? When was the last time you were afraid to go into hostile territory? When was the last time you could hardly sleep because you had nightmare after nightmare and would wake up screaming?"

"You shouldn't be here then," Fargo said.

Weaver let go of the bridle and gestured. "What else would I do? Scouting and tracking is all I know.

And I can't pass up a chance to spend the rest of my life in cozy comfort as far from redskins as I can get."

"What if someone else finds Gideon Zared first?"

"I'll cross that river when I come to it. But it won't make a difference. I'm through scouting, come what may."

"I wish you luck," Fargo said, and meant it.

Kip Weaver smiled. "For which I thank you. But you should know by now that a man makes his own luck." He raised the bottle in a salute. "Take care out there, you hear, pard? Don't let what happened to Pike Driscoll happen to you."

"I won't."

The grove where the Picketts were camped was quiet. Too quiet. Fargo suspected what he would find before he saw the charred embers of their campfire. The Picketts and Walker and the other bodyguards were gone. They had left early that morning, judging by the tracks.

Fargo was puzzled. Silky Mae had not said anything about leaving early. When he escorted her back at midnight, her brother and Walker had been by the fire.

Billy Bob had shot to his feet. "Where the hell have you been? Do you have any notion of what time it is?"

"I'm a grown woman," Silky Mae had snapped. "I can stay up as late as I darn well please."

"Is that so?" Billy Bob spun on Fargo. "And you! Gettin' her to waste money on that dress, and keepin' her out until all hours. You sure as hell are no gentleman."

"That will be quite enough," Silky Mae said sternly. "If you keep this up, our trackin' days together are over."

Shock evaporated Billy Bob's anger like dew under a blazing sun. "You would do that? Leave me for *him*?"

"Did I say that? You never pay attention." Silky Mae hunkered by the fire and held her hands to the flames to warm them. "I won't be treated like a child—not by you, not by anyone."

"But, sis, I'm only thinkin' of your virtue."

"That's sweet of you," Silky Mae said in a manner that did not make it sound sweet at all. "But it's *my* virtue, and *my* life, and you have no say over either. I've stuck with you because I like trackin', and the money we earn, but I will not keep stickin' if you don't grow up."

"I need to think," Billy Bob said, and walked off into the dark.

"And I need to shed this contraption and get ready to turn in." Taking her everyday clothes and her rifle, Silky Mae went into the dark in the opposite direction.

Jim Walker grinned. "There is never a boring moment with those two around." He indicated the coffeepot. "If you're staying, I'll pour you some."

"I'm not," Fargo had said.

"That was slick, how you lost me when you ducked into that alley," Walker complimented him.

Fargo grinned. "I have no idea what you are talking about."

"I suspected you would end up at the hotel. So I waited in the doorway of the butcher shop down the street, and lo and behold, along you came. But I didn't follow you inside. Mr. Zared wants me to watch these two like hawks but I figured she was safe in your hands." Walker chuckled.

Shortly after that, Silky Mae came out of the trees, and Fargo said good night. Now they were gone. He had some catching up to do.

Kellogg was northeast of Lewiston. It would not take as long to reach as it had to reach Lewiston from Fort Hall, but the country was just as rugged and there were several ranges to cross.

The Clearwater River system drained most of the

area, and there were a number of forks and tributaries to choose from. Walker and the Picketts were sticking to the main trail, no doubt to make better time. But it also put them in greater danger. No-Nose Smith was up the trail somewhere, maybe waiting for them to come along.

In due course Fargo met up with a party of prospectors heading the other way. Yes, they had seen three men in black and a young man and a young woman wearing peculiar hats, about five hours ago.

Fargo did not want to push the Ovaro too hard, not after all the pinto had been through already. So he compromised. He rode faster than he normally would but not so fast that he would exhaust the Ovaro before they were halfway to Kellogg.

Walker and the Picketts were pushing hard. The afternoon waxed and waned and the sun relinquished its reign of the firmament to a host of stars, and still Fargo rode on. He was tired and hungry, but whenever he was tempted to stop for the night and overtake the others in the morning, he thought of the six men in black who had already been murdered, and of Silky Mae Pickett.

It was close to nine when a campfire lit the distant darkness. Half an hour more and Fargo was close enough to the clearing that he could see figures huddled around the fire, and their picketed horses. He was all set to ride into the open when he had a change of mind. Reining north, he circled the clearing until he was almost to where the trail continued on toward Kellogg. Halting, he dismounted and slid the Henry from the saddle scabbard.

If Smith had seen their campfire and came to investigate, Fargo would be waiting for him. He made himself comfortable with his back to an oak, facing the trail, the Henry across his lap, the Ovaro right beside him. He was counting on the stallion to forewarn him if Smith, or anything else, approached.

The hours dragged. Fargo was glad he had had a good night's sleep the night before. Still, by one, his eyelids were heavy and he was constantly forcing them open and stifling yawns.

By three, Fargo was confident enough that Smith would not show that he bent his chin to his chest and drifted off. He slept fitfully, and when the first birds stirred and chirped in anticipation of sunrise, he stood and stretched and climbed back in the saddle.

Clucking to the stallion, Fargo continued toward Kellogg. Now that he was ahead of the Picketts, with a little luck he would run into Smith first.

At the back of his mind, troubling him, was the fact that Smith had twice spared his life. Why was still a mystery. *What if Smith spares me again?* Fargo asked himself. What if Smith let him ride on by and waited for the others? He had to hope the other times were flukes.

Fargo grinned at the irony. Here he was, deliberately riding into a killer's gun sights and hoping the killer squeezed the trigger. How loco was that?

The morning proved uneventful. Fargo met up with a few people bound for Lewiston. None had seen a buckskin-clad rider since they left Kellogg. That puzzled him. One possible explanation was that Smith was paralleling the trail instead of using it, or else Smith always left the trail when someone came along and hid until they went by.

By four o'clock, Fargo was having second thoughts. At six he came to another clearing that saw regular use, and when five weary riders and their packshorses caught up with him an hour later, he had a fire going, with fresh brewed coffee for them to wash down the dust.

"Skye!" Silky Mae flew off her horse and rushed over to hug him. Impulsively kissing him, she stepped back from him at arm's length. "Land sakes. This is a surprise. I thought you were back in Lewiston."

"It's mighty strange he got here ahead of us," Billy Bob commented, still in the saddle, "seein' as how we left before he did."

"It's not me you need to worry about," Fargo said, but he was wasting his breath. Her brother would no more believe him than he would believe cows could fly.

Walker shook Fargo's hand. "That was you who passed close to our camp last night, wasn't it?"

"You heard me?" Fargo was impressed.

"The horses did. I remembered you saying that horses are better than watchdogs, so I kept an eye on them, and when they all stared into the trees, I figured someone or something was out there."

"You're learning," Fargo said.

"No sign of Smith, I take it."

"Not yet."

It was a somber group that ringed the fire. They never knew but when the night would explode with gunfire and one or more of them would be blasted into eternity. The roars and snarls and screams that came out of the night were not nearly as hard on their nerves as the occasional snap of a twig or furtive rustling.

"I hate this," Silky Mae commented toward midnight. "It's like bein' a wooden duck in a carnival shootin' gallery."

"The rest of you can turn in," Fargo offered. "I'll keep watch."

Walker would not hear of it. He and his men were there to protect them, and they would take turns standing guard.

The night stayed peaceful. Nor did anything happen the next night. Or the next. Whenever they encountered anyone coming from Kellogg, they asked about Smith, but no one had seen anyone answering his description.

Billy Bob was convinced they were fretting over

nothing. Smith was not bound for Kellogg, he insisted, but had gone elsewhere. They were perfectly safe.

Eight days out they made camp beside one of the many small, nameless streams in the Palouse Range. Silky Mae excused herself and curled up under her blankets early. Since Billy Bob always turned in when she did, he followed suit. Soon only Fargo and Walker were up.

Fargo had come to know the man better over the past week. Enough to persuade him that Walker could be trusted. "I have something for you to see," he said, and handed him the letter he had found on Pike Driscoll.

Walker was quiet for a while after he read it. Then he said thoughtfully, "This explains a lot. I always wondered why Gideon favored Pike over the other bodyguards. Whenever Gideon left the estate, he always wanted Pike along."

"He was paying Driscoll to look the other way while he secretly met with Tabor."

Walker folded the letter and gave it back. "I never did buy the story that Gideon had gone after gold. That boy is city-bred, through and through. He doesn't know the first thing about panning or prospecting."

"What about his friend Asa?"

"Cut from the same spoiled cloth. Between the two of them, I doubt they've ever done a real day's work their entire lives. Everything was always done for them by the butler, by the maids, by the other servants. That's how it is when people are as rich as the Zareds."

"And Tabor Garnet?"

"As pretty and sweet a girl as ever lived, and madly in love with Gideon. But her family is poor. They come from what Mr. Zared calls the wrong side of town. He never did like her, not from the very beginning. To someone who has worked for Mr. Zared as long as I have, it was obvious in how he looked at her and spoke to her."

"Yet Gideon went on courting her?"

"The boy was young and in love. I don't think he realized how his father felt until he announced that he intended to marry her."

"You were there?"

"No. But I talked to the bodyguard who was. Mr. Zared bit a cigar clean in half. Then he sat Gideon down and tried to get it across that people like the Zareds do not marry people like the Garnets. Zared wanted his son to marry someone from a better family. But Gideon wouldn't hear of it. He said he loved Tabor and that was that. His father refused to give his blessing, and warned that if Gideon didn't heed him, he could cut off Gideon's inheritance."

"How did that go over?"

"About as well as you would expect. Gideon walked out in a huff. A few nights later, at the supper table, Mr. Zared forbade Gideon from ever seeing Tabor again. I was there, and I never saw Gideon so mad. He used language I never heard him use before. That only made his father madder. There they were, yelling at each other and pounding the table, and Edrea sitting between them and smiling like the cat that ate the canary."

"She was happy they were fighting?"

"Of course." Walker glanced at the other two bodyguards, apparently to assure himself they were asleep. "What I'm about to tell you goes no further. I could be fired if word ever got back to Mr. Zared that I was speaking ill of the fruit of his loins." He paused. "Gideon and Edrea hate each other. I'm not sure why. A lot of brothers and sisters can't get along. But those two have loathed each other since they were knee-high to a foal."

"It's not because Zared is leaving his fortune to his son?"

"You've heard about that, have you? Yes, he's leaving millions to Gideon and a few paltry hundred thousand to Edrea. But he only announced that about three years ago. No one saw Edrea for a week afterward. She was too upset to show herself, a maid told me. When she did come out of her room, she was as polite as could be to her father and her brother, but something had changed—something deep down inside of her."

"She hated Gideon before that, though?"

Walker nodded. "There is a secret in that family. A deep, dark secret that no one will talk about."

"What makes you say that?"

"There was an old black servant who had been with them since before Zared himself was born. The servant did light work. Brought in wood for the cook, and helped tend the flower gardens and whatnot. They called him Matthew but his real name was Matuka. He was born in Africa, in a small village in the jungle. He and his parents were caught by slavers when he was five years old and sent to America."

Fargo was reminded of the growing war of words between the North and the South over the slavery issue.

"I talked to him a few times. I wanted to hear about the Dark Continent but he didn't remember very much. He was too young when he was taken. But he sure knew a lot about the Zareds. He had been with the family so long, he knew things no one else did. Now and then he would drop hints. I tried to pry more out of him but he wouldn't betray their trust. All I can say for sure is that when Edrea was about ten and Gideon was eight, something happened that turned her father against her."

Fargo's mind ran wild with dark imaginings.

"Ever since, Zared has favored his son. Oh, he lets Edrea have a say in the family's business enterprises.

She has a good head on her shoulders, that woman. But as long as I have been there, he has always been more loving toward his son than toward her."

"She must be glad her brother ran off with Tabor Garnet," Fargo observed.

"Glad, hell. She's giddy with glee. A maid told me that when Edrea heard the news, she laughed until she had tears running down her face. Her brother has hung himself, and she couldn't be happier."

"Why doesn't Zared let his son go? What difference does the marriage make now?"

"You've met Benjamin Zared," Walker said. "Does he strike you as the kind to forgive a slight? He can't stand it when anyone stands up to him. Everything has to be his way and only his way. Whoever bucks him, he destroys."

"Even his own son?"

"Especially his own son. To Zared's way of thinking, if he doesn't punish Gideon, it will be seen as a sign of weakness. He has made a lot of enemies who would like nothing better than to bring the Zared business empire crashing down, and if they see he can't keep his own house in order, they might figure the time is ripe to strike."

"What about Gideon's friend Asa Chaviv? How does he figure into this mess?"

Walker sipped some coffee. "Asa's father is rich, but nowhere near as rich as Zared. The boys were playmates when they were small. Benjamin never did like having other children around but he made an exception in Asa's case so Gideon could have at least one good friend."

Fargo reached for the coffeepot. He thought he heard a slight sound off in the woods but neither the Ovaro nor any of the other horses so much as pricked their ears. It was the wind, he figured. "So Asa is only in this to help Gideon?"

"As far as I know. When they were growing up, they did everything together: played, rode, fished, hunted—all the usual things boys do."

"They fished and hunted?" Fargo's estimation of their chances rose a notch.

"A few times. But Gideon was too soft. He didn't like using bait. He couldn't stand to thread a worm on a hook. He shot a deer once, but the servants had to skin it and butcher it. He tried but he had to stop. It made him sick to his stomach."

"And they think they can make it to Canada?" Fargo marveled.

"That wasn't their plan originally, I understand. But I only have what Mr. Zared and Edrea have told me to go by."

"What else did they say?"

"That Gideon was trying to make it to Oregon but his father's agents traced them to Fort Hall, so Gideon decided to head for the border. His father doesn't have business holdings in Canada. Gideon must believe he will be safe there." Walker paused. "As if Mr. Zared will let a thing like that stop him. He won't rest until he's caught them, and I wouldn't want to be in Gideon's shoes when he does."

"What will Zared do to them?"

"Your guess is as good as mine. Probably have Gideon hauled back east and offer Tabor money to stay away from him."

"He would buy her off?"

"He would try." Jim Walker sighed. "Mr. Zared thinks that the answer to every problem is to throw money at it. However much it takes to make the problem go away. He'll offer Tabor enough to put her up in luxury but she won't take it. She loves Gideon as much as Gideon loves her."

Fargo sat back. He raised his cup to his mouth but he did not swallow. He had heard another indistinct sound. It could be anything: the flutter of a leaf in the breeze, an animal cautiously skirting the camp. Or it could be that someone was out there, someone like No-Nose Smith.

"What's wrong?" Walker asked.

"Maybe nothing." But Fargo set down the cup and stood, picking up the Henry. The horses were dozing. He took a dozen steps to the northeast and stopped to let his eyes adjust.

Walker came up next to him, holding his own rifle. "I hope it's Smith," he whispered. "Pike Driscoll wasn't much of a friend but Lattimer and those others were. I'd like to avenge their deaths."

Fargo was listening for alien sounds: the scrape of a boot, the scratch of brush on buckskin, anything.

"Why Smith is only killing bodyguards is beyond me," Walker whispered. "What did any of us ever do to him?"

Just then the Ovaro whinnied. Fargo looked and saw the stallion staring at the woods to his left. He started to turn but suddenly Walker shoved him and shouted, "Look out!"

The night erupted with gunfire.

17

The two slugs that struck Jim Walker in the center of his forehead cored his cranium from front to back and burst out the rear of his head in a shower of hair and bone. Walker was dead on his feet but his legs took a short shambling step before buckling.

Fargo had seen the muzzle flashes. He responded in kind, firing the Henry as fast as he could, four shots one right after the other. Then he crouched and darted toward a birch to his right. Over his shoulder he shouted to the others, "Stay down!"

But the other two bodyguards did not listen. They had jumped to their feet when the shots boomed, and now, seeing Walker fall, they rushed toward him.

That was exactly what the killer wanted. Twice more the rifle spoke, and at each retort, a man in black fell.

Again Fargo fired at the muzzle flashes. The killer was down low to the ground, maybe prone, and Fargo aimed at where he thought the man must be. The Picketts joined the fight, Billy Bob spraying lead fast and furious, Silky Mae firing more selectively.

In the silence that ensued, they all heard the patter of racing footsteps and the shrill laugh that mocked them.

Fargo gave chase. He ran recklessly, crashing through the brush like a crazed bear. The smart thing to do was to make as little noise as possible but he did not care. He was not worried about blundering into the killer's gun sights because now he knew beyond any shadow of a doubt that the man did not want him dead. He had been an easy target back there in the firelight, and the assassin had shot Walker, instead. Yet again, for reasons he could not fathom, his life had been spared.

"Skye!" Silky Mae shouted. "Wait for us!"

Fargo was not waiting for anyone or anything. He was only fifteen or twenty yards behind the assassin. All he wanted was one shot, one clear shot. More than that, he wanted to see who it was. All the evidence pointed at No-Nose Smith, but it could be anyone.

"Skye! Where are you?"

Fargo did not reply. He was focused on one thing and one thing alone: catching the killer before the killer reached his horse. The man had stopped laughing, and from the crack and crackle of undergrowth, he was as intent on getting away as Fargo was on overtaking him.

"Fargo?" This from Billy Bob. "Answer us, damn it!"

Ahead, through the trees, came a glimmer of dusky color against the inky backdrop. Buckskins, possibly, and the suggestion of a hat. On the fly. Fargo snapped the Henry to his shoulder, but in the instant it took, the glimmer was swallowed by the gloom of night.

Frustration twisted Fargo's gut. He spied the figure again and, past it, a larger silhouette that could only be the man's mount. *No!* he inwardly roared, and reached deep into his wellspring of stamina to pour on extra speed. He was so close! Another six or seven yards and he would have a shot.

The man came to his horse and vaulted into the saddle without breaking stride. Whooping like a Comanche, he slapped his legs against his animal.

Fargo had his shot! The man's buckskin shirt was bathed in starlight. Fargo threw the Henry to his shoulder and thumbed back the hammer. He was smiling, thinking that at last luck was with him, at last he would end the killings and find out who was behind them.

Suddenly the tip of Fargo's left boot hooked on something. A root, a rock, Fargo did not see what it was but he felt himself falling. His elbows smacked the ground hard, searing his shoulders with pain. He fired anyway, knowing even as he squeezed the trigger that he was wasting the lead and missed.

Another taunting laugh confirmed it. Hooves pounded, their drumming a taunt in itself. Yet again, the killer had murdered with impunity. Yet again, the killer had gotten away.

The bile that rose in Fargo's gorge was not from his fall. Bitter disappointment was to blame. He did not like failing at anything and he had failed several times now to put windows in the killer's skull.

Out of the vegetation behind him charged the Picketts.

"Did you get him?" Silky Mae breathlessly asked. "Is No-Nose Smith finally dead?"

Billy Bob answered, "You have ears, don't you? Your wonderful friend has let Smith slip through his fingers *again*."

"Damnation!" Silky Mae declared. "What does it take to feed him to the worms?"

"Someone who can shoot straight," Billy Bob said.

The Southerner would never know how close he had come to losing some teeth. Fargo hefted the Henry but did not swing. He could not blame Billy Bob for saying out loud what was going through his own mind. The blame was his and his alone.

"It's not easy to hit something at night," Silky Mae came to his defense. "You ought to know, all the coon huntin' we've done."

"If you say so," Billy Bob said.

His tone sliced through Fargo like a knife. But again

Fargo did not say anything, because again the younger man was right. An experienced hunter, an experienced marksman, did not make the mistakes he had made. Now three more men had lost their lives—one a man he liked.

"Don't be so mean," Silky Mae scolded. "I'd like to have seen you do any better."

"What I don't get," Billy Bob said thoughtfully, "is why Smith only kills Zared's men. Why does he keep sparin' your friend here?"

"That's not fair," Silky Mae responded.

"Ask your friend if he thinks it's fair," Billy Bob said. "Ask him if he thinks it isn't a mite peculiar."

Fargo had to remember that whatever else Billy Bob Pickett might be, he was no fool. "Your brother has a point. I'd like to know why myself." He turned to head back. "I'll bury the bodies."

Silky Mae caught up and touched his elbow. "Don't listen to my brother. He likes to hear himself jabber." When Fargo did not comment, she plucked at his sleeve. "Did you hear me? Don't let him get to you."

"Walker had a wife and two children."

"Don't blame yourself. He was doin' his job. Guardin' others is dangerous work. He accepted that." She was trying her best to cheer him up. "For his family's sake, he should have found another line of work. We never think it will happen to us but it rains on everybody, just like Scripture says it does."

"If you say so," Fargo unintentionally mimicked her brother.

There was a shovel on one of the packhorses. Selecting a brand from the fire, Fargo walked to the tree line and bent to his task. Thankfully, the soil was not hard, but there were rocks, and whenever the shovel hit one, the *ching* of metal on stone rang loud and clear.

Silky Mae hunkered nearby to watch him and slowly

rocked on her heels. "It's a cryin' shame," she said as another clod of dirt joined Fargo's growing pile, "all these people dyin' over a few pitiful handfuls of gold."

Fargo revealed the truth to her, ending with "Benjamin Zared has a lot to answer for."

"If you ask me, so does his son. They are both as contrary as goats. If Gideon had any sense, he would have run off to Florida or someplace."

The three riderless horses were added to the string, and on they rode. Fargo was not in the best frame of mind. He almost wished Billy Bob would prod him so he would have an excuse to knock him senseless, but Billy Bob hardly uttered ten words the rest of the day, and only to his sister.

The mountains through which they passed were spectacular. Douglas firs were the most common trees. There were also spruce, ponderosa pine, and larch. In the valleys grew the ubiquitous cottonwoods. Here and there were stands of aspen, their leaves quaking in the slightest of breezes.

Dogwood and elderberry grew in profusion. Huckleberry was by no means rare. Purple heather lent splashes of color. So did buttercups, fireweed, and violets.

Fargo had seldom seen so much animal sign. Deer were everywhere, elk abundant. He came across moose tracks, and several times spied mountain sheep high on rocky escarpments. Along the streams were tracks of otter, mink, and muskrats. Raccoons flourished.

The territory was a fisherman's paradise. On several occasions Fargo took line from his saddlebags and tried his hand in the rushing waters or in deep, quiet pools. Almost always, he hooked fish for supper.

Under different circumstances, he would have enjoyed the scenery and the wildlife. But the killer was still on the loose, and he never knew but when the man would strike again.

As the days went by, each as peaceful as the next, Fargo fought a sense of complacency. Just because the killer had spared him so far did not mean the killer would spare him forever.

The Picketts were cold to each other. For a while Silky Mae tried to get her brother to talk and joke with her but she gave it up as a lost cause. Billy Bob was in a funk to end all funks.

Fargo wished Silky Mae and he were alone. The nights were long and chill, and it would have been nice to share his blankets. But it was not to be. She would not touch him with her brother there.

This far north, the gold camps were fewer and a lot farther between. At each one Fargo went from saloon to saloon asking bartenders if they had seen anyone with a nose patch. At each saloon he received the same answer: no.

They were still several days out of Kellogg when they came to yet another gold camp on Wilbur Creek, named after the prospector who first found gold in its rushing waters. A single saloon provided liquid refreshment. Fargo ordered a drink and asked the bartender if he had seen anyone resembling No-Nose Smith. The bartender hadn't.

Sighing, Fargo washed the dust down with a gulp of redeye. He paid little attention when a grizzled prospector bellied to the bar and asked for a beer. But his interest was perked by the prospector's next remark to the bartender.

"I hear tell you had a shooting affray in here last week, Fred."

Busy pouring a drink, the bartender nodded. "That we did. A sassy pilgrim from back east had the gumption to insult Otto Pierce."

The prospector whistled. "Not a healthy practice. How did it come about?"

Fred looked both ways, then leaned toward his friend. "Pierce has been spending a lot of time here the past couple of weeks. No one knows why, but I have a feeling he is waiting for someone."

"I wouldn't want to be in the boots of whoever Otto Pierce is after," the prospector commented.

"That makes two of us," Fred said. "Pierce is as mean as the year is long, and will kill you as soon as look at you." Fred lowered his voice. "As for the shooting, Pierce was playing cards and a gold seeker from back east had the gall to accuse him of cheating."

"Was he?" the prospector asked.

"Whether yes or no isn't the point," Fred said. "The point is that for opening his fool mouth when he shouldn't have, that pilgrim is now buried in an unmarked grave in the woods."

"Jackasses always get their due."

"Tell that to the man's wife," Fred said. "We found a letter from her in his pocket."

"You say Pierce and his men have been hanging around?"

"Not his men. They're up in the high country somewhere. Only Pierce and that spooky breed he's always with."

"Red Moon?" The prospector shuddered. "I can do without those two, thank you very much."

"Keep your voice down," Fred admonished. "The tent has ears. And Pierce and the breed could walk in at any minute."

As if that were a cue, a hush fell. Nearly everyone stopped talking, or spoke in whispers.

Two men had entered. One was as stocky as a bull, with shoulders broad enough to hoist a Conestoga. A wedge of sandy hair jutted from under a flat-crowned hat. Around his waist were a pair of Colts and a butcher knife in a brown sheath. He strode into the tent as if he owned it, and those in his path hastily moved aside.

Fargo read fear on many a face, although the men tried not to show it.

The other man was of mixed lineage. His black hair and dusky complexion, contrasted by blue eyes, marked him as a half-breed. He wore buckskins and had a buckskin band around his long hair. His armament consisted of a Remington, a bone-handled hunting knife, and a tomahawk. Not a trace of friendliness animated the cruel stamp of his features. The looks he cast at the saloon's customers were scornful. A sneer was fixed on his thin lips, as if he were daring someone to say something.

"Mr. Pierce!" the bartender nervously exclaimed. "This makes, what, ten days in a row?"

Fargo's skin prickled. So these were the men Otter Tail insisted had been trailing Gideon Zared's party. Leaning his elbows on the plank bar, Fargo shammed an interest in his drink.

"You don't hanker after my business anymore, Fred?" Otto Pierce asked. He had a voice like gravel rattling in a metal drum.

"Of course I do! Where did you ever get a notion like that?" The bartender's laugh was much too shrill.

"A bottle," Otto Pierce demanded, thumping the plank with a hand as big as a ham.

"Right away."

Red Moon stood with his back to the bar, one hand on his revolver and the other on his tomahawk. His sneer of contempt seemed chiseled into his features.

Pierce did not bother with a glass. He upended the whiskey and chugged. Smacking his mouth, he wiped it with the dirty sleeve of his wool coat. "Has there been anyone in asking after me?"

"You ask that every day and the answer is always the same," Fred said. "No, sir, there sure hasn't."

Otto Pierce slowly lowered the bottle and regarded the bartender as he might an insect he was about to squash. "I didn't realize you have been keeping track of how many times I've asked or how many days I've stopped in. Should I take that as an insult, Fred?"

"Heavens, no!" Fred bleated. "I would never insult you, not in a million years."

"I hope not, Fred," Otto Pierce said. "Remember what happened to that jackass who accused me of dealing from the bottom of the deck?"

"You shot him. Eight times."

"He made me mad," Pierce said simply.

Fred broke out in a sweat. It did not help his disposition any that Red Moon was staring at him and fingering the tomahawk. He sought to change the subject. "Are your men still up in the high country?"

"You let me worry about them. The thing for you to remember is that if anyone shows up looking for me, you are to let me know pronto."

"I will, Mr. Pierce. You can count on me." Fred wrung his hands and shifted his weight from one foot to the other. "Do you mind if I go about my business?"

Pierce wagged a thick finger and the bartender scurried down the bar. To Red Moon Pierce said, "I reckon we have to wait a while yet. Go out and keep watch. Maybe they were delayed."

"They better not be," Red Moon said.

"Relax. We'll get the money. No one would dare try to cheat us of our due. Not after all we went through."

Fargo watched the breed saunter out. Otto Pierce took another swig of whiskey and gazed about him with the air of a grizzly among sheep. Fargo was careful to turn away and not look back until a minute had gone by.

Pierce was no longer at the bar. He was pulling out a chair by a table near the front flap.

Fargo nursed his drink. He wanted to learn what the pair were up to. It could be that Pierce held the answer to the fate of Gideon Zared.

The atmosphere in the saloon was subdued. No one went anywhere near Pierce's table. Newcomers were quick to note his presence, and to give him a wide berth.

Over half an hour had gone by when the flap parted once again, framing Billy Bob Pickett, who stood there scanning the card players and those at the bar.

Otto Pierce squinted against the sudden glare. "Close the flap, boy," he gruffly commanded.

Billy Bob was new to the territory. He had never heard of Pierce or he would never had done what he did next, namely, open the flap even wider and say, "I'll do as I damn well please, mister."

In the silence that fell, Fargo could have heard the flutter of a butterfly's wings. He stepped from the bar so he had a clear view of the table.

Strangely, Otto Pierce was smiling. "Well, well, what do we have here—a Son of the South?"

"And proud of it," Billy Bob said. He had not lowered the flap.

"I don't see why," Pierce commented, with a deceptively polite smile. "Southerners are inbred idiots. It comes from having relations with their cousins and their sisters."

The barb struck a nerve. Billy Bob took a couple steps, his hand hovering above his revolver. "You take that back, you Yankee polecat."

"You have it backward, boy," Pierce said. "You're the one who better get down on his knees and beg me for his life."

"The hell I will."

Fargo started toward them but he had only taken a couple of steps when the flap framed a new face, that of Red Moon. The half-breed did not say anything. He did not utter a single word of warning. He walked up to Billy Bob and, as swift as lightning, drew his knife and pressed the tip to Billy Bob's nape.

"Want me to kill him for you, Otto?" Red Moon

asked as casually as he might ask if Pierce wanted another drink.

Fargo did not have a clear shot. Customers were in the way. Trying not to be noticed, he sidled to the right.

Billy Bob had gone rigid with surprise, but he was too smart to draw with the blade jabbing him. "What's this?" he said to Otto Pierce. "Do you always have someone else fight your fights for you?"

"Not hardly, boy," Pierce said, and laughed. "Ask anyone. They'll tell you I tree my own painters."

"Painter" was another word for mountain lion, but rarely used. Fargo had a few more steps to take when Red Moon's dark eyes darted in his direction. Fargo promptly stopped.

"So do I," Billy Bob was growling. "So what do you say we step outside and settle this like gentlemen?"

Pierce chuckled. "Where in hell do you think you're at, boy? Atlanta? They're aren't any gentlemen in these parts, only the quick and the dead." He was more amused than anything else so far.

"And the stupid," Billy Bob said. "Don't forget the stupid."

"Oh, I won't," Pierce responded, staring straight at him. "I run into stupid everywhere I go."

Always easy to rile, Billy Bob clenched his fists. "Give me a fair chance. That's all I ask."

"Easily remedied," Otto Pierce said, and snapped his fingers. Just like that, Red Moon lowered the knife and stepped back. "See?"

Billy Bob glanced at Red Moon, then at Pierce. He did not appear as sure of himself. "This is a fine how do you do," he muttered. "Zared never said anything about the likes of you two."

Pierce's eyes narrowed. "What was that?"

"I was talkin' about the man I work for: Benjamin Zared." Billy Bob squared his shoulders. "Whenever you are ready, mister."

Incredibly, Otto Pierce spread his hands on the table and said, "Tell you what, boy. If you walk out right this second, I won't turn you inside out and hang your hide out to dry."

"What?" This was from Red Moon, not the Southerner. "No one talks to us as he talked to you. Kill him and be done with it."

"Let's not be hasty," Pierce said.

Red Moon was not the only one puzzled. So were Fargo and, to judge by their expressions, half the men in the saloon.

"I do not ride with weaklings," the breed declared. "If you will not kill him, I will do so for you."

Billy Bob did not have the sense God gave a turnip. He spun, his hand dropping to his six-gun, and snarled, "I would like to see you try, you mangy son of a bitch. Only this time I'm facin' you."

Red Moon still had the knife in his hand. Rumor had it he was so skilled with blades he could stick his knife in a target no bigger than an apple at ten paces, ten tries out of ten. "You are eager to die, white boy."

Billy Bob did not know that he would have cold steel in his heart before he cleared leather. "We'll see who does the dyin', breed. And I can tell you right now, it won't be me."

"Fool," Red Moon said.

Fargo shouldered a man aside. But even as he moved, Otto Pierce heaved out of his chair and came around the card table with a speed belying his bulk— a speed that attested to his reputation as one of the deadliest men on the frontier.

Billy Bob never noticed Pierce come up behind and tower over him like a redwood over a willow. "What are you waitin' for, breed?"

Red Moon was looking at his partner.

"Some people never learn," Otto Pierce said, and struck.

18

Otto Pierce was a killer many times over. The number of those he had shot, stabbed, strangled or beaten to death was reputed to be anywhere from twenty to two hundred. Granted, saloon gossips had a tendency to embellish. Tall tales were their stock in trade. But there was no denying that whatever the tally, Otto Pierce shed blood as casually as other men shed their clothes.

Fargo knew of one incident, sworn to be true by the muleskinner who witnessed it, where Pierce slit a man's throat after the man inadvertently blew cigar smoke in Pierce's face.

So it was all the more startling when Pierce smashed the butt of a pistol across Billy Bob Pickett's head instead of blowing Billy Bob's brains out. The Southerner folded like wet paper.

Ironically, Red Moon asked the question uppermost on Fargo's mind, and no doubt the minds of many others: "Why did you spare him?"

"The trouble with you," Otto Pierce said, "is that you never listen. Clean the wax out of your ears sometime."

"I heard him insult you. I heard him insult me. What more did I need to hear?" Red Moon challenged. "Sometimes you make no sense."

Pierce laughed and twirled his pistol into his holster. "I make enough sense that you have stuck with me going on seven years now."

Contrary to popular belief, Red Moon had a sense of humor. He smiled and said, "I stick with you because you don't mind when I kill other whites." He stared at the figure on the ground. "Or at least you never did until now."

"Come with me." Pierce strode to the flap. "We have some palavering to do."

A collective sigh of relief filled the saloon. Several men gathered around Billy Bob and rolled him over.

Fargo went to the flap and peered out. Pierce and Red Moon were walking down the rutted track that passed for Wilbur Creek's main street. They were having an animated talk. He closed the flap.

"Anyone know this youngster?" a man asked.

"Whoever he is, he was born under a lucky star," commented another. "I never thought I'd see the day when Otto Pierce spared a living soul."

"Me neither," said someone else.

By then Fargo was on one knee, running a hand over the back of Billy Bob's head. There was a nasty bump and a little blood but the Southerner would be fine once his head stopped hurting. "Fetch some water."

Fred brought a glass filled to the brim. "Is he a friend of yours, mister? You ought to learn him better than to stick his head in the mouths of grizzly bears."

"Maybe he's feebleminded," suggested another.

Fargo held the glass over Billy Bob's face and upended it. Almost immediately Billy Bob coughed and sputtered and his eyes blinked open. He gaped in confusion. Then, as his memory returned, he abruptly sat up, and groaned.

"My noggin! What hit me? Why am I seein' double?"

"Death on a holiday," Fred said. "Count your blessings it's only your head."

"Did that make no kind of sense or is it me?" Billy Bob squinted at Fargo. "You! I came in to find out what was takin' you so long, and some fella called me an idiot."

"You are." Fargo helped him to stand. "Can you manage or should we wait a while?"

Shrugging off Fargo's hand, Billy Bob declared, "I can manage!" He took a step, and would have pitched forward had Fargo not caught him. "Then again, maybe I'd best rest. I feel woozy."

"It comes from having curdled brains, boy," Fred said. "But if you can count your toes, no real harm done."

Billy Bob scowled and asked, "Who *is* this jasper and why is he babblin' like a lunatic?"

Fargo had something more important to ask. "I told you to stay with your sister. Where did you leave her?"

"With the horses. Where else?" Billy Bob said defensively. "She can take care of herself, if that's what you're worried about."

Fred took the words right off the tip of Fargo's tongue. "Sonny, I hope to heaven your sister takes better care of herself than you do of you. That performance of yours was downright pitiful."

"I swear I will shoot him if he doesn't stop," Billy Bob vowed.

A husky prospector warned, "You'll do no such thing, boy. This here is the only saloon in camp, and Fred runs it. Shoot him, and the rest of us will treat you to a strangulation jig from the nearest cottonwood."

Fargo went to the flap. Otto Pierce and Red Moon were nowhere to be seen. "Come on." He beckoned, and did not wait to see if Billy Bob followed. He went left and only had to go a short distance when he saw the string, and the shapely figure leaning against a packhorse with her arms folded.

"I told you she was all right," Billy Bob said sullenly.

"Don't you care for her?" Fargo asked.

"What kind of damn fool question is that? Of course I do. We might have a spat now and then but she's my sister. Where we come from, blood kin counts for more than anything else in the world."

"Do you know how many women there are in this camp?"

Billy Bob surveyed the dirt street and the motley assortment of tents and other temporary structures. "I don't see any at the moment but there have to be a few here somewhere."

"Your sister is the only one."

"What?" Billy Bob started. "You're joshin'. Why, if she was the only female in these parts—" He stopped. "Oh, my God. The only female? Why, there are hundreds of men here, and they probably haven't been with a woman in—" Again he stopped. "Damn me to hell. My thinker sure is puny sometimes."

Silky Mae came to meet them. She was so intent on them that she did not notice that every man she passed gazed at her as a hungry wolf might gaze on a helpless fawn.

Billy Bob swore. "Look at them! Why, I'd shoot the whole lot if I had enough bullets."

"Where have you two been?" Silky Mae asked. "I was gettin' worried." She glanced around. "And the looks some of these jaspers give me! Why, you would think I was a Saint Louis dove dressed in satin instead of a country gal in homespun."

"We are glued at the hip from now on," Billy Bob informed her.

"What on earth are you on about now? Why would you want to do that?" Silky Mae asked.

"To make up for bein' plumb stupid."

"What purpose brothers serve is beyond me. I swear, Billy, the older you get, the less sense you make."

Fargo was on the toes of his boots, craning his neck for sign of Otto Pierce and Red Moon. Instead, he spotted a pair of riders, entering the gold camp from the north. Both wore black from head to toe. "What do you make of them?"

"I wonder what they're doing here?" Silky Mae said. "Didn't Walker tell us that the rest of the bodyguards were with Mr. Zared in Kellogg?"

"Maybe he sent them to look for us," her brother guessed.

The men in black drew rein a hundred yards away and were about to climb down when a broad-shouldered bull in a flat-crowned hat and a half-breed with a wide leather band around his hair came out of a tent and greeted them.

"Do you see what I see?" Billy Bob blurted.

"Who are those two?" Silky Mae wanted to know.

Fargo grabbed the siblings by their arms and pulled them between two tents. "It's best those bodyguards don't spot us."

"Why is that?" Silky Mae's confusion was growing. "One of you had better start talking, and right quick."

Never taking his eyes off Otto Pierce and Red Moon, Fargo explained who they were and related some of the more vile deeds attributed to them.

"But what would Mr. Zared's bodyguards be doing with men like that?" Silky Mae scratched her head. "It makes no sense."

"Somethin' sure ain't right," Billy Bob said.

Pierce and one of the bodyguards were having a long conversation. It ended with Red Moon going down the street and returning with two horses. Pierce and Red Moon climbed on and the quartet headed west, out of Wilbur Camp.

Fargo stepped from between the tents. "You two go on to Kellogg with the string. I'll catch up as soon as I can."

"Like hell," Billy Bob said. "I owe that big one for the wallop he gave me. I'm comin' with you."

"If you are, so am I," Silky Mae said.

Fargo did not have time to argue. "Your brother is going to Kellogg and so are you." He focused on Silky Mae since she was the more levelheaded. "Those men might give us a clue to where Gideon Zared is. Alone, I have a better chance of shadowing them without being seen."

Billy Bob shook his head. "You're not leavin' me here no matter what you say."

"If Tabor Garnet is still alive," Fargo said to Silky Mae, "it could be that Otto Pierce has her."

"A man like that?" Silky Mae pursed her lips. "I savvy. Very well. My brother and me will go on to Kellogg like you want."

Billy Bob was his usual pigheaded self. "I'll do no such thing, sis. You didn't see what that coyote did to me."

Placing a hand on his, Silky Mae said softly, "Please." When Billy Bob growled like a kicked dog, she said it again, even more softly. "Please, brother. Fargo is right in this."

"Damn all women to hell," Billy Bob fumed.

Trusting in her to keep him there, Fargo ran to the Ovaro. The trail up into the mountains saw steady use thanks to the gold seekers. No one had made a really big strike up there yet, but greed sprang eternal.

Fargo came to the first bend and dismounted. Poking his head past a tree, he verified Pierce and Red Moon and the men in black were up ahead. When Red Moon started to twist in the saddle, he ducked back. The rest of the afternoon, Fargo let them get far enough ahead that he need not worry about Red Moon spotting him. Their tracks were plain enough: three shod and one unshod.

Half an hour before sunset, Fargo realized their

tracks were no longer there. "Damn," he said, and drew rein. They had turned off somewhere and he had missed it. Reining around, he noticed a dry wash he had not paid much attention to. Sure enough, their tracks led into it.

The wash led steeply upward. Its bottom was littered with loose dirt and stones, and Fargo had to exercise caution that the Ovaro's hooves did not dislodge a lot of it and give him away. He climbed so slowly that it was full dark when he beheld flickering flames a quarter of a mile above. Pierce and the bodyguards had stopped for the night.

Fargo rode up out of the wash and found a suitable spot. Swinging down, he wrapped the reins around a branch. He removed his spurs, stuck them in a saddlebag, shucked the Henry, and headed higher on foot, thankful for the gusty wind that had sprung up with the setting of the sun. The clearing they had picked was sheltered on three sides by thickets. Fargo crawled within earshot and parted the brush.

Otto Pierce and the men in black were chewing jerky and drinking coffee. Red Moon was not there, although his horse was.

Unease crept over Fargo. The half-breed was the wariest, a panther in human guise. Fargo kept waiting, in vain, for him to reappear. Nor were Pierce or the bodyguards saying much.

The bodyguards interested him. Zared had close to two dozen in his employ. Fargo did not know the names of these two but he vaguely recollected seeing them before. He thought it important he remember exactly where but he couldn't.

Then the taller of the two raised his head and said, "If anything happens to us, the deal is off."

Otto Pierce grinned over his coffee cup. "Why, Jansen, what makes you say a thing like that? Can it be you don't trust me?"

"What I think doesn't matter," Jansen said. "I'm

only following orders. Were it up to me, I would not have any dealings with you whatsoever. You are a scoundrel, Mr. Pierce, and that is putting it mildly."

Pierce was a while answering. When he did, his eyes were glittering spikes of simmering violence. "I've been called a lot of things. Bastard. Son of a bitch. Outlaw. Killer. A preacher I shot called me a misanthrope, whatever the hell that means. Scoundrel is new. It's a polite Eastern way of calling a man scum without really calling him scum."

"I never implied any such thing."

"That's all right," Pierce said with a dismissive wave. "I should shoot you but I won't. It would make your boss mad, and I can't afford to do that until I have the money I'm owed." He chuckled at something, then said, "This makes twice today I've had to keep my gun in its holster."

"You will have the ten thousand dollars once the rest of the details have been agreed upon," Jansen said.

"What is left to work out?" Pierce asked. "I have the merchandise. I have been true to my word, and I expect your boss to be true, too."

"Never fear in that regard. But I need to see them with my own eyes. Once I report back, you will get your money."

"I hope so," Otto Pierce said. "I hope your boss doesn't decide to double-deal me. I'll put up with a lot, but not that. Never that. Double-deal me and not one of you will make it back across the Mississippi River."

"There is no need for idle threats," the bodyguard said.

"Unlike you Easterners," Pierce responded, "I always say what I mean and mean what I say. Ask anyone. I might kill and steal and treat myself to ladies whether they want me to treat myself to them or not, but I am always as good as my word."

Jansen shrugged. "That's something, I suppose. But again. What I do is not up to me. It's up to the person who pays me."

"Ever killed anyone?" Otto Pierce abruptly asked.

"What sort of question is that? My job is to save lives. I would only kill if I had to, and so far I have been spared from having to."

"Amazing," Pierce said, and refilled his cup.

Fargo lingered, hoping to learn more, but Pierce stayed silent. All the bodyguards did was exchange a few words about the weather and how hard the riding was on their back sides.

Red Moon's continued absence was disturbing. Fargo could not explain it. Then it hit him that Pierce might have sent the half-breed down the trail to see if they were being followed, in which case Red Moon might find the Ovaro.

As silently as he had crawled up to the clearing, Fargo now backed away from it. Once he was far enough, he rose and cat-footed along the rim of the wash until he came to where he had left the pinto. He did not go right over to it but stood looking and listening until he was convinced it was safe.

Unwrapping the reins, Fargo slid the Henry into the scabbard and started to lead the Ovaro deeper into the trees, saying, "Come on, boy."

The sudden touch of metal to the side of his neck froze Fargo in his tracks. He did not look around. Any movement, however slight, could prove fatal.

"You know who I am?" Red Moon asked.

"Yes," Fargo said.

"Do not move unless I say so. If you do, I will kill you. Do not speak unless I say so. If you do, I will kill you." Red Moon stepped back. "Lift your arms out from your sides."

Fargo did, and felt his Colt snatched from its holster. A hand patted his buckskin shirt, searching for other weapons. It patted around his waist and under his right arm and then under his left arm. It patted down his leg but did not pat the top of his right boot.

"You will walk ahead of me up the wash. If you stop, I will shoot. If you run, I will shoot. If you try to jump on your horse, I will shoot you and the horse."

Anger boiled up in Fargo, not at the renegade, but at himself. Like a rank amateur, he had let Red Moon slip up on him. He told himself it could have happened to anyone, but he was not just anyone.

"How are you known?" Red Moon asked. He was to Fargo's right and a step or two behind.

Fargo said his last name.

"Why do I know that name? I have heard it somewhere." Red Moon might as well have been a ghost for all the noise he made walking. "Do you have an Indian name?"

"Several."

"Is one of them Rides With The Wind?"

"I was known by that name once, yes," Fargo admitted. In his travels, he had stayed with various tribes at one time or another, and each had given him a name they felt fit him.

"You scout for the blue coats." It was a statement, not a query. "You are the one who rubbed out Blue Raven. You are the one who killed High-Backed Bear."

"They were renegades, and they were trying to kill me at the time," Fargo mentioned, and received a sharp jab in the ribs from Red Moon's rifle.

"Did I say to speak?"

Fargo took a calculated gamble. "If you are going to shoot me, do it. But don't treat me like you would a woman."

"I have heard you are brave," Red Moon said. "I have also heard you always speak with a straight tongue. But that I do not believe. Every white dog I have met speaks with two tongues."

"Otto Pierce, too?"

"Pierce is my blood brother. He is the one white man who does not look at me with hate in his eyes because I am half and half."

"Not all whites hate half-breeds—" Fargo began, and received a harder jab than the first one.

"It is not wise to remind me of their hatred. When I think of it, I lose my head. I want to kill, and kill some more."

Fargo gauged the distance between them. He could spin and spring but Red Moon would get off a shot before he could reach him. He had to wait and see how things played out.

Otto Pierce and the bodyguards heard them, and rose. A pistol appeared in Pierce's hand as if out of empty air, and he said, "Well, now, what do we have here? So there was someone on our back trail. Good work, Red Moon."

"He is a hunter of men," the half-breed said. "I think he hunts us for the blue coats."

"Bring him into the light so I can have a look at him before I bed him down with the worms."

Jansen and the other bodyguard showed only mild interest until Fargo came close to the fire. Then Jansen blinked and exclaimed, "I know him! He's one of the scouts Benjamin Zared hired. His name is Fargo."

Otto Pierce's thick eyebrows pinched together. "You don't say. That brat down in the gold camp was also hired by Zared. What was that boy's handle again?"

"The one you described? Billy Bob Pickett."

"I don't believe in coincidences," Pierce remarked, and switched his gaze to the bodyguards. "How is it Fargo followed you up here?"

"What are you talking about?" Jansen rejoined. "This is the first I've seen him since he left Fort Hall."

"He sure wasn't trailing Red Moon and me," Pierce said. He wagged his six-shooter at Fargo. "Have a seat while I work this out in my head. Nice and slow, if you please. Red Moon, if he so much as twitches, put lead in him. Cripple, don't kill. He has some talking to do."

"We should report this," Jansen said.

"Go all the way back to Kellogg? That would take days. I want this over with so I can get the money we're owed." Pierce holstered his pistol but kept his hand on the butt.

Jansen fidgeted and said, "It wouldn't take us that long."

"I can count as good as most. Even if you ride your horses into the ground, it's three days there and three days back. That's the better part of a week."

"It wouldn't—" Jansen started to repeat himself, but stopped when the other bodyguard nudged him. "Fine. Whatever you say."

"Something is wrong here," Otto Pierce said to Red Moon. Planting himself in front of Fargo, he tapped his fingers on his Colt. "Make this easy on yourself. How much do you know?"

Fargo had no reason to keep silent. "You and your men were seen chasing Gideon Zared."

"I told you!" Jansen exclaimed. "He was following you, not us!"

Otto Pierce ignored him. "Seen by who?"

"The Nez Percé."

"Now why would they be keeping an eyes on us?" Pierce wondered. "And how is it they let you know?"

"I do not like this," Red Moon said.

Jansen was a few apples short of a bushel. "What difference does it make? From what I've heard, the Nez Percé are friendly. So what if they saw you?"

"If the Nez Percé told him," Otto Pierce said, wagging a thumb at Fargo, "who else have they told? Some have turned Christian. What if they tell a minister or some other leaky mouth, and word gets back to Benjamin Zared? He could bring in the army to hunt me and my men."

"I do not like this," Red Moon repeated.

Otto Pierce drew his butcher knife from its sheath and held the blade close to Fargo's face. "Mister, start wagging your tongue or lose it."

19

Skye Fargo had been tortured by Apaches once and had the scars to prove it. The Apaches wanted to know about troop movements. Was the army planning a campaign against them? How many soldiers would come? Would the soldiers bring cannons? Fargo refused to say. The troops would have been massacred if he talked. So a warrior commenced to carve on him. The pain had been excruciating but Fargo refused to cry out. He bit his lower lip until it bled. If a friendly Apache had not intervened, he would have died that day.

Now Otto Pierce was threatening to do the same. Only this time it was different. No one's life was at stake except his. Fargo had no qualms about saying, "I'll tell you whatever you want to know."

"Explain the Nez Percé."

"I met up with a hunting party. I told them I was looking for Gideon Zared. A warrior mentioned seeing Red Moon and you," Fargo summed it up.

"A tame Indian, I take it," Pierce probed. "What was his name?"

"He never said and I didn't ask," Fargo lied, and had an inspiration. "He mentioned telling a minister about you."

"Hell in a basket!" Otto Pierce glowered. "All the trouble I went to, and what good did it to me?" He scowled at Red Moon. "I thought you told me there wasn't a Nez Percé village within a hundred miles?"

Jansen had been listening with rising impatience. "Will you forget about the Nez Percé? You'll be long gone before word that you were involved can reach Benjamin Zared, if it ever does. You have nothing to worry about."

"I'm an hombre who likes things neat and tidy," Pierce said. "How else do you reckon I've lasted so long?"

"You came highly recommended in certain quarters," Jansen remarked. "It's why you were sought out. It's why you were offered so much money."

"I'm flattered," Pierce said, although he did not sound flattered. "But ten thousand isn't anything. Not when I have ten men who ride with me. When we divide it up, we'll have barely nine hundred dollars between us."

"How you split it is your business."

"I always treat my men fair," Pierce said. "It's why they ride with me." He paused. "As a matter of fact, now that I think about it, after I show you the whelp and prove I have him, I want you to ride back and let your boss know the price has gone up."

Jansen appeared shocked. "What are you up to? You agreed to ten thousand, remember?"

"That was before I knew all the particulars," Otto Pierce said. "Zared is rich. To him ten thousand is a little drop in a large bucket."

"You can't change the terms halfway through," Jansen persisted.

"Why can't I? You still want him, don't you? Well, he's yours, but not for no measly ten grand." Pierce smiled. "I want one hundred thousand or the deal is off."

"You're crazy," Jansen said. "Gideon and the others aren't worth that much."

"Then I might as well let them go. I'll give them their horses and send them on their way. If they're lucky, they can be in Canada in a month or so."

Jansen came partway around the fire. "You can't do that. We have an agreement. You shook on it. You gave your word."

"I've done what I said I would do. I found the boy and his filly and their friend and I'm holding them for you. But I never said I was happy with the amount you offered. At the time I figured it was the most you were willing to pay." Pierce smiled. "Now I think you're willing to pay more."

"You will take the ten thousand and like it."

Otto Pierce laughed. "How do you like this?" he asked, and drawing both Colts, he shot Jansen in the chest. Jansen flew back as if he had been kicked by a mule, and lay quivering like so much pudding. Pierce shot him again, then swiveled toward the other bodyguard. "How about you, Baxter? Do you think I should be happy with the ten thousand?"

Baxter had gone as white as a sheet. "How much you get isn't up to me. I just work for them."

"Then how about if you get on your horse and go tell the big fish that I want more money? And if I don't get it, the little fish goes free."

"You want me to leave now?" Baxter gazed anxiously at the benighted forest. "In the dark?"

"You can leave or I can shoot you."

Baxter's Adam's apple moved up and down as he backed toward the horses. "I'll relay your message. But it won't go over well. Neither will your killing Jansen."

"I'll meet you five days from now, at noon, in Wilbur Camp," Pierce said. "Make sure your boss shows up in person, with the money."

Baxter was not a horseman. He fumbled with his saddle blanket and saddle, and took forever cinching up. As it happened, a wolf howled somewhere near, and as he reined past the campfire, the whites of his eyes were showing.

"Don't wet yourself," Pierce said.

Fargo thought he saw his chance. Red Moon had turned as the bodyguard went by; his rifle was trained on Baxter. But Otto Pierce suspected what he was about to do and thumbed back the hammers of his Colts.

"I have plenty of pills to spare if you're that eager to push up daisies."

"We do not kill Fargo anyway?" Red Moon sounded disappointed.

"Never kill your chickens until you're ready to eat," Pierce said. "He might be of use. We'll take him with us. But to keep you happy, you can tie him up."

Fargo did not understand that last remark until Red Moon was done. The breed took perverse delight in binding his wrists and ankles so tightly the circulation was cut off.

Red Moon also found a dirty rag somewhere and held it next to Fargo's mouth. "Open."

Fargo did no such thing.

"Otto says we must keep you alive. He did not say you must keep your ears or your fingers."

Fargo opened. He nearly gagged when Red Moon shoved the rag halfway down his throat. He tasted dirt, sweat, and other stains. He would have spit the rag out except that the half-breed removed his bandanna and tied it around his mouth so he couldn't.

"What about the body?" Red Moon asked Pierce.

"Drag it into the brush. Coyotes have to eat, too."

The numbness in Fargo's wrists rapidly spread. Soon his shoulders were tingling. He lay on his side, totally helpless and hating it. The ace up his boot was his one hope. But the wily outlaws took turns sleeping, and he could not move without them noticing. His fingers were inches from his boots but he dared not slide the Arkansas toothpick out.

Pierce and Red Moon were in no great hurry. The sun was an hour high in the sky when they finally saddled up. Red Moon untied Fargo's legs and re-

242

moved the gag and roughly threw him onto the Ovaro. Fargo could barely feel the saddle. The reins were placed in his fingers but he could barely feel them, either.

Red Moon rode ahead, Otto Pierce behind. Fargo's perch was precarious. He nearly fell off six times in twice as many minutes. With infinite slowness, sensation returned. But with the sensation came sharp, stabbing pains in his thighs and calves.

Fortunately, they did not have far to go. After climbing steadily for only a couple of hours, they came to a broad, grassy tableland. In the center was a pristine lake, seldom seen by human eyes, and on the shore were tethered horses, two campfires, and nine of the meanest-looking curly wolves Fargo ever set eyes on.

A lean-to made of pine boughs sat off by itself. Two burly brutes hauled Fargo over to it and threw him to the ground inside, then left without a word.

Pierce's gang was gathering around their leader, but they were of no interest to Fargo. Sitting up, he faced the other occupants of the lean-to.

All were worse for wear. All were worn from lack of sleep and worry, their once expensive clothes in need of washing and mending. All had their wrists tied. And all three of them studied him as he was studying them.

It was easy for Fargo to guess who the nearest young man was since his features were the spitting image of his father. "Gideon Zared," Fargo said. Beside Gideon lay a fetching young woman, her hair a mess, her cheeks marked by the many tears she had shed. "You must be Tabor Garnet." On the other side of her, on his back, lay the third member of their party. "And Asa Chaviv," Fargo finished.

"Who are you?" Gideon asked. "And how is it you know our names?"

"Your father hired me to find you." The reaction

Fargo received was not that of a loving son glad his father cared enough to mount a search.

Stark fear gripped Gideon Zared, and he glanced sharply at Tabor Garnet. "Dear God. Is there no end to our nightmare? I'm sorry, darling. You were right. We should have fled to Europe instead."

Tabor stayed calm. "Do you know what these ruffians intend to do with us?" she asked Fargo. "Why have they held us so long? All the big one will say is that we are worth a lot of money to him."

"It's the reason you are still alive," Fargo said.

Gideon could scarcely contain himself. "But who is paying him? And why haven't they shown up yet?"

"That I don't know." Fargo had his suspicions but he would keep them to himself.

Asa Chaviv finally spoke. "Who cares who is paying these animals? We're dead, all of us."

"Quit saying that," Gideon snapped. "We have no idea what this is about. If my father is behind it, he'll send Tabor and you home and do all in his considerable power to see to it that I never see either one of you again."

"Or have us murdered," Asa said.

"My father is a lot of things I do not like. He is headstrong and arrogant and thinks he has the God-given right to run my life, but he is not a murderer!" Gideon's shoulders slumped. "I just want this awful ordeal to be over, for Tabor's sake." Gideon slid closer to her. "No matter what my father does, he can't keep us apart now that we are man and wife. I will move heaven and earth to reach you, and next time, we won't make the same mistakes."

"I love you so much," Tabor said.

"And I love you."

They touched their foreheads together, and Gideon whispered, "I won't let anything happen to you. I promise. Whatever my father has cooked up, we can overcome him."

"Wait a second," Fargo interjected. "Did I hear that right? The two of you are married?"

Gideon beamed. "By a justice of a peace. And there isn't a damn thing my father can do."

Fargo saw Asa Chaviv frown and open his mouth and close it again, and then say, "How much longer before you come to your senses, Gideon? Hasn't this taught you anything?"

"What do you mean?"

"There is no escaping your father. He has too much money. He is too powerful. He will find you wherever you run, and he will find a way to break you and Tabor up. It will always end the same." He held out his bound wrists. "Look at us, for God's sake."

"We almost made it to Canada," Gideon said. "A few more weeks and we would have been over the border."

"So what? Canada, Oregon, Europe, Asia. What difference does it make? Your father can buy as many men as he needs to track you down." Asa shook his head. "Why I let you talk me in this, I will never know."

"You helped us because you are the best friend any man ever had," Gideon said.

"We'll always be grateful," Tabor added.

They had forgotten about Fargo. He had some questions he wanted to ask but they could wait.

Otto Pierce had detached himself from the rest of the cutthroats and was sauntering toward the lean-to with his thick thumbs hooked in his gun belt. Pierce had an extra shadow, as usual, in the form of Red Moon.

"Oh, no," Tabor gasped. "Here comes that awful man again."

"They won't lay a hand on you. I promise." Gideon moved so he was between her and the front of the lean-to.

Pierce had overheard, and he laughed. "Quit your

fretting, boy. She's not my type. Some of my men are interested but they won't touch her so long as I say they can't."

"Am I supposed to be grateful?" Gideon sarcastically asked.

Without warning, Pierce kicked him in the ribs. The force bowled Gideon over and he writhed in torment in the dirt. "Ungrateful whelp. Keep a lock on that mouth of yours."

"You animal!" Tabor burst into tears and reached for her husband. "What have we ever done to you?"

"Not a blessed thing, girl," Otto Pierce said. "As if that matters." Taking a swift step, he brought his right boot down on Gideon's forearms, pinning them to the ground. "Enough blubbering, boy. I can't abide weaklings."

"But you hurt him!" Tabor cried.

"And I'll hurt him worse if he doesn't start behaving like a man." Pierce removed his boot. "Now sit up. And be careful how you talk to me." He glanced at Fargo. "Kids, huh? They think they know it all but they are dumber than tree stumps."

Tabor could not resist. "And you have room to talk—a beast who kidnaps others for money, a killer who brags about those he's killed?"

"I only mentioned a few so you would understand I'm not to be trifled with," Pierce replied. "I could have cut off one of your ears to make the same point."

Asa Chaviv had not tried to help Gideon. He stared at the boughs, his attitude that of someone who had given up all hope.

Otto Pierce had more to say. "I came over to let you know that by the end of next week I should have my money and you'll be turned over to the person who hired me."

"You still haven't told us who it is," Tabor said.

"I gave my word I wouldn't, girl. They want it to

be a surprise." Wheeling, Pierce stalked off, his ever-present shadow at his side.

"I hate him," Gideon said. "I hate him more than I have ever hated anyone." He rose onto his shoulder. "It's my father who is behind this. I'm sure of it. I will never forgive him, not as long I live."

Fargo pointed out the flaw in the younger man's thinking. "If it's your father, why did he hire me and other scouts to find you?" They had no answer. Leaning toward them, he said quietly, "How would you like to get out of here sooner than next week? How about tonight, after most of them are asleep?"

"They tie our legs at night," Tabor told him. "And they always have one or two men on guard."

"Mister," Gideon said, "if you can do it, I'll pay you ten times whatever my father is paying you to let us go."

Asa Chaviv mumbled something, then said, "When will you learn? You can never beat your father. Never."

"Are you with us if we try to escape?" Gideon asked him.

Asa eased onto his side. "I've stuck by you this far. I'll stick by you until the end, whatever it may be."

Fargo spent much of the rest of the day answering questions, and asking a few of his own. He learned that Gideon and his father had never really gotten along, that Benjamin Zared treated his children as he did business associates.

"I've often thought he would make a great Roman emperor," Gideon commented. "He would love to throw people to the lions."

The strained state of affairs had worsened when Gideon became old enough to be interested in the fairer gender.

"None of the girls I socialized with met with my father's approval. In his eyes they were not good enough for me."

Then Gideon met Tabor, and the two fell hopelessly in love. For over a year Gideon hid his budding relationship from his father for fear of how Benjamin would react.

"When I eventually told him, he was nice enough at first. He had me invite Tabor over for a Sunday meal so he could get to know her. Or so he said. No sooner had we sat down at the table than he announced she was not the right one for me and I should stop seeing her." Gideon gazed adoringly at his wife. "But I could no more stop seeing her than I could stop breathing."

"So we snuck around behind his father's back," Tabor took up the account, "stealing precious moments when we could."

"Have you ever been in love?" Gideon asked Fargo, then did not give Fargo a chance to answer. "It is exhilarating. I was never so happy in my life." Reaching out, he brushed his fingers across hers. "I decided to ask her to marry me. She insisted I tell my father. She said it wouldn't be right not to. So, like a fool, I did."

"It was the worst mistake you ever made," Asa remarked.

"My father would not hear of it. He was furious that I had continued to see her after he expressly forbade me to. When I told him that I was marrying her whether he liked it or not, he rose up out of his chair and struck me." Gideon shook his head in disbelief. "He knocked me to the floor, right in front of the servants."

"So she and you ran off together," Fargo said.

"What else could we do? I would be damned if I would let him separate us. Tabor and I talked it over and figured Oregon Country was the place for us. We could start a family and live happily ever after."

Tabor's eyes were misting over. "Is there really such a thing? Or is it a fantasy that never comes true?"

Gideon concluded his account. "We made it as far as Fort Hall. I learned there were men asking about us, agents of my father. They were watching the road to Oregon, so we did the last thing they would expect."

"You fled for Canada." Fargo sat back. "And your father sent for me and some of the best scouts in the country to track you down."

"Don't forget that pig over there." Gideon stared at Otto Pierce. "My father hired him, too. Now here we are, trussed up and waiting for my father to take his spite out on us. But I don't care what he does. Tabor is my heart, my soul, my very life."

At sundown they were brought beans, bread and water. As Red Moon untied them so they could eat, five of Pierce's men lined up in front of the lean-to to keep them from trying anything. They were given fifteen minutes to eat. Then their hands and ankles were bound and Pierce's men ambled to the campfires.

Fargo was glad they had not been gagged. "Listen to me," he whispered. "Pretend to fall asleep like you normally would. But be ready. When we move, we'll have to move fast."

"I couldn't sleep if I want to," Tabor whispered. "I'm so nervous and excited, I can't stand it."

Earlier in the day Red Moon and another man had gone off to the south, leading an extra horse. When they came back they brought a dead doe. Now the doe's haunches were rigged on spits over the fires, and Pierce's men were hungrily awaiting their feast. They were joking and smiling and laughing, and of them all, Otto Pierce talked and laughed the loudest. A lion among jackals, he lorded it over the others.

Red Moon hunkered on his heels, rarely speaking.

The mantle of night shrouded the mountains. Stygian darkness claimed the lean-to.

Fargo had waited long enough. He hiked at his right pants leg but it would not slide up. The rope around his ankles was too tight. He found the knots and pried at them with his fingernails but it was slow going. Two hours later his fingers were sore and stiff. He was bleeding from under one of his fingernails, but his dogged persistence had paid off. The first knot came undone. After that, the rest were easier.

Fargo's pant leg came free. He was about to slide his fingers up under it to palm the Arkansas toothpick when the crunch of footsteps warned him not to. Lying completely still, he peered from under his hat brim.

"I came over to tuck you in," Otto Pierce joked. "Anything else you need tonight?"

"A gun to shoot you," Gideon Zared said.

Pierce sighed and motioned at Red Moon. "See? You try to be nice to some folks and they throw manure in your face."

"We would like to be set free," Tabor said, "but there's no chance of that, is there?"

"Not a chance in hell, girl."

Fargo held still until Pierce and Red Moon were back at the fire. In moments he had the toothpick out and cut the rope around his wrists.

"Don't forget us," Gideon whispered.

"Slow and quiet does it," Fargo said, passing the hilt to him. "Each of you take a turn, then give it back."

The meal was soon over. Cards and dice were brought out, and one man produced a flask but Pierce told him to stash it.

By midnight only Pierce and Red Moon were still up, besides the pair chosen to stand guard.

"How much longer?" Gideon Zared eagerly asked.

"When Pierce and Red Moon fall asleep and not before," Fargo whispered. Then he would spirit the newlyweds and their friend out of there, or die in the attempt.

20

The horses were on the other side of the campfires. One fire had been allowed to burn low but wood was added to the other from time to time, and it cast a yellow glow in a large circle. Apparently it would be kept burning all night.

As near as Fargo could tell, everyone except the two men on guard were asleep. Many were snoring. Others were buried under their blankets. Otto Pierce was on his back with his blanket pulled to his chin and his hands folded on his chest. His hat was over his eyes, and his chest slowly rose and fell.

Red Moon, even in sleep, was at Pierce's elbow. The half-breed did not use a saddle for a pillow, or even a blanket. He lay on his side on the ground, his head resting on his left arm. He had removed his leather band and his long hair hung across his face.

At the moment, one of the guards was warming his hands at the fire. The other had his back to the lean-to.

The time had come. Fargo rose into a crouch and whispered, "Stay close and don't make any noise." He crept from the lean-to and sidled to the left, never once taking his gaze off the guards, and slipped around the end of the lean-to. From there the forest was only a dozen strides away. He led the Easterners in a wide loop, staying clear of the circle of firelight.

None of the sleepers stirred. The guard with his

back to the lean-to stretched and seemed to be admiring the stars.

Fargo was as silent as a wraith but he could not say the same about those he was trying to save. Gideon tried hard, but if there was a twig to be stepped on, he stepped on it. Asa had a knack for rustling the brush. Only Tabor moved quietly enough to earn his respect.

They were halfway around the clearing when Gideon snatched at Fargo's sleeve and pointed. The one outlaw had turned and was strolling toward the lean-to, his rifle in the crook of an elbow.

"He'll see we're not there!" Gideon whispered. "We should run for it while we can."

"Do as I do," Fargo growled. He did not go faster. They were making too much noise as it was.

The guard stopped a pebble's toss from the lean-to. He gazed at it, but the opening was too dark for anyone to see inside unless they were right in front of it. Instead of entering, he drifted to his right, making a circuit of the clearing.

Fargo came to the string. Most of the horses were dozing. The Ovaro was tied at the middle of the string, and he saw that no one had seen fit to strip the saddle. Hoping against hope, he checked the scabbard but the Henry was not there. Undoing the reins from the picket rope, he turned, and realized none of the others had picked a horse. "What are you waiting for?" he demanded. "Mount up!"

All three gave him blank looks, and Tabor whispered, "You want us to ride one of these?" She sounded greatly surprised.

"Unless you can flap your arms and fly." Fargo put a hand on the saddle horn and raised his leg to the stirrup.

"But none of us have ever ridden bareback."

Fargo lowered his leg again. "What?" He had heard her; he simply could not believe what he heard.

"We have never ridden bareback," Gideon confirmed. "We wouldn't want to fall off in the dark and break our necks."

Fargo reminded himself that Easterners did not rely on horses to get around as much as people who lived west of the Mississippi. Rich Easterners rode even less; they were shuttled everywhere in carriages, surreys, and buggies. "Clamp your legs tight and hold on to the mane. You'll do fine."

"I'm not so sure about this," Tabor whispered skeptically, but she was the first to chose a horse and lead it from the string.

Fargo glanced toward the fire. The one guard was still warming his hands and the other was halfway across the clearing. Fargo forked leather, and as he did, his gut balled into a knot. Red Moon was on his feet, staring in their direction.

"Hurry!" Fargo whispered to the others.

Gideon and Asa were gazing uncertainly at the bareback animals. Then Gideon shrugged, said, "What the hell?" and chose a claybank.

A war whoop rent the night. It brought all the outlaws to their feet with their revolvers drawn or rifles in their hands.

"There!" Red Moon screeched, pointing at the string. "They are getting away!"

Fargo and Tabor and Gideon were ready to ride but Asa could not get the bay he had chosen to stand still long enough for him to mount.

A gun boomed. Fargo braced for more but Otto Pierce roared, "No more shooting, you lunkheads! We need them alive or we don't get the money!"

There was a rush toward the horses.

"Damn." Fargo reined over to Asa Chaviv, hooked an arm under Chaviv's, and swung him onto the bay, all in one smooth motion. "There! Now light a shuck!"

All three gaped at him, and Gideon asked in bewilderment, "Which way do we go?"

Fargo assumed the lead. He flew around the lake and off across the tableland to the east.

Back in the camp, Otto Pierce was roaring like a madman, "After them! Move, damn you! Move!"

Shifting in the saddle, Fargo saw that Asa had fallen a bit behind. "Keep up with us!" he shouted. He did not want to lose any of them in the dark.

A grassy slope marked the end of the tableland. Confident in his horsemanship, and in the Ovaro, Fargo galloped down it. But the others were not as sure of themselves, and when he came to the bottom and looked up, they were descending much too slowly. "Hurry!"

To the west, artificial thunder rumbled. That would be Pierce's gang, out to recapture them at all costs.

Gideon came to the bottom first, and drew rein. Tabor was next. Asa Chaviv followed last. "Whew! That scared me half to death!"

If he thought that was scary, Fargo grimly reflected, he had not seen anything yet. "Keep going!" he shouted, and spurred the Ovaro into the trees. A deeper darkness enveloped them. They could not see more than ten feet ahead, and what they did see were vague shapes and indigo shadows.

Fargo had ridden in the forest at night before, many times, although not always by choice. It was experience that now stood him in good stead as he reined around a pine, vaulted a log, and ducked under a low limb.

Gideon was cursing. Tabor cried out. But they stayed on their horses, and kept up with him. Asa was farther back.

Fargo counted on the woods to slow down the outlaws. Not a lot, but he and the others should be able to stay ahead until daylight. Then he would ride like hell for the gold camp. He needed a rifle and a pistol. Once he was armed, let Otto Pierce and company come.

Another tree loomed, and Fargo expertly skirted it. The others were struggling to maintain his pace. Occasional shouts from their pursuers goaded them on.

Each minute was an eternity. Fargo could not say how many eternities had gone by when Tabor Garnet screamed his name. She had reined up, and Gideon was quick to do the same, leaving Fargo no choice but to rein around and race back to investigate. "Why did you stop?" he demanded, none too pleasantly.

"It's Asa!" Tabor cried, and pointed.

Chaviv's horse had halted. That was because Chaviv was no longer on it. Fargo flew to the spot and rose in the stirrups. A few yards away something was thrashing madly about in a thimbleberry thicket. Swinging down, Fargo ran to Chaviv and tried to grip him by the shoulders to hold him still but it was like trying to hold a bucking bronco.

Asa's hands were to his throat and he was gurgling and sputtering and gasping. Suddenly he reached up and grabbed Fargo's buckskin shirt. He went to say something but all that came out was a strangled whine. Asa arched his back, convulsed, and was still.

Fargo bent lower, and only then saw Chaviv's throat. It looked as if it had been smashed by a hammer. Glancing up, he saw a low limb a few yards from where Chaviv lay.

Gideon and Tabor had dismounted. They came running up, and Gideon anxiously asked, "What's wrong with him? Why is he lying there like that?"

"He's dead," Fargo said simply.

"Dead?" Tabor said in stunned disbelief. "That can't be. What killed him?"

Fargo pointed at the limb. In his mind's eye he imagined Chaviv galloping at full speed to keep up with them, and in the dark not seeing the limb until it was too late to duck. It was just Chaviv's luck that the limb caught him full across the throat.

Gideon knelt and shook Asa. "Please, no. He's my best friend. He can't be dead. He just can't." He bent and placed an ear to Chaviv's chest, then lifted a limp wrist and felt for a pulse. "I can't feel it beating." He was on the verge of tears.

"We must keep going," Fargo said, rising. He listened but did not hear sounds of pursuit. Could it be Pierce had lost them? Or was Pierce being smart and taking his time to conserve his horses?

"How can you suggest such a thing?" Tabor asked. "We're not going anywhere until we bury poor Asa."

"That would take half an hour," Fargo noted. "Have you forgotten about Pierce and his men?"

"Surely you're not suggesting we leave Asa lying there?" Gideon said, appalled. "That would be uncivilized."

Fargo wondered where Gideon thought he was. "Every minute we waste is a minute closer Pierce and his men are to catching us."

Gideon slowly rose, his face ashen in the gloom. "Poor Asa. All he wanted was to help me."

"Then don't let his death be for nothing, which is what it will be if Pierce gets his hands on you again."

That did it. Gideon tossed his head as if rousing from a horrific dream, and turned to Tabor. "Fargo is right. We must push on. Otto Pierce won't rest until he has us. We're worth too much to him."

"But to leave Asa there," Tabor said sorrowfully, tears trickling down her cheeks. "It's barbaric."

"We have to, dearest." Gideon hugged her. "Please. I don't want to lose you, too, and if Pierce turns us over to my father, that is exactly what will happen." He kissed her forehead. "For me. Before it is too late."

Tabor let him guide her toward her horse. She moved woodenly, unable to take her eyes off Asa Chaviv. Gideon boosted her up, and she sat there weeping profusely.

Fargo swung astride the Ovaro and brought the stallion alongside her dun. "Shed your tears later."

"How can you be so heartless?" Tabor asked, blinking. "What kind of man are you?"

"The kind who wants to keep you alive." Fargo started off and looked back to make sure she followed. She did, but she was still crying and not watching where she was going.

Gideon reined his mount into step beside hers. "I'll keep an eye on her," he assured Fargo. "Don't worry about us."

Fargo held to a walk. One accident was enough, and it would not do to wear out their own horses.

An hour went by—an hour of weeping and sniffling and then more weeping and more sniffling. Gideon sought to console her but Tabor cried until she had no more tears to shed.

Listening for the beat of hooves was futile until Tabor finally stopped. Fargo strained his ears but heard nothing to indicate the outlaws were anywhere near. He should have been elated, but their good fortune was too good to be true. A man like Otto Pierce did not give up easily, not with one hundred thousand dollars at stake.

Another hour dragged past, the benighted woodland rife with menace. Once, at a faint sound to the south, Fargo placed his right hand on his holster, where his Colt should have been, and frowned. The sound was not repeated, nor did he hear anything else of consequence until the eastern sky began to brighten and somewhere a bird stirred and warbled.

"Can't we rest?" Gideon Zared asked. "Tabor is about done in."

Fargo supposed it couldn't hurt. He came to a stop in a small glade. "Fifteen minutes is all we can spare."

Gideon climbed down and helped Tabor to dismount. She sagged against him, as much from grief as from fatigue. He assisted her to a log and they sat arm in arm, her head on his shoulder.

Fargo scanned the forest before sliding off. He was tired and sore, and it felt good to stretch his legs. He roved the edge of the glade, and became aware that Gideon Zared was staring at him. "Have something on your mind?"

"Be honest with me. What are our real and true chances?"

"Fifty-fifty," Fargo said, shading it ten points in their favor, "provided we reach the gold camp before they catch us."

"I can't stop thinking about Asa. He was the best friend anyone ever had. He came all this way with us out of the goodness of his heart. Now he's gone, and it's all my fault."

"If you have to blame someone, blame Otto Pierce."

"But Asa would not have been here if not for me. Oregon and Canada were my ideas. I dragged him clear across the country to die a needless horrible death in the middle of nowhere."

"You just said he came because he wanted to," Fargo reminded him.

"I appreciate what you are trying to do. But I *am* to blame, and nothing you say can change that."

Tabor raised her head from his shoulder. "Don't ever let me hear you say that again. I'm as much at fault as you are. I couldn't wait to be married. I couldn't wait to start a family and a new life."

"If my father only knew," Gideon said bitterly. "All he's gone through to stop us from being husband and wife, and he's too late."

"I wonder if it would make a difference to him?" Tabor said.

Fargo doubted it would. Benjamin Zared was accustomed to having his way. Zared would not let a little

258

thing like marriage keep him from tearing Gideon and Tabor apart.

"The happiest moment of my life," Gideon was saying, "and look at all the misery it has bought us."

"Are you saying you regret it?" Tabor asked, clearly hurt.

"Never in a million years," Gideon said softly. "If I had it to do things all over again, I would do them exactly the same. I could not imagine life without you by my side."

"The worst is behind us," Tabor said. She looked at Fargo. "I'm sorry for how I behaved. I'm better now." She smiled, then went as rigid as a board, her smile transformed into an expression of stark terror.

Fargo whirled.

Red Moon stood a dozen paces away. In his hands was a leveled rifle—Fargo's Henry. He did not say anything. He did not have to. His vicious smirk said it all.

"Not him!" Gideon exclaimed.

"But how?" Tabor marveled.

Fargo had the answer. "Pierce sent you on ahead."

"Otto sent me on ahead," Red Moon said. "And now we will wait for him."

Clasping Tabor to him, Gideon shot to his feet. "Damn you! Can't you leave us alone? This isn't fair!"

"What does fair have to do with anything, white boy?" Red Moon sneered. "Life is cruel. Then we die." He stayed well out of reach, the Henry centered on Fargo. "You tried your best, eh?"

"Please," Tabor pleaded. "Let us go. We won't tell anyone. Your friends need never know."

Red Moon's sneer widened. "How the white eyes have lasted so long is a mystery."

"You have white blood in you," Gideon said. "I heard someone say so."

"Do not remind me," Red Moon warned.

259

Tabor pulled free of Gideon, balled her fists, and walked toward Red Moon, her voice rising to a shrill pitch. "I won't take this anymore! Do you hear me? I have had all I can stand!"

Red Moon swung the Henry toward her. "Stop."

"Or else what?" Tabor railed. "You can't kill us! If you do, you won't collect your precious money!"

Fargo tensed. She was going to get herself shot. She was right that Pierce needed them alive, but there was nothing to stop Red Moon from putting lead into her leg or her arm.

"That is far enough," Red Moon said.

"You vile, despicable man! I am going to scratch your eyes out! Do you hear me!"

Gideon grabbed her from behind but Tabor shook him off and stalked toward the last person in the world she should have antagonized. "I dare you to fire! Go ahead! I dare you!"

"Tabor, no!" Gideon cried.

"Stupid cow," Red Moon said. "Let's see how much scratching you do with your kneecap blown off."

It was the moment Fargo had been waiting for. He hadn't really expected a savvy killer like Red Moon to take his eyes off him, but Red Moon did. Fargo sprang. He thrust one arm at the Henry.

Instantly, Red Moon pivoted, but he was a shade too slow. The Henry went off, the slug digging a furrow in the dirt.

Fargo wrapped his hand around the bone-handled hunting knife at the half-breed's waist and streaked it from its sheath. Red Moon skipped backward so he could level the Henry but Fargo foiled him by slashing the hunting knife at Red Moon's hands. The keen edge sliced open two knuckles. Swearing, Red Moon dropped the Henry. Almost in the same breath, Red Moon clawed for his revolver, and Fargo slashed again. This time the blade opened Red Moon's forearm, and the revolver joined the rifle on the ground.

Furious, Red Moon bounded out of reach, drew his tomahawk, and coiled. "For cutting me, I will kill you the Blackfoot way. Your scalp will go in my saddlebags with the other white scalps I have taken."

"Are you sure you are part Blackfoot?" Fargo taunted. "You talk as much as a white man."

Hissing between clenched teeth, Red Moon attacked, swinging the tomahawk in tight arcs.

Fargo retreated. The tomahawk was longer than the knife, giving Red Moon greater reach. When Red Moon suddenly swung high, at his head, he stabbed low, at Red Moon's chest. He missed a killing stroke but the blade sliced through Red Moon's shirt and glanced off a rib.

The half-breed recoiled, but only for a split second. Voicing a feral snarl, Red Moon unleashed a whirlwind of blows. He sought to split Fargo's skull, but Fargo blocked the tomahawk with the blade.

Twisting, Red Moon cleaved the tomahawk at Fargo's neck. Fargo ducked but lost his hat.

Red Moon began circling. Scarlet drops fell from his knuckles, and a dark stain was spreading across his shirt. "You are the fastest white I have ever met. But that will not help you."

Nearby lay the Henry and the revolver. Gideon could easily reach them, but Gideon and Tabor were riveted in place.

"It's not too late to do as the girl wanted," Fargo said, knowing full well Red Moon would never agree. He only mentioned it to distract Red Moon as he reversed his grip on the knife, which he held low against his leg.

"I expected better from you," Red Moon said, continuing to circle. "We are not like these silly ones, you and I. We are wolves. They are sheep."

"You are not a wolf," Fargo said. "You are a mad dog." On "dog," he whipped his right arm in a throw he had practiced many times. The hunting knife flashed between them, spinning smoothly. By rights it should have imbedded itself to the hilt in Red Moon's chest. But quick as thought Red Moon flicked the tomahawk and the hunting knife went flying.

"Now I have you," Red Moon crowed, wading in.

Unarmed, Fargo had to give way. He skipped right; he skipped left. He nearly lost an eye and almost had his neck split. Suddenly he glimpsed the Henry and the revolver, almost at his feet. He dipped toward them, only to jerk back when Red Moon aimed a terrific blow at his face. Dropping flat, he scrambled for the revolver, palmed it, and rolled. Beside him came a thud. He kept rolling and heard a second thud, and a third.

Then Fargo was on his back with Red Moon rearing above him and the tomahawk rising for a killing stroke. Fargo fired as it started to descend. He fired as Red Moon staggered. He fired as Red Moon screeched like a cougar and leapt at him, and he fired as Red Moon pitched forward.

The tomahawk missed by a whisker and bit into the earth.

Pushing off the ground, Fargo thumbed back the hammer, but another shot was not needed.

Gideon and Tabor came over to gape at the body. In a tone that implied it was an unthinkable act, Tabor said, "You killed him!"

"A lot more will die before this is over with," Fargo predicted. The revolver was a Smith & Wesson, not a Colt. He did not have ammunition for it but he found five cartridges in Red Moon's pocket. Reloading, he shoved the Smith & Wesson into his holster. Then he picked up the Henry and brushed dust from the brass receiver. "Otto Pierce is in for a surprise."

"He is not the only one," said a female voice behind him.

Once again Fargo whirled.

Edrea Zared wore a smart riding outfit complete

with short-topped boots, a wide-brimmed hat, and a quirt. Strapped around her slender waist was a pearl-handled Remington.

"Sis!" Gideon happily exclaimed. "Are you a sight for sore eyes! But what in God's name are you doing here?"

Edrea did not answer. Instead, she gestured with the quirt, and out of the trees in a skirmish line advanced seven men in black, with rifles. "You will be so kind as to drop those guns you just picked up," she instructed Fargo, "or I will give the order to have you shot to pieces."

21

Even then, Gideon Zared did not see the truth. "What are you doing, Edrea? Fargo is on our side. Father sent him to find me. Have these men lower their guns."

"Father might want you found, you simpleton," Edrea said, "but I don't." She fixed her icy gaze on Fargo. "Why aren't those guns on the ground yet?"

Left with no recourse, Fargo set them down. Her bodyguards covered him, prepared to blast him into oblivion if he tried anything. "Satisfied?"

"Not until I'm running the Zared business empire," Edrea answered, "which will be sooner than anyone suspects."

Gideon wore his confusion on his sleeve. "I don't get this. I don't get any of this. Why are you treating us as if we are your enemies? And what's that about you running things?"

"You are really rather pathetic—do you know that?" his sister rejoined.

Dawning horror seized Tabor Garnet. "I think I understand. God help me, but I think I do." She paused. "Your sister isn't here to rescue us. She's the one who hired Otto Pierce."

"What are you talking about?" Gideon glanced in bewilderment from one to the other. "Edrea would never do anything like that." He looked at her, and something in her features sparked uncertainty in his. "You wouldn't, would you?"

"Listen to yourself," Edrea said scornfully. "Would I eliminate the one obstacle that stands in the way of my acquiring a fortune?"

"But I'm your brother!" Gideon exclaimed.

"Don't remind me." Edrea touched the tip of a fingernail to his chin. "Have you any idea how much I hate you, how much I have hated you for years, how much I hate the fact that father always loved you more, how much I hate it that he plans to leave millions to you and a few paltry hundred thousand to me?" She suddenly dug her nail in deep, breaking skin and drawing blood. "Well, I have plans of my own."

"But I'm your brother," Gideon repeated, his turmoil transparent. "I love you. I have always stood by you, no matter what."

"Liar," Edrea said icily. "Where was your love when father announced how he was dividing up the estate?"

"I spoke to him on your behalf," Gideon said. "I told him it wasn't right. You heard me."

"Yes, I did. I heard a few feeble protests that changed nothing. It convinced me that if I wanted my rightful share, I had to take steps of my own." Edrea smiled. "What do you think of them?"

"It's true you hired Pierce and his men to kill us?"

"If I had wanted that lout to dispose of you, you would already be dead," Edrea said. "No, I want the privilege of doing that myself."

At long last the full truth hit Gideon Zared like a club between the eyes. Swaying, he took a faltering step back. "This can't be happening."

"It most definitely can." Edrea drew her pearl-handled pistol. "I made up my mind to kill you the day after father told us about the will. But I had to find a way to do it so that suspicion did not fall on me. Then you obligingly confided that you were running off to Oregon with your precious Tabor. I had Pike Driscoll keep an eye on you and—"

265

"Pike?" Gideon interrupted. "He was my friend. He helped me arrange everything."

"Idiot," Edrea said in contempt. "Pike wouldn't so much as blink without my say-so. He and I were lovers. I was the one who had him help you secretly meet with your sweetheart. I was the one who had him set things up so you could leave without father knowing." She saved the best for last. "I was the one who had him go to father a day after you left and say that you were missing, and he had found a letter in your room hinting Tabor and you were on your way to Oregon."

Gideon was a portrait of the most abject despair. "So that's how father found out so fast?"

"And it was Pike who got word to Otto Pierce after hearing about Pierce at Fort Hall," Edrea revealed. She looked at Fargo. "Where is the ever-efficient Mr. Driscoll, by the way? He was supposed to be watching you."

"He's dead. Shot, along with eight more of your father's bodyguards."

"They're not all my father's," Edrea said with a sweep of her arm at the seven who flanked her. "He only thinks they are."

Fargo had to hand it to her. She had worked it out as slick as could be.

"And after you dispose of me, what then, sis?" Gideon asked. "Will you dispose of father as well?"

"Need you ask? Oh, I'll wait a while—until after he draws up a new will naming me as his sole heir." Edrea pointed her expensive pistol at her brother. "He'll be devastated when he hears how Otto Pierce killed you."

"You're going to blame it on Pierce?"

"Why do you think I retained his services? As a scapegoat, he is marvelously convenient."

Fargo laughed. He knew something she didn't, and he exploited it to bring her down. "Does Pierce know you are using him? It takes a lot to pull the wool over his eyes."

"I already have," Edrea said. "The man isn't exactly a genius. I never had any intention of paying him a cent."

"Then what are you doing here?" Gideon asked.

"You haven't been paying attention, brother mine. Two days ago I left father in Kellogg under the pretext of having learned where you might be. I camped near Wilbur Camp and sent in two of my men. As you are probably aware, Pierce shot one and sent the other to me with a demand for more money. The fool."

Folding his arms, Fargo said, louder than he needed to, "Let me guess the rest. You planned to track Pierce to his camp, wipe out him and his men, kill your brother, and be back in Kellogg with your father in a few days with no one the wiser?"

Tabor broke her silence to say, "And to think I liked you and felt sorry for you. But you're a diabolical witch."

"That I am," Edrea proudly agreed. "And in a year or so I'll be the richest witch who ever lived."

"If you're still alive," said one of the shadowy shapes that had been slinking toward the glade from all sides.

Edrea Zared spun, then froze, overcome by shock. "You!"

"Me," Otto Pierce said, striding from the vegetation. The rest of his men were ranged in a crescent, their guns trained on Edrea's bodyguards. "The scapegoat. The fool. The jackass who trusted you to be as good as your word. I should have known. Women aren't to be trusted. Ever."

"Let me explain—" Edrea began.

"Shut the hell up." Pierce was staring at the crumpled form of Red Moon. "Is this your handiwork, too, bitch?"

"I can't claim credit, no."

Fargo tried to catch Gideon's eye but Gideon and Tabor were listening to the exchange between his sister and the scourge of the northern Rockies. He glanced at Edrea's bodyguards; they were watching Pierce's men.

"Don't do anything rash, Mr. Pierce," Edrea said. "I can still pay you the money you want. One hundred thousand, isn't it? Would you accept a draft on a bank in New Jersey?"

"The only thing I want," Otto Pierce said, "is to have you choke to death on your own blood—or better yet, stake you out naked and skin you alive, then wait for the ants and the buzzards and the coyotes. You will take a long time dying, I promise you, and I will enjoy every minute."

"Think again," Edrea said, and shot him.

It was hard for Fargo to tell who was more surprised: Edrea's men, Pierce's men, or Pierce himself. Her slug cored him high in the left shoulder. Where most men would have fallen then and there, Otto Pierce showed why he was widely feared from Denver to San Francisco. Pierce drew his two Colts and repaid Edrea Zared, with leaden interest.

For a moment the tableau froze. To a man, Edrea's bodyguards were too stunned to retaliate. The outlaws were staring at their leader, awaiting a cue as to what to do. His iron will always directed them, and they would not act without his say-so.

Their lapse was Fargo's gain. For as Pierce stared down at the crumpled heap that had been Edrea Zared, Fargo squatted and reclaimed the weapons at his feet. He shoved the revolver into his holster, then turned to Gideon and Tabor, who were stock-still in shock. "Head for the trees!" he whispered.

Neither budged. Tabor glanced at her beloved. Gideon's mouth moved but no sounds came out.

Then that which Fargo dreaded came to pass.

One of the bodyguards shook himself and bellowed in fury, "They've killed Miss Zared! Wipe them out!" He shot first, into the gut of the nearest outlaw, and at his blast, thunderous chaos ensued.

The men in black and Pierce's men concentrated on one another. Fargo seized the moment and pushed Gideon and Tabor toward the undergrowth, shouting, "Run, damn you!"

But Gideon only took a couple of steps, then stopped and gazed in horror at his sister. He did not seem to care that she had been about to kill him. It did not seem to matter that she was responsible for all he had been through. She was his sister, and he the grieving brother.

Tabor came to Fargo's aid. She grabbed Gideon's wrist and started toward the woods. "You heard him! Come on or we will end up like her!"

But Gideon dragged his heels, too numb to realize the peril they were in.

An outlaw swung toward them, raising his rifle, and Fargo cored the man's temple. As he fed another round into the Henry's chamber, Tabor hauled on Gideon with all her might while screaming his name over and over, and at last Gideon moved.

Protecting them, Fargo backpedaled. He shot an outlaw who jerked a pistol in their direction but the outlaw did not go down. Tottering like a sailor on a storm-pitched deck, the man gripped his revolver with both hands, grit his teeth, and tried to take aim. This time Fargo shot him in the face. The slug shattered the man's teeth, spraying bits and pieces every which way, and ruptured out the rear of his skull, taking a good portion of it along.

By now the unequal clash was nearly over. Outnumbered at the outset, most of the men in black were on the ground, a few in their death throes. Only one was still upright, and he was shot to ribbons, with blood-rimmed bullet holes in his chest, arms, and legs.

The bodyguards had given a good account of themselves, though. Only three of Pierce's men were unscathed. Pierce himself had been hit again, in the thigh, and was finishing off the bodyguard who had shot him by standing over the man in black and firing again and again into his head.

Tabor entered the forest, pulling Gideon after her.

A few more steps and Fargo was there. "Keep going!" he urged, and heard Otto Pierce say something he did not quite catch. More shots resounded as the remaining bodyguards were disposed of.

Gideon's legs were moving normally but he could not shake off his shock at the turn of events. "They murdered her!" he bleated to Tabor. "Did you see? That bastard killed my sister!"

"She shot him first," Tabor mentioned, but Gideon wasn't listening.

"We have to find my father!" Gideon declared, attempting to pull from her grasp. "We must get him to avenge Edrea."

Tabor placed her hands on Gideon's cheeks. "Snap out of it! You are not thinking straight. Your father wants to break us up, remember?'

"She was my sister," Gideon said forlornly. "I can't let the man who killed her get away."

Shadows were gliding after them.

Fargo caught up and gave Gideon a hard push toward a log. "Get down! We're not out of this yet!" No sooner were the words out of his mouth than a rifle cracked and Gideon lurched forward, his arms out flung. A slug had smashed between his shoulder blades.

"Gideon!" Tabor screamed.

Fargo sank onto his left knee and fired at the shadow responsible. Down it went. Several more guns belched lead and smoke. A slug sizzled past his ear. Another struck a pine with a loud *thwack*. Crouching, he banged off several shots.

Gideon was on his belly, flapping his arms like a bird trying to take wing. Blood gushed from his nose. Tabor dropped to her knees and clasped him to her, heedless of the fact she was out in the open. "Gideon! Oh, Lord, no! Speak to me?"

"Get down!" Fargo shouted again, and nearly lost his head to a shot from out of the brush. He answered in kind, twice, and an outlaw keeled into sight, fumbling at a neck wound. Blood spurted in a mist, and nothing the man could do would stanch it.

Tabor had Gideon's head in her lap and was rocking back and forth in misery, tears streaming down her cheeks.

Dashing to them, Fargo hooked a hand under her right arm and tried to haul her to her feet and get her out of there. But she resisted, blubbering, "He's dead! He's dead!" over and over.

Another outlaw burst from the vegetation, firing a rifle from the hip. Fargo snapped off a shot that lifted him onto his bootheels.

"Look out!" Tabor suddenly shrieked. "On your right!"

Fargo's scalp prickled at the sight of Otto Pierce holding a pistol pointed at him. Moving almost too swiftly for the eye to follow, Fargo worked the Henry's lever and fired. But instead of a welcome blast there was only a *click*.

"Empty," Otto Pierce said, and smiled. He was holding his other hand to the wound in his shoulder. "Drop it. And lose the gun belt."

Fargo hesitated. He could draw, but Pierce would put a shot into him before he cleared leather, and at that range, Pierce could hardly miss. Fargo let the Henry fall, then unfastened his belt buckle.

"Smart hombre," Pierce said. He glanced at the bodies, and frowned. "It's all gone to hell," he said quietly. "Red Moon dead. My men dead."

"All that trouble you went to," Fargo said.

Pierce nudged Gideon with a toe. "I told them not to shoot him. A stray bullet must have done it."

Tabor slapped Pierce's leg. "Don't touch him, you vile pig! Do you hear me? Or so help me, I will scratch your eyes out!"

"Hush, girl," Otto Pierce said.

Something in Tabor Garnet snapped. She came up off the ground in a rush, her fingers hooked to rip and rend. Maybe she forgot who she was dealing with. Maybe she did not care now that Gideon was gone. Whatever the case, she had not quite reached Pierce when his Colt went off.

Fargo took a step but stopped when Pierce pivoted toward him. "You could have spared her."

"I could have," Pierce admitted. "I wasn't in the mood." He removed his hand from his shoulder. His fingers were slick with blood.

"So what now?" Fargo stalled. He could dart for the undergrowth, or he could try for any of the weapons on the ground, but neither option was promising.

Pierce wiped his hand on his pants. "I owe you for Red Moon. He was my friend. But I want you to suffer. I'll start with your knees, then between your legs. You'll beg to be put out of your misery before I'm through."

"Not if I can help it," Fargo said. Brave talk, but he was as human as the next person. He could only endure so much.

"You can't," Pierce said, and lowered the barrel so it was trained on Fargo's right knee. "I wish Red Moon was here to see this. He wanted to skin you and make a tobacco pouch of your hide." Pierce smiled at the recollection. "That breed was the best damn friend I ever had."

"He said your name right before he died," Fargo lied, sliding his right leg a couple of inches toward Pierce. He had to get Pierce mad, boiling mad, and pray it affected Pierce's aim—a feeble hope, but it was the only hope he had.

"He did? What else did he say?"

"Not much," Fargo said, tensing. "Only that you were about the most worthless partner a man ever had, and it was too bad you didn't die before he did so he could spit on your grave."

Otto Pierce blinked, and Fargo charged. He saw Pierce's trigger finger tighten and threw himself to the right as the Colt went off. A whang on his arm went flying but otherwise he was unhurt. Another bound brought him to Pierce, and he swung at Pierce's right hand.

Fargo had assumed that since Pierce had been shot in the left shoulder and had not used his left arm since being shot, the arm had been rendered useless. He was mistaken. Pierce clamped his left hand on Fargo's throat, and squeezed. At the same time, Pierce sought to bring the Colt to bear.

In desperation Fargo caught hold of Pierce's left wrist. He pried at the thick fingers closing like a vise on his throat.

Otto Pierce's mouth curled in a vindictive sneer. "I will enjoy snuffing your life out."

Fargo could not respond. The breath in his windpipe was choked off. He gasped for air that was not there. He wrenched hard at Pierce's fingers but it was like wrenching at iron bars. All it did was provoke a cold laugh.

"Is that the best you can do?" Otto Pierce asked. "I've had grandmothers put up a better fight."

An image of Pierce strangling a gray-haired old woman popped into Fargo's head. He punched at Pierce's left wrist with no effect. Then he realized that Pierce was slowly but inexorably turning the barrel of the Colt inch by gradual inch toward his abdomen.

As if Pierce could read Fargo's thoughts, he asked,

"Ever been gut shot? They say it hurts worse than anything."

Fargo had heard the same thing. His lungs were aching, his throat was a molten pit of pain. He would black out soon, or take lead, unless he did something, and did it right then.

Fargo didn't hesitate. He kicked Otto Pierce in the right kneecap with all the strength he could muster.

If being shot in the stomach was the most painful wound, being struck in the knee was a close second. Knees were fragile. Knees were much more susceptible to breaks than the shin bone or the thigh bone. It did not require a lot of force to break one.

Otto Pierce opened his mouth but did not cry out. His right leg nearly buckled. Straightening, he hissed and rasped, "Do that again and you will wish you had never been born."

Fargo kicked him in the right knee again. A howl was torn from Pierce. He lurched back, struggling to stay upright, bracing his left leg for extra support. Fargo kicked him in the left kneecap.

"Damn you!"

Pierce sagged. His grip on Fargo's neck lessened enough for Fargo to suck air into his lungs. But it was far from over; Pierce was still trying to point the Colt at him. That was when a thought hit Fargo: *Only one Colt, and Otto Pierce is a two-gun man.*

Fargo swooped his right hand to the other one. He had it out before Pierce could guess his intent, and pressing the muzzle to the big man's stomach, he thumbed back the hammer and fired. Pierce was jolted backward. Fargo kept firing, shot after shot, until the cylinder was empty and Otto Pierce was a disjointed pile of flesh at his feet.

Pierce's huge arms fell to his sides. His Colt thudded to earth. Glazed eyes fixed on Fargo, and somehow he was able to say, "Sneaky bastard." Then his eyes rolled up into his head and he died.

"Well done," someone said.

His neck throbbing, his chest on fire, Fargo turned.

"That was some scrap, pard," Kip Weaver said. He was smiling and friendly but the smile did not reach his eyes, and his friendliness was belied by the rifle he held.

"I was wondering when you would show up."

"Is that so?"

"What I don't savvy," Fargo said, "is why you did it—and why you spared me when you had the chance to kill me."

"You knew it was me the whole time?" Weaver was skeptical. "You're joshing. I'm good at covering my sign, as good as you are."

"It wasn't your tracks," Fargo said. He was bone-tired and battered but he had to stay sharp or end up beside Otto Pierce.

"Then what?" Kip Weaver asked.

"First tell me why you killed all those bodyguards." Fargo was becoming a master at stalling.

"You haven't figured that part out?" Kip circled to the right until he was near Gideon's and Tabor's bodies. He glanced at Gideon's and frowned. "What a shame. A million dollars up in smoke."

"The bounty is twenty thousand," Fargo reminded him.

Kip laughed. "For those who think small. I had a better notion. One that would set me up in rich style for the rest of my days." He poked Gideon Zared with his foot. "I was going to take the boy here and hold him until his pa paid me a million dollars."

"You're loco."

"Am I? Benjamin Zared is one of the richest coots alive. What is a million dollars to a man who has ten or fifteen?"

"You would never get away with it," Fargo said. "Even if Zared paid, every lawman in the country would be after you."

"Give me more credit. Do you really think I would let Zared live after I had that million?"

"Others would know. His daughter. His bodyguards—" Fargo stopped. "So that's way you killed them."

"Partly that, partly to whittle the odds," Kip said. "There. Now you know all there is worth knowing. Suppose you tell me how you knew it wasn't James."

"His nose patch," Fargo said.

"That won't wash. I wore one in Lewiston when I pretended to be him for a day to throw you off the scent, and everyone fell for it."

"Not there. When Walker was shot, I chased the man who did it. I was close enough to hear him crash through the brush, close enough to hear his feet as he ran. But I didn't hear him breathing."

"I've lost the scent," Kip admitted.

"When James breathed through what was left of his nose, he made noise—so much noise, people would stare. So he had the habit of breathing through his mouth." Fargo prepared for his leap. "But when James ran, he couldn't help breathing through his nose, like that time some Comanches were after us. He sounded like a blacksmith's bellows."

"I see. So when you didn't hear loud breathing when you chased Walker's killer, you knew it wasn't Smith. But it could have been anyone, not just me."

"The killer had to be someone who knew bodyguards were trailing each of us. Benjamin Zared knew but he wouldn't have his own men killed. Edrea knew, but if she killed them, she drew suspicion to herself." Fargo shook his head. "No, the killer had to be one of us."

"You think you are pretty smart, don't you?"

"Not really," Fargo answered. "At first I thought it might be No-Nose, just like you wanted me to think. Then I suspected the Picketts were involved until they proved they couldn't be." He paused. "It took a while but I worked it out—all except why you spared me."

"I reckon I should have blown out your wick back in Fort Hall that night you were with the filly from the wagon train—or that night at the boardinghouse."

"That was you?" Fargo remembered something. "But I saw you aim your rifle at her, not me."

"I figured you were fond of her," Kip explained, "and that if she took a bullet, you would stick around Fort Hall until she was on her feet again." He shrugged. "I had already talked to Edrea Zared and had some idea of why her father sent for us. I wanted you out of the way. You're the best scout there is, whether you will admit it or not. You were the one who stood to beat me to the boy."

"When did you decide to kidnap him yourself and demand a million dollars?"

"Before you reached Fort Hall. I got to thinking about how rich Benjamin Zared is, and how it was a shame he has all that money and I don't have any, and how stingy he was, only offering us twenty thousand when he could afford to pay us ten times as much."

"What about James? I take it he was the first one you killed?"

Kip nodded. "I left Fort Hall about an hour after he did. I saw Lattimer and those other bodyguards following him. I circled around and caught up with James shortly after he made camp for the night. He never suspected a thing. He even invited me to share his coffee and stew."

"How did you do it?"

"I stabbed him when he turned to fill my cup. Got him right above the heart. You should have seen the look on his face. He tried to draw his pistol, so I stabbed him again. But that still wasn't enough. He was a tough coon, Smith was. In all, I think I had to stab him nine times before he gave up the ghost."

Fargo had all the answers. Now all he had to do was stay alive. "Then you buried his body, ran off his horse, and waited for Lattimer and the other two bodyguards and took care of them."

"They were easy. City folk are like fish out of water."

"All those people dead," Fargo said, "and now you don't get a cent. You should be proud of yourself."

"Sticks and stones," Kip said. "As for sparing you, chalk it up to old times' sake. You and me go back a ways, pard."

"That's all there was to it?" Fargo was genuinely surprised. They had played a lot of cards together and drunk a lot of whiskey together and done scouting for the army together, and he had always considered Weaver a friend, but no more so than many of the other scouts he knew.

"What else? Maybe I was trying to arrange things so you would take the blame?"

Fargo had not thought of that, but now that he did, it made more sense than the first reason. "I would like to be there when they hang you."

"Afraid not," Kip said. "You know too much. I'll tell Benjamin Zared it was you all along killing everyone. I tried to take you alive but you forced me to shoot you—after you shot his son, of course."

"Of course," Fargo said.

Kip Weaver smiled. "Go ahead. Try. I'll give you that much. And to be nice, I'll shoot you in the head so it's quick."

"You are all heart." Fargo had run out of words. For what it was worth, he would go down resisting to the end.

Kip was in no rush. "Any final requests from one pard to another?"

"Go to hell."

"You first." Kip wedged the stock to his shoulder

and took a precise bead down the barrel. "Send me a letter, why don't you?"

The shot was like a thunderclap.

His left temple erupted in a shower of flesh, blood, and hair, and Kip Weaver was flung backward. He dropped his rifle and doubled over, the furrow the slug had dug a red slash from his eyebrow to past his ear.

Amazed at his deliverance, Fargo turned to see who had saved his life. Tabor Garnet was on her elbows by the prone form of a dead outlaw, his six-gun grasped awkwardly in both hands. The whole front of her shirt was stained dark, and she was sprinkled with drops of sweat. Licking her lips, she smiled weakly and asked, "Did I do good?"

The crash of underbrush made Fargo want to kick himself. Snatching the revolver from Tabor, he said, "I'll be back." Then he was off after Kip Weaver, who had a ten-yard lead and was running like a man who realized his life depended on it.

Fargo almost snapped off a shot. But he did not know how many cartridges were in the revolver and he did not want to waste one.

Kip was racing east down the mountain, moving with remarkable agility for someone who had just been shot. He was bleeding profusely. Again and again he wiped a sleeve across his brow to mop blood out of his eyes.

After all Fargo had been through, all his muscles ached. His legs protested every step. But he would be damned if he would give up, not with the end literally in sight.

The trees began to thin. Kip ran faster. A mocking laugh was borne on the breeze.

"Think again, pard," Fargo said under his breath.

Suddenly Kip came to an abrupt stop. Throwing out his arms to keep his balance, he swore luridly, and spun. His hand stabbed for a six-shooter at his waist but both his holsters were empty. "Not like this!" he cried.

Fargo was close enough that he could do something he rarely did; he fanned the revolver, the heel of his hand slapping the hammer three times, his trigger finger tight around the trigger. Three bullet holes appeared in Kip Weaver's buckskin shirt and he fell straight back—and disappeared.

Fargo warily stepped to the exact spot. He was at the brink of a sheer cliff over sixty feet high. He got there just as Kip Weaver crashed to earth amid a cluster of jagged boulders. Weaver's body burst like an overripe sausage and half his face was ripped off, including, fittingly enough, his nose. The body would make a fine feast for the buzzards and the coyotes.

Unbidden memories washed over Fargo. Memories of happier times: of Kip laying down a full house and laughing as he raked in a pot; of Kip smacking a dove on the fanny and telling her to bring them another round of drinks; of Kip before fear and greed destroyed him.

Fargo hurried back.

Tabor had crawled to Gideon, and her cheek was cushioned by Gideon's chest. Her eyes were closed.

"Tabor?" Fargo found a vein in her neck and held his fingers there for a long while. Then he bowed his head and said softly, "Damn."

Benjamin Zared took the news hard: not the news about Asa, not the news about Tabor, nor the news about his daughter. "My son! Not my son!" he wailed, and buried his face in his hands.

Fargo had five thousand dollars in his poke and a hankering to light a shuck for Denver or San Francisco or anywhere he could drown himself in life's simple pleasures, and forget.

He had a lot of forgetting to do.